FRECKLED VENOM
SKELETONS

D1607433

by

Juliette Douglas

Best Wishes &
Happy Trails!
Juliette Douglas!

FRECKLED VENOM
SKELETONS
by Juliette Douglas

Cover design and layout Rob Krabbe, Noon at Night Publications,
Copyright © 2015

Published by Noon at Night Publications,
Galveston, TX

ACKNOWLEDGMENTS

The author would like to thank the following:

God has truly blessed me in this new adventure/midlife crisis, *whatever*, in my life. And I thank Him everyday for giving me the opportunity by placing the right people in my path to guide me and pass along these stories so that others may enjoy my over-active imagination.

Rob Krabbe and Noon At Night Publications

Muchas Gracias, Debra Wagner, Editor

Collin and John Case Shadowen. The prototypes for my characters, Cotton and Ben in this story.

Jeff Holley, for keeping my 'puter running when I screw it up.

To my wonderful supportive readers...Thank you...Thank you!

And to the Marshall County, KY businesses who so graciously offered to sell these books. Marshall County Co-op and Shop-a-Rama, I thank you from the bottom of my heart.

Megson Farms, Marshall County, KY for allowing the photo shoot with your beautiful Rare White Thoroughbreds

In Memory

Evelyn Bleidt

Paul Megson

Myrla Glidersleeve

Sandra Vied Ford

DEDICATION

William Joseph
Jared Cutter
Mason Eldin

Even though you are too young to read...yet.

I hope that you will come to love the many adventures you will find between the covers in the wonderful world of books, allowing your imaginations to soar within your mind, flying you places where you physically can not go.

Other works by Juliette Douglas

Freckled Venom Copperhead

Freckled Venom Copperhead Strikes

Freckled Venom Skeletons

Works in Progress

Perfume Powder & Lead * Holy Sisters

Pocketful of Stars

Bed of Conspiracy

Chapter One

Summer 1888

Hearing the stage rattle from up the street, Ezra Shemwell stepped out of his newer and larger mercantile store and stood at the edge of the steps. He watched dust churn beneath the wheels and hooves leaving a hazy trail behind that settled across everything in its path like yellow-brown flour.

Marty Abrams, the stage driver, yelled as he threw the mailbag to Ezra, "Talk at ya, when I come back through, Ezra."

Catching the heavy bag, Ezra threw a wave as the stage clattered toward Luke's stable for a quick exchange of horses before Marty continued his journey on to Medicine Bow.

No passengers today, the shop owner noted, turning his back on the circling plume of dust floating onto his walk. Ezra hurried inside and over to the counter. The heavy canvas bag slammed the top with a solid thud. Walking around the counter, he sniffed appreciatively at the scents inside his store. The fragrance of fresh coffee mixing with the cinnamon he'd just ground, mingled with the tangy, smoky aroma of tobacco twists and new harness leather. His store still carried that new smell of fresh cut wood, even after eight years. Shaking his head, his mind retrieved the memory of when White River had almost been totally consumed by fire. Some sick bastard had decided to get back at Lacy Carrigan by burning down the town. The fire was the reason that when Ezra decided to rebuild he added living quarters off to the side. He'd kill the next sum-bitch who broke into his store.

But that wasn't the only reason for the addition. Ezra Shemwell was still a reasonably nice looking man, pushing fifty. He stood at a little below six feet and Ezra's brown hair now showed traces of silver above his ears. His shoulders, still muscular from lifting fifty to one hundred pound grain sacks over the years, were encased in his ever pristine white shirt. The colorful garters remained above his elbows. He had a different color for every day of the week; the only color in his otherwise drab appearance. Black sleeve protectors kept his shirt white. A dark leather belt, crafted by Luke Castleberry the livery owner, circled a trim waist above dark britches. This was covered by a light colored canvas apron.

Eagerly unlatching the buckle holding the canvas mailbag closed, he dumped the contents on his counter. His hands quickly shuffled through the mail. Finally he spotted the item which he had been searching for. His hands stilled. Nondescript brown eyes looked intently at the neatly flowing script gracing the face of the envelope.

B. Hudson

15 River Street

St Joseph, Missouri

Mr. Ezra Shemwell

General Delivery

White River, Wyoming

He picked up the envelope and sniffed, hoping for the least little bit of feminine scent. *Nuthin',* except for the dusty smell of paper, Ezra sighed wistfully. He'd subscribed to the Denver Post and the St. Joe Chronicle just for the ads. He found one in the Chronicle that piqued his interest and that's when he began corresponding with Mrs. Beth Hudson, a widowed teacher with a ten year old son named Ben. Ezra Shemwell was tired of being a bachelor and wanted to get married. The western territories still lacked enough women to go around and ads offering mail-order brides were common.

The last letter Ezra had sent to Beth had contained travel expenses along with his proposal. Staring intently at the envelope he held in his hand, Ezra knew the letter contained either a yes or a no. Opening his pocket knife, he slit the envelope. Pulling the folded pages out, Ezra opened them and began reading the fine neat script.

Dear Ezra,

I hope this correspondence finds you well.

His eyes quickly scanned the words, looking hopefully for the ones he wanted to see. After doing a little jig behind the counter, he settled down. Placing elbows on the scarred top, Ezra leaned over them and began reading Beth's letter from the beginning.

I have enjoyed receiving your letters as with each one you have filled us in on the residents and every day life in the west. White River sounds like a very nice town to re-locate, so, yes, I accept your proposal. I have resigned my position with the St. Joe school system and will be arriving by train in Medicine Bow, Wyoming on August the 17. Then we will take the stage the rest of the way, hopefully arriving the 19 or the 20th.

Ezra looked up, today was July 28, just a few more weeks. He resumed reading.

Ben is so excited to be moving west, where he thinks cowboys and Indians still roam. He has been devouring the Ned Buntline's Dime Serials, which I am not particularly fond of but at least he is reading.

Ezra smiled. He couldn't keep Ned Buntlines storied lies in stock, even the adults read them.

He wants to make sure 'the code of the west' still exists, but maybe once we arrive he will drop that foolish notion.

We will be traveling light, just one trunk and a few smaller valises. My credentials are all in order. Hopefully, the town council will see fit to hire an eastern educated woman to teach the community's children. Do you have a library within the city limits? If not maybe we can set one up in your business.

City limits, library? Thought Ezra, scratching his head. He looked around his store, and then resumed reading.

I look forward to finally meeting you and the residents of the town of White River. Even though we have yet to meet, I feel that you have been honest and forthright with me in your letters. I hope I won't be

9

disappointed, or you with me or my son.

> *Fondly,*
>
> *Beth Hudson*

    Ezra thought, *Finally, I will have a family, and a ready-made one at that!* There weren't many single women in White River. The ones that did live there were already spoken for or way too young for him anyway. He had already spoken to the town council and school board about Beth Hudson becoming the new schoolmarm. They had been delighted after the last schoolmaster disappeared in the middle of the night, for whatever reasons he had. Olivia Johnstone had stepped in to finish out the last of the school year.

    He began whistling a happy tune as he stuffed the mail into their correct boxes over by the telegraph. He was the one in charge of maintaining the telegraph, receiving and sending the messages, but most days the keys remained quiet.

Chapter Two

"Mister Rawley, Mister Rawley!" Lanky fourteen year old, sandy brown-haired Chad slid in the open door of the Marshal's office. He and his brother Thad were the first set of twins Doc delivered in White River. "You gotta come quick! It's Hanah! She's got Dobie Litchfield down and is beating up on him sometin' fierce!"

"Why didn't you bigger boys just haul her off him?"

"You gotta be kidding! She'd just turn on us and beat us up. We're not that stupid!"

Tall and broad shouldered, Rawley Lovett just exhaled noisily. He rose quickly, following Chad out the door. His daughter had gotten into another scrape again. Shaking his head as he ran behind Chad, he accepted the fact that Hanah had inherited her mother's freckles, temper and feisty ways just as Doc predicted seven years ago on the night she was born. He may have a daughter, but one would never know it with as many fights as he had to break up.

Voices cheering on their favorite reached Rawley's ears. His eyes swept the scene as he came into the school yard. Hanah sat on Dobie Litchfield, yelling at him as she hit him. Coming up behind her, Rawley Lovett stuck a big paw down the back of her britches. Grabbing belt and cloth, he hauled his daughter off the poor kid. His muscular limb held Hanah out at arm's length, which helped Rawley to avoid being hit by her hands and feet still swinging and kicking in mid-air.

"I'll get you for this, Dobie Litchfield!" Hanah yelled, as her fists swung through the air, "I'll get you for this!"

Dobie Litchfield scrambled up and took off.

Rawley grabbed a thin arm, settling his daughter down on her feet. When he looked up, the remaining kids scattered as his stern gaze scanned the small group.

Knowing she was in trouble now, Hanah still managed a defiant stance. She folded her arms with a jerk. Her mouth forming a pout, she stared at the dirt.

Rawley tucked thumbs in back pockets, and stared down at his other redhead. Between the two of them, he really didn't know how he survived, but he did. *Sorta.*

Heaving a huge sigh, he knelt in front of his daughter. Hanah quickly looked at her Daddy, then back at the dirt.

Trying to prevent the grin from spreading, he clamped his lips into a tight line. Hanah's freckled face was dirt smudged. Burnished copper tendrils were pulled out of her braid. The sleeve of her green-checkered shirt was ripped, exposing a tiny freckled arm. Dirt caked her tan canvas britches. His daughter was tall for her seven years, but small boned like her Mama. Her temper gave her the strength her body did not.

Smiling, Wyoming sky blue eyes tried to look stern as Rawley asked quietly, "You wanna tell me what this is all about?"

Another set of blue eyes still flashed anger as they peeked out from under dark red-gold lashes. "He called me freckle face and...and carrot top!"

"Oh..." Rawley's face remained deadpanned, "Well...that's not so bad, is it?"

A pouting mouth within a red face shouted, "My name is Hanah Marie Lovett! Not freckle face or carrot top!"

Sometimes Rawley just ran out of words and patience with his daughter and this was one of those times. Sighing, he stood. Hanah remained in her defiant stance. Watching Hanah grow over the years made Rawley realize even more how Lacy must have been a handful when she was young. He saw so much of Lacy in Hanah. Like the time Hanah had found a pretty little black and white kitty behind Luke's stable. She'd kept it in a box hidden in her room. Neither he nor Lacy knew anything about the little black and white kitty until it let loose with both barrels, suddenly becoming a skunk. The house had reeked for weeks, including Hanah. But he loved both his redheads and wouldn't trade those years for anything.

"It's almost suppertime, guess we'd better head home and tell your Mama what happened," he said holding out his hand.

Hanah looked up at her Daddy and then unfolded her arms. She nodded as she slid her small freckled hand into his big one.

* * *

Anyone watching the tall, black-haired lawman walking peaceably down the street holding the hand of a little redheaded girl, probably wouldn't think much of that image. One would have to know the history of how another redhead had showed up in White River, Wyoming almost ten years earlier and set this town on it's ear.

And how a lawman, who didn't know quite what to do with the girl, had married her. Oh, he had fallen deeply in love with his little copperhead and she with him. But that didn't mean things had settled down in White River. No. Between folks showing up out of his and Lacy's past, the town growing by leaps and bounds and the railroad coming through in Medicine Bow making transporting cattle easier, Marshal Rawley Lovett had his hands full. And now, besides the two boys he and Lacy had taken in, they had a feisty, hot-tempered, redheaded daughter to ride herd on.

Not much rattled Rawley Lovett. He was an affable sort; quick to laugh, easygoing, and had the patience of a saint. And he had needed every drop of that patience in dealing with his two feisty redheads. Through the years that patience had been stretched mighty thin; more than once in fact.

Lacy Carrigan Lovett, a/k/a Lacy Watson had been a bounty hunter when she had ridden into White River looking for her prey. Exhausted and wounded, she fought the Marshal every step of the way. She even ran away on her wedding day, really setting the town in a tizzy. Then along came Hanah Marie Lovett.

No, the town of White River had never been the same and wouldn't be as long as the Lovetts were around.

* * *

"Sunshine, we're home!" Rawley called as he and Hanah entered the house.

Coming out of the kitchen Lacy stopped abruptly, seeing the ragamuffin who was her daughter. Hanah stood sulkily in front of her Father, her eyes cast down.

Mouth dropping, Lacy glanced at her husband.

Rawley rolled his eyes.

Walking over and kneeling in front of her disheveled daughter, Lacy asked, "Hanah Marie Lovett, what happened to you?"

Silence filled the room.

Lacy looked at Rawley.

Rawley looked at Lacy. Rolling his eyes again and sighing inwardly, he took two fingers and nudged his daughter, "Go on, tell your Mama what happened."

Snapping blue eyes cut a hasty look, way up.

Two fingers poked the miniature firebrand again, "Go on, tell her."

Mouth still in a pout, Hanah's arms folded tight across her slender chest, she glared at her Mama. "It was Dobie Litchfield! He called me freckle face and carrot top!"

"I see," Lacy said as dimples began to peek through a smile, surrounded by a million freckles mimicking her daughter's face. "Well, did you win?"

"No! Daddy stopped me before I could make him cry uncle!"

Rawley rolled his eyes again, settling them on the ceiling.

"I see. Well, go get washed up," Lacy said standing. "It's almost time for supper."

She watched as Hanah raced up the stairs and then turned toward her husband with her hands resting on still slender hips. "Why did you

14

stop her? Dobie Litchfield is a bully. He needed to be taught a lesson."

"And you would have let her continue to fight him?"

"If I'd known, I'd have been there cheering her on!"

"Sunshine, I'd like our daughter to be a young lady. She can't get that way fighting every boy who calls her names!"

"I did."

"Yeah…well, that was different. You didn't have a Daddy or a Mama to guide you. Hanah does. She needs to find other ways to deal with that temper of hers. You need to talk to her."

"Me? Shoot, I'd just show her all my best fighting moves, so she could defend herself better."

"You better not, Sunshine. That's playing dirty," he said, remembering what his wife almost did to him when they had first tangled.

Burnt coffee eyes began to dance with merriment. Lacy knew what Rawley was thinking. "You'd better talk to her then. I just might make her into a worse tomboy." Turning, she strode back into the kitchen, mumbling, "Damn, why do I always seem to miss the good stuff! I hope Dobie Litchfield learned his lesson."

Rawley shook his head. Hanging his hardware by the door, he cast eyes up the stairs. Blowing air through his lips, he decided that after supper he'd have a talk with Hanah.

Rawley walked into the kitchen. Wrapping muscular arms around the spunky firebrand that was his wife, Rawley nuzzled and kissed her neck.

Lacy leaned back into his embrace, Rawley could still set her insides on fire.

"I want you," he whispered.

"Now?" Lacy turned.

"Later, I want to make love to you all night long," he said, taking those delectable lips in his and kissing her thoroughly.

15

Lacy's arms slid around his neck. "Umm, that sounds like a plan," she said, kissing him back. "You better wash up, supper's almost ready."

"Yes, Ma'am." Releasing her, Rawley slapped her tight rump. His wife smiled.

* * *

Lacy glanced around the dinner table. Bill was twenty-two now. He wanted to be a Marshal like his adopted father. Rawley was teaching him the ropes. Bill had a quiet demeanor, much like Rawley. Bill was about six feet, two inches. Handsome, with dark brown hair and eyes with a medium build. Even though he had an easygoing personality, he still had no girlfriend. Angela, a girl he had fancied, married someone else and left town.

Lacy's eyes settled on Cotton. At thirteen, he still had that shock of white blond hair and jovial blue eyes. He had decided he wanted to be a lawyer when he got older. He always read any law book he could get his hands on. Cotton also had a wicked sense of humor and could debate anyone under the table, even Doc. He had become an apprentice to Adam Brinkhoff, a lawyer in town after school. For only thirteen, Cotton was one sharp little bugger.

Yes, she was one lucky woman, Lacy decided, glancing around the table, listening to the happy banter. Her eyes settled on the man she loved so dearly. All of this would not have been possible if he had not forced her to face her past, teaching her how to live and love again. Lacy owed this man her life and she loved him dearly for that second chance he had given her.

Rawley caught Lacy's tender look and smiled at her. Lacy returned the smile.

"Hey, Punkin, you gonna teach me some of those moves you used on Dobie Litchfield today?" Cotton asked.

Billy looked up from his second helping, "Yeah, how 'bout teaching me some of those moves, Punkin? Never know when they

16

might come in handy to a Deputy Marshal," he grinned.

Hanah continued to spread mashed potatoes inside a biscuit. She took her hand and smashed the top of the biscuit down on the potatoes. Taking a bite, she answered around a full mouth, "I might."

"Hanah, don't talk with your mouth full."

She swallowed twice before answering, "Yes, Daddy."

Gazing around the table at her brothers, Hanah said, "If you show me how to use a rifle, I'll teach you how to fight."

Rawley and Lacy cut a swift glance at each other hearing Hanah's remark.

"Honey, you're just a little too young to handle a rifle," Lacy said.

Her mouth full of more mashed potatoes and biscuit, she mumbled, "Am not." She glanced at her Daddy and quickly swallowed the food. She continued to look at her Mama, saying, "You knew how to use a gun when you were my age, why can't I?"

"I was fourteen when I learned how to use a gun and that was still too young."

Bail me out here, Lacy's eyes told Rawley.

His blue ones replied, *She's your child.*

Lacy's shot back, *She's yours too!*

She's got your temper, his eyes gleamed.

But you were the only one who could tame that temper, her eyes returned.

Rawley rolled his eyes and then settled them back on his wife. *Alright, Sunshine, but you're gonna owe me big time, tonight!* They said.

Lacy just let a smile slide across her face, exposing two dimples.

Clearing his throat, Rawley said, "Punkin, I think we need to have this conversation later, when you're older."

"But why, Daddy? Everyone else in this family knows how to use

17

a gun, 'cept me," Hanah argued.

"It's not exactly what a young lady would need to know right now," he returned.

"Why? Mama's a lady and she knows how to use a gun? Why can't I learn?" Hanah insisted.

Lacy rose, gathering the plates. She whispered in Rawley's ear, "Let's see how you get yourself out of this." She gave him a swift kiss on his shiny black hair.

Hanah piped up, "I bet I'd be good, too."

"I'm sure you would, Punkin. But, we'll talk about this later, okay?" Rawley glanced up as Lacy brought in an apple pie. She gave him a smug look. He sent one of his own blistering looks her way.

Lacy grinned back at him.

* * *

Sitting in her Daddy's lap, dressed in her nightgown, Hanah snuggled against her Daddy's chest. Rawley's arms were wrapped around her as one hand tangled and untangled itself through Hanah's copper curls.

Lacy loved these moments at the end of a day and never got tired of them. Hanah was really her Daddy's girl, following him everywhere and trying to mimic him. Just as Cotton used to do when he was younger.

"Daddy?"

"Hum?"

"Why do you call Mama, Sunshine?

Rawley glanced at Lacy and smiled. "Well, when I first met your Mama, she was as sour as a bucket full of lemons and acted like she had been eating them all her life."

Hanah sat up, "Did you, Mama?"

18

"No."

Rawley grinned, "So since she was so sour all the time, I just started calling her Sunshine. Now, she's the Sunshine of my life." His eyes glowed with love across at Lacy.

His look was making her insides flip-flop again. Oh, how she wanted this man tonight.

Lacy cleared her throat and said, "Honey, I think it's time you went to bed."

"Okay," Hanah replied, hopping off her Daddy's lap and then skipping up the stairs.

"I'll be right up to tuck you in," Lacy added.

Hanah stopped. "Why? I'm a big girl now, I can tuck myself in." She flicked a glance from one parent to the other. "Night," she said, skipping up the rest of the steps.

When he heard a door close softly from upstairs, Rawley stood and walked over to Lacy. Removing the sock she was darning from her hands and laying it aside, he pulled her into his arms. Speaking over the top of Lacy's own copper curls, he said, "She's got your independence."

"She's got your intelligence and I think your intuitiveness," Lacy replied.

Pushing Lacy's head back a tad, he gazed into her eyes, the ones he'd grown to love so very much, "Just like Fancy, the best of both Sire and Dam...huh?" He grinned.

Wrapping arms around his neck, Lacy kissed him deeply for her answer. Pushing herself away from the man who could still turn her world upside down, she whispered in that soft, husky voice of hers, "I've got to do the dishes." She turned and began heading toward the kitchen.

Reaching for his wife, Rawley surprised her by swinging her into his arms. "Hang...the dishes!" his voice harsh with emotion as he strode toward their bedroom. "We got more important things to do...than the damn dishes." And with that, he kicked the door shut to their bedroom with the heel of his boot.

19

* * *

Their bodies reflecting the heat of passion, Rawley and Lacy remained entwined. Rawley's fingers continued playing with Lacy's braid. Abruptly, she sat up and asked, "Does it bother you that I couldn't give you more babies?"

Taking that copper rope, he twisted it around his finger. Sliding his hand down the braid, it stopped at the end where red-gold feathers lay outside of her constant braid resting against her stomach. His hand gathered the feathers and lightly brushed them across Lacy's breast. Rawley smiled when she gasped. "Sunshine, I figured God gave us all we could handle with Hanah. And no...it doesn't bother me. We have a houseful with the boys." And with that he pushed her against the bed clothes and began making love to his wife, again.

Chapter Three

Cody Brown rested his forearms on the scarred counter in Shemwell's Mercantile. His hands lightly clasped together as he watched Ezra Shemwell fidget nervously, pacing back and forth across the open double doors of his store as he waited on the stage. Ezra's finger reached between his neck and collar and attempted to loosen the restrictive material. Often he'd roll his shoulders back as he straightened himself tugging here and there on the new coat that Lydia, Cody's wife, had made him. Then he would walk over to the looking glass, hands smoothing down his thick brown hair, one last time *again*. Cody grinned.

Glancing over at the clock hanging on the wall, Cody noted a half hour remained before Ezra's bride arrived from Medicine Bow along with her son and luggage. *If Ezra lasts that long,* he thought, noting the beads of sweat glistening across the man's forehead. *Why, he's as nervous as a long-tailed cat in a room full of rocking chairs.*

Stepping from behind the counter, Cody walked into Ezra's living quarters. Glancing around, he noticed how pristine the rooms were. Even the wood floors shined with the wax Ezra had vigorously rubbed into them.

Plucking up a glass and the bottle of rye Ezra kept in the cabinet, he walked back into the store. Standing behind the counter once again, the glass tapped the wood. The cork squeaked as Cody twisted it out of the bottle. Amber liquid splashed into the glass. Replacing the cork, it squeaked again. Cody pushed the tumbler toward the outer edge of the counter, saying, "Ezra...come swill some of this down your throat."

Ezra flicked a gaze at his business partner, then at the glass of rye. He walked toward it and then slowed his pace. Throwing his hands up in a stopping motion, Ezra backed off. "No...No," he began, "I don't want the smell of liquor on me. I don't want Beth thinking she's marrying a drunken store keeper." Gesturing toward the glass, Cody said, "You're losing it Ezra. It'll settle your nerves."

Brown eyes snapped, "Well...it ain't everyday an old fart like me gets the chance to marry for the first time!"

Cody rolled his eyes and sighed while scratching his head, "Suit yerself, Ezra."

Chapter Four

It is beautiful out here, Beth Hudson thought as she gazed out the window of the stagecoach. Every bone in her body ached from the constant swinging and swaying of the leather braces as the coach bounced and clattered along the dusty road. *Nothing but wide open spaces...and loneliness...and dust. So much dust,* she thought, as her fingers continued to caress her sleeping son's hair.

Beth Hudson had been a widow for three years. Her husband had been killed in a card dispute. *Aces and Eights,* they'd called it. She didn't know what that meant and didn't care to. She'd scrambled trying to make ends meet while taking care of her son and paying off her husband's gambling debts. After receiving her teaching certificate, Beth Hudson took a position in the St. Joe School District in Missouri. The pay wasn't much, but she and Ben had survived.

Reading the *St Louis Chronicle* one day looking for part-time work to help pay the bills, Beth noticed the ads placed by women looking for husbands, as well as men looking for wives. One read; *Good husband wanted: pretty-looking 24 year old wants to move west. Can cook, clean, sew. Not afraid of hard work. Send inquiries to...*

The ad planted a seed in her mind that had set her plan in motion. Beth Hudson wasn't looking for love; she'd made that mistake once and wouldn't fall into that trap again. No. The only reason she was marrying Ezra Shemwell was purely for the economics of the union. However, that would forever remain a secret she would keep to herself.

Chapter Five

Metal rimmed wheels clattered, accompanying the rocking motion of the stage as it crossed the wooden bridge over White River. The sudden noise woke Ben Hudson. He sat up and rubbed his eyes with the heel of his hands. Peeking out of the open square space the stage line called a window, he asked, "We almost there, Mom?"

Beth smiled at her ten-year-old son, "I sure hope so. I don't know how much longer I can stand this coach."

Ben gave her a toothy grin, returning his attention to looking out the window.

The driver began slowing the three teams as the coach pulled into the outskirts of White River. Marty Abrams juggled and pulled back on six reins, three to each hand as he stuck his boot into the loop of rope controlling the brake. Slowly pressing the brake, he called out to his lead team, yelling, "Ho...Bob. Ho...Bill."

Marty slowed the team down more and the stage pulled up next to the steps of Shemwell's Mercantile. The thick brown powder swirled around the coach in a dusty fog. Beth coughed as the swirling mass filled the coach. It continued floating, reaching across the walk and steps, covering the mercantile storefront and settling into the cracks and crevasses of the walk before dissipating.

The driver leaned down from the seat, directing his words toward the two passengers in the coach, saying, "White River...Ma'am."

Hearing the stage clatter from up the street, followed by Marty's raucous hollering at the team, Ezra's eyes grew round as the metal wheel rims of the coach. Ezra stepped to the counter in his store and reached for the glass of rye. Picking up the glass, he poured the amber liquid down his throat. He coughed, then swiped the back of his hand across his mouth. As he moved toward the open double doors, Cody watched him and smiled.

Opening the opposite side door of the coach, Ben Hudson hopped down first. Sharp brown eyes gazed around his new home. White River had one street. New buildings were mixed in with the old. One building was encased in red brick, but the rest were clapboard siding or logs. A large tree sat by the brick building, while a smattering of smaller trees surrounded the livery and pens. A sign above the stable's open sliding door identified the building. Ben could see the saloon. That was one place he planned on exploring. He'd never been in a saloon before. The log building across the street said Marshal's Office. He'd have to explore that too. He'd never been in a jail before, either.

Ben was a medium framed young lad with brown hair that accented his square face and sharp pointed chin. A coat covered the cream colored muslin shirt his mom had made for him. The shirt was tucked into dark blue britches. He smiled, pleased with his new home. The town looked just like Ned Buntline described in his dime novels. Jamming hands into his britches' pockets, he rocked back and forth on his heels. Ben knew he was going to like it here.

Taking a deep breath, Ezra slowly descended the steps. Peering cautiously inside the window of the coach, he gazed at the woman sitting on the wooden seat. His bride-to-be, Beth Hudson, was dressed in a grey traveling suit. Kidskin gloves encased her hands. A triangular grey felt hat perched jauntily on shiny dark brown hair, complementing her ensemble. *She's pretty,* Ezra thought. Opening the door and clearing his throat, he held out his hand, "Miz Hudson? I'm Ezra."

Beth gazed at the man whose hand was waiting to help her down. She nodded, greeting him, "Mr. Shemwell." Beth liked what she saw. Brown hair with a touch of grey barely covered her future husband's ears. Brown eyes gazed out of a pleasant face, which continued to carry a questioning look as he waited on her to take his hand.

Delicately placing her hand in his, Beth stepped from the coach. Gazing around White River, Beth noted the dusty single street the town boasted. *Dust, dust everywhere,* she thought as she absentmindedly brushed the powder that had accumulated on the sleeves and skirt of her grey suit. Beth was accustomed to the cobblestone streets of St. Joe with it's green vistas. A trunk landed with a thud next to Beth causing her to jump. More dust rose into the air. Another bag landed next to it. *More dust,* she signed inwardly.

Mike hollered into the kitchen of his saloon, "Maddie! The stage is here...we need to go welcome Ezra's bride!"

Coming to stand in the doorway, Maddie replied, "Aye...ya don say." Fingers reached up and began tucking frizzy curls behind her ears, "Let me chust freshen up a bit."

Mike touched her arm, making Maddie turn back toward him. "Nah...you're beautiful, chust the way, ya are," he assured her.

Already rosy cherubic cheeks turned brighter as green eyes twinkled, "Ach...Mr. Stewart. Ye do have a way wit words."

Mike grinned and taking her hand, the pair headed to greet Ezra's bride.

Standing in the door of his office, Rawley leaned against the jamb and watched as folks came out of their businesses and converged on the coach, welcoming the passengers to White River. He even observed old Miz Birdy Dawson among the welcoming town folk.

Glancing over his shoulder, he directed the words at his daughter, "C' mon, Punkin, let's go welcome the newest residents to White River." With that, Rawley stepped through the doorway and down the steps.

Hanah dropped her pencil and slid off the desk chair. It didn't squeak as it usually did. Hanah didn't weigh much more than a thimble. She ran, jumping over the steps, then catching up with her Daddy, she took his hand. Glancing down, Rawley smiled.

When Rawley and Hanah arrived, Ezra had already begun making introductions. Spying Rawley, he said to Beth, "And this is our town Marshal, Rawley Lovett, and his daughter Hanah."

Two fingers brushed the brim of his felt hat. "Ma'am," Rawley said. "I hope you enjoy living in our fair little hamlet," adding as an afterthought, "And congratulations. Ezra is a fine man and runs a good business."

Beth just nodded, overwhelmed by the town's exuberant welcome.

Letting go of her Daddy's hand, Hanah wandered over to stand next to the boy whose hands were stuck in his pants' pockets. Blue eyes framed in long red-gold lashes drifted up and down the length of the boy, scrutinizing him. Finally sticking freckled hands into her own pockets, mimicking the boy, she sidled closer saying, "My name is Hanah Marie Lovett. What's yours?"

The boy glanced at the girl whose height was the same as his. *Boy...oh...boy,* he thought. His mind began conjuring up the mischief he could get into with that bright red pigtail swinging down the girl's back, as well as words he could say to tease her about all those freckles. But he came back to earth, minding his manners as his Mom would expect him to do. "Uh...Ben...Ben Hudson."

Chapter Six

Supper time was the silent affair it had become during the short time Ezra and Beth had been married. Ben looked at his Mom, then Ezra and back down at his plate as he pushed the food around on it. Finally giving up Ben asked, "Mom..can I be excused?"

Without glancing up Beth automatically said, "May I..." then looked at her son. "You have barely touched your meal..." her hand reached out to touch his forehead. Ben shied away from her touch. "I'm not hungry," he replied.

Ezra remained quiet, watching.

Beth gave her son a shrewd gaze. "I suppose you want to go find that Lovett girl?"

Ben shrugged his shoulders.

"I'll not have you associating with that...that heathen!"

Ben spoke quietly, "Hanah is not a heathen, Mom. She's nice and so is her Mom and Dad."

"Ha!" Beth intoned disgustedly. "That family has the social graces of a...a cow!"

"Beth..." Ezra's voice carried a warning, "I'll not have you speaking ill about my friends."

Narrowing her eyes, Beth taunted her husband, "You call a half-breed a friend?"

"That's enough, Beth," Ezra responded.

Ben's eyes bounced from one parent to the other.

Beth puffed out like a mating prairie chicken. "I have never seen the likes...until I moved to this town. In Boston and St. Joe everyone knew their place! This is just ludicrous...half-breed's marrying white women. Toting weapons like gunslingers...and the children that are spawned are good for nothings...."

Ezra slammed his fist on the table, dishes rattled and jumped as did Beth and Ben. "That's enough of your foul mouth, woman! You will not speak about the citizens of this town like that ever again!" Ezra leaned threateningly toward his wife, his eyes sparking with anger. "Do you understand me...Beth?"

Continuing to stare boldly back, Beth could barely contain her rage at the man she married. "You are rabble, scum and a poor excuse for a man...Ezra Shemwell!" With those words Beth threw her napkin on the table and rushed from the kitchen to the sanctuary of her bedroom.

Two sets of eyes followed her retreat, then refocused on each other.

Ezra breathed in deeply, "I'm sorry you had to see and hear that, Ben."

The boy shrugged. "Mom used to get that way before with my Dad, too. I guess that's why he drank so much and gambled away our money. But I was littler then and it used to scare me so bad, I would take a pillow and cover my head, hiding in the closet so I couldn't hear her screaming at him. And then someone killed him saying he cheated at cards or something," Ben finished quietly.

"I'm sorry, son."

Shrugging again, Ben answered Ezra, "T'wern't your fault. Pops? Something is wrong with Mom...don't 'cha think? I mean...I've never seen her like this before...even with Dad..."

Lifting the cup to his lips, Ezra swallowed bitter, now cold coffee. Replacing the cup in the saucer with a slight clink, he gazed at Ben. He had come to like the boy, hell he might even love the kid as far as he knew. Ezra's eyes softened. "Son...why don't you go git yerself two pieces of stick candy and take one to Hanah...okay?"

Nodding, Ben slid off the chair, "Thanks, Pops."

Ezra smiled halfheartedly watching the boy scamper through the store and out the entrance. His eyes then turned toward Beth's closed door; sighing heavily, he rose.

* * *

Agitatedly Beth marched back and forth across her small room, her mind flicking images so fast, she felt blind and confused. Finally she stopped in front of the one window, staring through the lace curtains into nothing. Absentmindedly, her fingers began caressing the material. Her mind calmed down going back to when she had first met Rod Hudson. He was a dashing young man who was attending Boston College at the time, studying finance, hoping to manage his own bank one day. They fell in love, married and had a son. Beth loved the city of Boston. The high society they were a part of, the parties, the nice flat they lived in. Then an opportunity presented itself to Rod to manage a bank in St. Joe, Missouri. So they moved. St. Joe's society was nothing like Boston's, but they were still able to move in the right circles which Beth treasured. Then Rod seemed to change. He began staying out later and later at the gentlemen's clubs, coming home drunk. He began gambling more and more until he lost his job at the bank.

Then suddenly Rod was killed in a card dispute. She hated him for losing his position with the bank, leaving her and Ben no better then the gutter-swipes she'd see in the streets. They had to find cheaper quarters in a section of town Beth despised, but she had no choice. The building stank of rancid cooking smells all day and night. The street and alleyway were littered with trash.

Her mind came back to the present. She thought by coming west and marrying a mercantile owner, she would regain her prestige within a community along with no more money worries. Beth's mind gritted at how foolhardy her idea had been. Instead of looking at the beauty, the wide open spaces and a good man by her side, Beth chose to focus on all the negatives. *Not a green patch in town,* she thought. *Either constantly blowing dust or mud when it rains.* There was no in-

31

between. Her mind flicked back to the green vistas of St. Joe when she and Ben would stroll through the parks on a Sunday afternoon, stopping often to speak with others doing the same. *Other folks who had class, not the animals I have encountered here,* she thought disgustedly. Beth's mind tumbled, looking for a solution out of her predicament, the nails of one hand digging into the soft flesh of her palm.

The abrupt knock on her door had Beth whirling.

Ezra cracked it open and announced, "Beth, we need to talk."

She stood rigid, her lace-edged handkerchief now clutched tightly in her hands. Beth answered curtly, "You may come in."

Pushing the door open further, Ezra stepped inside Beth's room.

He gazed at the woman he had brought to White River, hoping for a harmonious union and a long marriage. He took his vows seriously and had waited a long time to say them. He wouldn't give up easily.

Ezra caught Beth's look of pure venom spouting poison through the air at him. He cleared his throat. Before he came into the room he knew exactly what he wanted to say...but now the words seemed to have flown from his mind. He stuck his hands in his pockets and shuffled his feet, taking a few steps closer.

Picking up on that, Beth spoke acidly. "I was taken in by your elegant letters. I thought I had found someone to carry on intelligent conversations with. I was a fool to believe your letters. You seem to be able to talk your *friends* just fine about the weather, their crops or cattle. But that's all. Why you don't even get a decent newspaper in this town from other cities." She threw one last dig, "You're a small-minded man, Ezra."

His lips drew into a tight line. "You sure do know how to talk down to folks Beth, since I can't see where you're any different then any of the good folks around here."

Beth gasped as her mouth dropped.

"I'm a quiet man, Beth. I'm not good with words, especially with a woman. Yeah...I pen a fair hand, but there hasn't been much time for

32

me to develop the so-called talking skills you think I need. I've been building my business and it is flourishing." Ezra leaned forward, "Something you choose not to recognize." Taking a few steps closer, Ezra continued, "You could have a good life here Beth, if you'd jus' stop all this foolishness. I'd do anything in my power to see that you and Ben were well taken care of..." he trailed off seeing the expression on Beth's face.

"Foolishness? You call my actions foolish?" The handkerchief in her hands became even more twisted. "I can't even get a good cup of tea! Foolishness? The children in this town have never seen what a globe looked like until I came! Foolishness? This place...this town is no better than some savage Indian camp!"

"Beth...think about what you are doing to Ben! He loves it here!"

"Ha! Cavorting with that Lovett girl? I didn't raise my son to play with a half-breed's daughter!"

"That's enough, Beth...The folks in this town is good folks, they'll do anything to help a neighbor...Why when that bastard almost burnt the town down some years ago...we all's pitched in to make it right again," Ezra said.

"You can't even speak proper English," Beth returned.

"Maybe not...but I get my point across. It's no use trying to talk to you...one of these days you're gonna fall off that high and mighty pedestal and break an arm or a leg. When that happens I won't come to pick you up." Ezra strode toward the doorway.

Beth spoke harshly. " I hate this town. I hate the people in it and I hate you."

Turning halfway around, Ezra gazed at Beth. "I'm sorry it wasn't what you expected, Beth. But it's the best we got."

33

Chapter Seven

Two child-like voices giggled, hunkered down behind the barrels on the porch of the Mercantile's store. A pair of blue and brown eyes smiled with mischief at each other. "Do you have them?" Hanah whispered.

Ben nodded and whispered back, "You get the matches?"

Hanah nodded.

The two youngsters crawled on their hands and knees under the Mercantiles big window, moving toward the open doors. Hanah pulled the matches out of her shirt pocket as Ben pulled the firecrackers out of his britches. Holding two up, he waited on Hanah to light them. When she lit the two firecrackers, he immediately threw them through the store's open doorway. Two faces peeked around the door jamb. Soft giggles erupted, waiting.

POP-POP!

Quickly, they lit two more, throwing those through the doorway.

POP-POP!

Ezra flew out of his storeroom, "Damn...kids," he muttered. The two mischief makers knelt beside the doorway fiddling with more firecrackers. The store-keep surprised them with his appearance. The kids tried to run, but Ezra was quicker. Grabbing the collars of the two culprits, he yanked them into a barely standing position with his strength. Hanah and Ben's legs danced in the air, twisting this way and that, in an attempt to get away. Settling their feet back on the walk, Ezra hauled them to the edge of the steps. Hanah and Ben were no match for Ezra's muscular hands and forearms.

He bellowed across the street toward the Marshal's office, "Rawley Lovett? Come Git...Yore...Damn...Kid!"

Rawley sat straighter in his chair hearing Ezra yell from the store.

He'd heard the firecrackers going off, but hadn't paid much attention to them. Now looking through the office window, he saw Ezra had corralled Hanah and Ben by the scruffs of their necks. The three of them were standing on the edge of the walk. The kids kept twisting in Ezra's clutch. *Ezra looks mad enough to spit nails,* Rawley thought. Sighing wearily, he stood and reached for his hat, jamming it on his head and out the door he went, making tracks across the street.

Hanah looked at Ben.

Ben looked at Hanah.

Ben nodded at Hanah and they both aimed a solid kick at Ezra's legs.

Yowling and releasing the two mischief-makers, Ezra hopped from one leg to the other rubbing his shins.

Hanah went one way, while Ben went the other.

Picking up his pace, Rawley hollered at Ezra, "I'll get Hanah! You get Ben!" Rawley saw Hanah skedaddle between the buildings so he headed in that direction.

A half-hour later with no sign of the kids, Rawley whipped off his hat in frustration, his fingers combing his dark hair. Ever since Ben Hudson had hit town, he and Hanah had formed an alliance that created holy mischief throughout the town of White River. Together they were worse than the tales he'd heard about preachers' kids. *My black hair is gonna turn white as Cotton's if Hanah keeps this up,* he thought. Turning, he rammed the hat back on his head as he strode toward the office. *I'll deal with those two later.*

About that time he heard the sound of child-like soft whispers and giggles. Tilting his head to the side, Rawley listened for the direction of the smothered sound. Glancing toward some large wooden crates, he walked towards them. The whispers were more pronounced now. Pushing his hat back on his head, he tucked a thumb into a back pocket as he pondered the situation. A smile spread across his features as a thought entered his brain. *I'll teach those two a lesson...* Whipping out his pistol, he sprung around the crate as he pointed the muzzle at two very surprised kids.

"All right...you two varmints...come outta there," Rawley growled.

Hanah's mouth dropped and then snapped shut at the surprising appearance of her Daddy. She swallowed, cutting a look at Ben. Her friend's eyes remained focused on the barrel of the pistol staring him in the face. Eyes round as saucers and his mouth open wide enough to catch flies, he didn't move.

Stepping back, Rawley gestured with his weapon, "You two varmints...crawl outta there." When the partners in crime continued to stare at the Marshal holding a gun on them, he bellowed, "Move it!" The two jumped, stumbling over each other in their hurry to obey. They stood in front of the Marshal and waited. Hanah knew she was in big trouble now. She wasn't sure about Ben, but he looked terrified as his eyes remained fixed on the muzzle of the gun her Daddy held.

Continuing in his gruff tone, Rawley ordered, "Turn around." After cutting each other a swift glance, they did. "Hands in the air!" Four skinny arms stuck themselves into the air reminiscent of fence posts leaning against the sky. "Now...march," he said. Four legs began an awkward high-step toward the street. Rawley did his darnedest to prevent a grin from spreading, but it didn't work.

Coming out of Ezra's Mercantile and carrying a paper sack of flour, Lacy stopped and did a double take of the scene before her. Her mouth dropped open as she stared in disbelief. The sack of flour slipped through her hands, splattering her britches, boots and the walk with it's fine white dust. Bewildered, Lacy couldn't believe her eyes. Her husband with his pistol drawn, was marching their daughter and Ben Hudson with their skinny arms stretched to the sky toward the jail. Her eyes turned venomous, narrowing into slits. She threw a black look at her husband.

Catching that familiar look from his peripheral vision, Rawley gave a slight shake of his head and threw one of his own dark looks at his spit-fire. *Don't you, dare, Sunshine.*

Lacy's mouth clapped shut.

Tossing his wife a wink, he smiled as four short legs continued their high-step march toward the jail, skinny arms reaching for the sky.

Chapter Eight

Camping in a watershed about ten miles from White River, Wyoming, Big Joe Kannon and his boys finally made it into the area. Taking a sharp bone from the leg of a prairie chicken they'd eaten, Big Joe picked at his tarnished, tobacco stained teeth, his mind on the next big payout. He hadn't finished working all the details out in his mind yet. So, he kept pickin' and thinkin'. Tall and lanky, Lenny squinted the permanently crossed eye at his boss, then slammed his tin cup against a rock, hoping to make Kannon jump with surprise. "Damn it! Kannon! When we's gonna move?"

His head swung around, hearing the tin ping against rock. Kannon's muddy eyes tapered drawing the dirt encrusted crows feet together as a line of bushy brow merged into an overhang. Lenny Jackson remained the hot-head in his boys. He'd had to put Lenny in his place several times...hard, in the past. *Might have ta do it 'gain,* Kannon thought. Out loud, his gravelly voice replied, "When...I'm ready."

"Shee-yut," Lenny mouthed, making rustling noises. Quiet anticipation filled the air as Kannon's other men waited. As Lenny picked up his saddle and began moving toward his horse, he announced "I'm goin' ta town, git me a couple of bottles."

Kannon pulled his pistol and fired a round at Lenny's boot heels. "Naw...ya ain't."

The saddle thudded against dirt as Lenny whirled, his weapon pulled, hand slamming the hammer back. He pointed the muzzle at Kannon. "Ya aiming fer a showdown, Kannon? I'd oblige ya...been wantin' ta git rid of ya fer a long time."

Muddy eyes narrowed further. He spoke to another of his boys, "Wheat...git them bottles I've been saving outta ma saddlebags,"

Kannon's eyes never left Lenny's for a second.

A grin busted out as Lenny put away his pistol and picked up his saddle. Walking back, he dropped the leather. "Now...yer talking ma kinda talk, Kannon," he said, reaching for his cup. He waited on the bottle that was being passed around.

* * *

A misty, half cloudy day followed eight men as they rode quietly into the town of White River. Eyes furtively skimmed the town's landscape under lowered brims of hats that had seen better days. Buckskin and dusters covered the backs of the various men riding except for one, who wore a moth-eaten buffalo hide. Lining up at the rails outside of Stewart's Saloon, leather creaked as they swung down. Boots thumped up the three steps then quieted as the men turned, gazing at the lack of activity within the one-street town. Seven sets of eyes swiveled toward their leader. Big Joe Kannon nodded toward the interior as his hand pushed at the bat-winged doors. Eight men walked into Mike's place.

Chapter Nine

The heady aroma of cinnamon teased her nose as Lacy slipped around the back of the business. She pulled the screen door open to Maddie's domain, the kitchen in the back of Mike's saloon. "Ohh...these smell wonderful...Maddie," Lacy said, when she picked up the box of cinnamon buns. "The Ladies' Aid Society really appreciates you making them for the bazaar."

"Ach...lass...t'wern't nuthin'," Maddie returned. Madeline Campbell had never rebuilt her Blue Bird Cafe after Lowell Taylor had destroyed it over eight years ago, preferring to work alongside Mike Stewart out of his saloon. This arrangement had worked out well; Maddie and Mike had unexpectedly fallen in love.

Backing into the saloon from the kitchen, Lacy added, "Many thanks...anyway, Maddie."

Turning and taking a few steps into the saloon, Lacy slowed as she caught the whiff of a long ago familiar odor. She glanced toward the bar. There, lined up like ducks in a row, were eight roughshod men, their bodies stinking like week old rotting elk carcasses in the heat of summer.

Mike looked her way and rolled his eyes toward the hole that remained in his ceiling that Lacy had put there ten years ago.

Catching Mike's glance, Lacy shifted the box, balancing it on one hand as the other touched the grip of her pistol. Her eyes narrowed when they traveled across the menagerie. Lacy found the one she remembered, the boulder-like man still wrapped in the ratty old buffalo hide. Her nose scrunched at the thought of wearing something that old and that stinky. She moved toward him. The still warm and fragrant box did nothing to erase the powerful assault on her senses as she rested the box on the bar. Breathing from her mouth to halt the flow attacking her nose, Lacy turned toward the stench. Her eyes tapered

41

even more taking in the man's different appearance from long ago. His grizzled mug now had a long, dirty grey beard, stained with tobacco juice. She wondered when he'd bothered to bathe last. The ratty buffalo hide had more bald patches on it, too.

Years ago when Big Joe Kannon came through White River, he'd been on the trail of the Dillard brothers, not realizing she and Rawley had caught them months before and had already claimed the bounty. He hadn't been happy with that news, but had left peaceably. Lacy wondered what he was doing in town this time.

Big Joe continued to watch the girl out of the corner of his eye. Finally turning, he allowed his muddy eyes to wander up and down the pretty redhead. The tin star remained pinned to a blue and cream-checkered shirt tucked into tan canvas britches. Sleeves rolled to her elbows revealed tan freckled arms. His gaze settled on the pistol belt notched around a trim waist with her weapon tucked under her left arm for a cross-draw.

Boldly staring back, Lacy's husky voice asked softly, "Mr. Kannon...what brings you back to White River?"

Instead of answering her, his mind continued tallying up the bills he could stuff into his pockets selling this one across the border. But his plans didn't include her.

"Mr. Kannon?"

Big Joe flicked eyes toward her, "Jus'...passin' through...sister. Jus' passin' through," he said. Turning away, he splashed more amber into his glass. Raising it, he poured the liquid down his throat.

Her eyes narrowed again, *Something's not right,* Lacy thought. A premonition had begun to grow, starting in her gut and flowing toward her shoulders, setting them to tingling along with the hairs on the back of her neck and arms. Lacy hadn't had that feeling in years but it was back now with these men. Her old bounty hunting sensations returned, making her body tense.

Leaning out and away from Kannon, Lacy's eyes traveled down the row of backs draped over Mike's bar swilling down the Kansas

42

Sheep Dip. *Rough and mean,* she thought. Leaning back in, her elbow rested on the edge of the counter. Her eyes flicked back to Big Joe Kannon, "Well...finish up here, and get whatever supplies you need and move on." Picking up the box of cinnamon buns Lacy cut a glance at Mike then made a move toward the door.

Turning, Kannon's muddy eyes followed her. Resting his spine against the edge of the bar and placing his elbows on the top, he challenged, "That a threat...sister?"

Stopping and slowly facing the man, Lacy threw her now famous blistering look his way. The one that would make a skunk roll over and play dead. Kannon's brow inched up a notch.

Mike rolled his eyes at Lacy's threatening glint.

Her soft throaty voice replied, "That's up to you, Mr. Kannon." And with that, Lacy pushed through the bat-winged doors and walked down the steps.

Muddy eyes narrowed. *Bitch*, he thought. Turning, Kannon spoke to Mike, "Fill us up, barkeep."

The cork squeaked as Mike did as he was told.

* * *

Instead of heading to Liv's house with the cinnamon buns like she promised, Lacy hurried toward the Marshal's office.

As the latch clicked, Rawley looked up. A big smile busted out as he saw his bride walk through carrying a big box. To Rawley, Lacy would always be his bride, no matter how many years they were married - almost ten now. He softly said, "Hi."

Usually when Rawley said that soft 'Hi', it would make her insides melt, but not today. Right now, she had something else on her mind. Looking around and continuing toward the desk she asked, "Where's Billy?"

Rawley watched as Lacy laid the box on his desk. As the fragrant smell of cinnamon teased his nose, his hands moved toward the box.

"No...you don't," she said, slapping his hands away. "That's for the Ladies' Society Bazaar." She asked again, "Where's Billy?"

Since he couldn't have a cinnamon bun, Rawley reached for his redhead instead. He pulled her into his lap and plastered her lips with a kiss. Leaning back, he gazed into that cute as a speckled pup face, saying, "I sent him to exercise the harses."

Lacy pushed herself off his lap, she had something important to say. "Oh..." She plunged into her next statement, "Guess who's back in town?"

Instead of answering her, his eyes flicked toward the tantalizing box on his desk. He reached again, pulling it closer. Lacy picked up the box and walked over to the table about ten feet away. She set it down way out of his reach this time. Rawley sighed.

Turning, she poked fingers down the back pockets of her britches, saying, "Guess...who's back in town?"

With his mouth watering at the thought of one of Maddie's cinnamon buns, Rawley had a hard time focusing on what Lacy asked. "What?"

Lacy rolled her eyes and repeated for the third time, "Guess...who's back in town?"

Sighing noisily again at the loss of a cinnamon bun, he asked, "Who?"

"Big Joe Kannon".

Black brows drew together, pulling a frown across his features. "What?"

Rolling eyes again, Lacy said in an irritated tone, "Sheesh...Lovett! I need to take you to Doc and have him clean out your ears. I said, Big Joe..."

Waving a hand, Rawley interrupted, "I heard ya...I heard ya the first time. I'm jus' surprised...is all."

Walking over, Lacy rested her hands on the back of the chair by his desk. The one she used to sit in long ago. "What are you going to do?" she asked.

Glancing at his wife, Rawley said, "Nuthin'...least-ways not yet."

Stepping around the chair, she sat. Her hands resting on her knees, she leaned forward and narrowed her eyes. "Seems like, I 'member you saying that once before. Then Jack Drake blew a hole through your shoulder."

He shrugged. Leaning back in his chair, it squeaked. Rawley laced hands across his still flat stomach. "That was different...I know Kannon," he said.

Lacy hissed, "Like...hell, Lovett!

Silence permeated the office as husband and wife faced off against each other.

Squeezing her eyes shut, Lacy let fly with a loud "Pffttt," as she flopped back in the chair. Taking a calming breath, her eyes opened, "Something is different this time...he...he's too, cocky."

Tilting his head, Rawley replied, "He's always been cocky."

Lacy shook her head. "No...no, it's different. Maybe...cocky isn't the right word." Freckles scrunched. "I can't put my finger on it...but, well...I felt like I was back on the trail, bounty hunting again."

Rawley blinked. *That is news,* he thought. "Really?"

Lacy nodded, "Uh-huh...and he's got more men with him this time, too. There's eight of them all total."

"Where?"

Nodding over her shoulder, Lacy replied, "Mike's place. Swilling down that Kansas Sheep Dip you men like so much."

A grin popped out. The chair squeaked as Rawley rose, stepping over Lacy's legs stretched out in front of her. He bypassed the table with the cinnamon buns, giving them one last wistful glance. Rawley plucked his hat and hardware off the pegs and moved toward the door.

45

Settling his hat on his head, his hands buckled on the belt.

Watching those big feet step over her legs, a weird thought popped into her brain. How she loved the feel of his muscular legs wrapped around hers when they made love. Sitting straighter in the chair and tossing that thought out of her head. Lacy turned slightly, her elbow resting on the chair back as her words stopped him. "I love you, Rawley Lovett."

Another grin popped out. "I love you, too, Sunshine," Rawley replied, opening the door and then disappearing.

Lacy exhaled noisily. Pushing herself out of the chair, she mumbled, "Better get this box to Liv." Picking up the box her eyes settled on the rifle rack. Her head swiveled, glancing over her shoulder through the open door and then back at the rack.

The box slapped the table. Running to the desk, a drawer scraped open as she retrieved the keys. Running back to the gun rack, Lacy stuck the key in the lock, it snapped open with a click. The chain rattled as she pulled it through the trigger guards. Plucking Rawley's Henry from the mix, she ran back to the desk pulling another drawer open; it too scraped from lack of use. Lacy pulled a box of cartridges out and began loading the Henry while her mind chanted, *Load it on Sunday and fire it all week. Sixteen brass rim-fire cartridges, two for each man.* Lacy ran out the door and headed for the exterior stairs going to the second floor of the saloon. Mike added them after Lowell Taylor almost burned down the town a little over eight years ago. He wanted to make sure folks had a way off the second floor if something like that should ever happen again.

* * *

Stepping through the bat-wing doors of Stewart's Saloon, the stench slammed into Rawley like he'd crashed into a brick wall, settling over his senses like oil. Stopping, his look skimmed the bodies draped over the bar. Rawley's eyes caught Mike's.

The barkeep rolled his eyes, focusing them on the hole again in his ceiling.

Walking further into the saloon, Rawley kept his languid gate. Now he too, was beginning to get the same premonition as Lacy. The hairs began tingling on the back of his neck, setting him on edge. He shook it off momentarily as he stepped up to the bar.

Automatically, Mike reached under his counter for Rawley's earthenware mug. It tapped the wood slightly, the noise loud in the extreme quiet. Reaching for the constant carafe of coffee that sat on the edge of his bar, Mike filled the cup.

Bringing the mug closer to his lips, Rawley sniffed the pleasant aroma. Even that didn't hide the over-powering odor coming from the right of him. Setting the cup down, Rawley turned toward the stench. The stench turned toward him.

A speckled grey beard now covered the face of Big Joe Kannon, stained brown with tobacco drippings. Muddy eyes peeped from under a bristly overhang of brows. They grazed over a clean-shaven, lean jawed face carrying bright blue eyes that were just a tad bit too frosty, Kannon noted. "Lovett," he greeted.

"Kannon," the Marshal answered back. "What brings you back to White River?"

Turning and hunching boulder-like shoulders over his arms, dirty palms cradled his glass. Kannon replied, "Ya always wuz a nosy sum-bitch, Lovett."

"Protecting this town is always my business," Rawley replied. "State yours, Kannon."

His head slowly turned as he gave the lawman a long look before answering, "Boys an'...uh, me...plan on takin' a l'il veecation...'round here...been riding hard, the last few weeks."

Kannon had always been a side-winding sum-bitch, Rawley knew. Lying was his best trait, besides stinking up the air. Eyes narrowed at the man in the ratty buffalo hide. "This is my turf, Kannon," Rawley began. "Take your carcass and your seven hide-hunters and go stink

47

up someone else's turf."

Muddy eyes turned ugly. "Them's fightin' words, Lovett."

One black brow cocked. Rawley waited, his body tensing in anticipation of what might come next.

Joe gave his counterfeit grin instead showing stained yellow teeth. "But I ain't in the mood ta fite ya," his voice and eyes lied. "Jus' got back from across the border, haulin' merchandise to them greasers." He grinned when he heard his boys snicker.

Rawley gazed down the backs lined up at the bar like a row of ducks. These men were rough and mean, born to fight and drink bad whiskey. He cut a sharp look at Kannon. "You running guns?"

"Who me?" Kannon deadpanned. "Naw...jus' purty l'il trinkets for them folks down there to play with." His boys snickered again, Big Joe grinned.

A sudden chill ran down Rawley's back. *Trinkets...hell,* he thought. *He's slave running.* He held down the shiver, but it still circled around his ribs and landed with a thud in the pit of his stomach. Rawley quickly picked up his coffee and swallowed back a slug washing the bile back down. Now he knew the reason for Big Joe Kannon's return to his sleepy little hamlet. And Rawley Lovett didn't like it one bit.

Tip-toeing across the upstairs hallway, Lacy stopped and listened. She could hear Rawley's smooth caramel baritone and Kannon's gravelly one. Moving toward the steps going to the main floor of the saloon, Lacy quietly sat on a step, the barrel of the Henry slipped between the balustrades. Pressing the stock into her shoulder, she waited.

Cold eyes sent shards of steel into the air, focusing on muddy brown ones. "Think again, Kannon. If you plan on using this town as your next big payout," he threatened, "I'll track you down and gut you like a hog at killin' time...you murdering sum-bitch."

His fists balled, Kannon swung.

Already anticipating the move, Rawley ducked, throwing a hard punch to Kannon's gut as his left rounded and connected with the man's chin, sending him spinning into the bar.

An expletive escaped Kannon's mouth.

Mike pulled the sawed off scatter gun from under the counter. The metallic click of two hammers cocked, stopping the flurry of hands reaching for pistols that had begun at one end of his bar. "Leave 'em be, boys. This is between them two."

The seven glimpsed at the scatter gun, then back at Kannon facing off against the Marshal. They knew what kind of damage that bird shot would do at close range; they backed off.

A balled fist swung again.

Agility against Kannon's lumbering frame had Rawley ducking again. Throwing out one long leg, he caught Kannon's ankles, pulling his feet out from under him. Kannon crashed to the floor. He pulled his weapon before Kannon had a chance to pull his. Dragging in air, Rawley gritted. "Pack your carcass and your men and get out of here, Kannon. You went and picked the wrong town," he said quietly. His eyes flicked briefly at the seven men facing him. His peripheral vision saw Mike riding herd on the outlaws with his scatter gun. No match there once Mike emptied the gun. A thought flickered briefly in his mind, *I sure could use Lacy's back-up right about now.* He tossed that aside, refocusing back on Kannon, still sprawled in front of him.

Gripping the edge of the bar Kannon slowly hauled himself up. Muddy eyes took on a venomous appearance. Standing, his gravelly voice ground out, threatening the Marshal, "Ya ain't heerd the last of me, Lovett." Backing away toward the bat-wing doors, his hand fingered his jaw while his eyes never left Lovett's face. When his back touched the doors, he threw a nod over his shoulder, indicating to his boys to follow him. "Ya ain't gonna win tha next time, Lovett," Kannon warned. Turning, bat-winged doors squeaked when he shoved them. His boots thumped across the boards and down the steps. The doors squeaked with each passing of Kannon's men, finally falling silent.

Rawley followed. Standing at the doors, his height towered over the top. Hard eyes watched while Kannon and his boys quickly swung into their saddles, then rode toward the outskirts of White River. Hoof beats clattered against the hard packed street, echoing off wooden buildings. Dust billowed and hung in the air a few moments before settling.

He exhaled slowly over the doors as his Colt whispered lightly against the leather, returning to its boot. Turning, Rawley saw Mike pouring two glasses full to the brim of amber liquid. He headed in that direction. That's when he saw Lacy, carrying his Henry and walking down the stairs. Rawley walked over to her. Glancing up the steps, his eyes settled on his wife, "You were here...the whole time?"

She smiled mischievously. Lacy patted his cheek, "Yep. I was covering your butt, once again Lovett." And with that Lacy skipped down the rest of the steps. Throwing Mike a wave, she walked through the bat-winged doors as they squeaked again.

Rawley grinned.

Chapter Ten
September 1888

The toe of a boot scruffed the hard ground outside the schoolhouse, stirring up a little dust. Ben Hudson looked across at Hanah, "I'm bored."

Ben was already tired of school. And what made it doubly hard was the fact that his Mom, Beth Shemwell was the teacher. She expected him to set the example for the other kids, always having the right answers when she called on him in class. Things weren't so hot at home right now either. The tension between his Mom and Ezra had grown to the point you could slice it with a knife like slicing through thick, creamy butter. That's why he liked hanging around Hanah so much. He'd walk into her house and it was like walking into a breath of fresh air. Her house was a happy home...not like his house.

"Let's play hooky," Ben said abruptly. His spit-plastered brown hair fluttered just a tad in the light breeze. Brown eyes gazed intently into a freckled pink face. His hands jammed into neatly pressed blue britches, Ben's ten year old frame leaned forward, waiting on Hanah's response.

Blue eyes grew round as wheel hubs. "You gotta be kidding," Hanah said. "You 'member the trouble we got into with those firecrackers? Daddy 'd really box my ears if he caught us playing hooky."

Ben shrugged. His head turned as he watched the other kids playing on this warm September day as his mind was already thinking ahead. Ben's head swiveled back to focus on Hanah, "You still got the string and box of hooks in your pockets...we could go fishing?"

"Nooo..." Hanah answered. "Mama made me clean out my pockets this morning. Said I was jingling like Fancy's bridle."

Hands still jammed into his britches' pockets, Ben rocked back and forth on his feet. "If we're gonna play hooky...we need to hightail it before Mom rings the bell showing recess is over," he said.

Hanah looked over the playground. It was just too pretty a day to be cooped up in a stuffy classroom. Glancing at Ben, she grinned and nodded.

Ben grinned back.

Emily Harrison looked up when she saw Ben and Hanah tear around back of the schoolhouse, disappearing into the brush. She continued pushing Emma Sue in the swing, thinking as she did so she'd have to tell Miz Shemwell those two went off to play hooky again. She sighed heavily, wishing she had the guts to pull some of the stunts those two did.

Chapter Eleven

Kannon knew that getting back at Rawley Lovett and his redheaded deputy after all these years was some reward. This was gonna be his biggest payout yet, capturing all the kids from the schoolhouse to sell to Del Rio. Yellow teeth showed themselves, *It was payback time.* Kannon ground out in his gravelly voice, "Time to move...boys. Git them mules hitched ta the wagon and saddle up," he said. "We's gonna kidnap us a passel of kids."

* * *

Giggling and laughing at their freedom, Ben and Hanah tore through the underbrush on their way to the river to spend the afternoon skipping stones across it's rippling, sun-drenched waters.

An arm suddenly snatched Hanah around her waist as a hand clapped over her mouth, stifling her surprise. Glancing around, she saw the same thing had happened to Ben. Both she and Ben struggled against their captors until she heard a gruff voice say, "Back to tha schoolhouse boys...we gotta collect the rest of them kids."

* * *

Beth Shemwell's toe tapped impatiently against the planked flooring as she glared across the faces of her students. Ruler slapping angrily against her hand, Beth sent a cold look toward Cotton. "Where's your sister, Howard?"

Not flinching a lick, Cotton returned her frosty look, giving a shrug for his answer.

Beth opened her mouth to say something, when the door of the schoolhouse shattered, tearing itself off the frame and settling with a soft whump against the floor. Six men filed through the busted doorway, pistols drawn, led by one wooly mammoth holding a bead on her and her students. Screams erupted as bodies half rose from their seats, shoes scraped against the floor as books were dumped from desk tops.

Dobie Litchfield rose from his seat muttering, "What the hell...."

Beth jumped back from the abrupt invasion. Her heart climbed into her throat cutting off her screams, her face paling to rice powder.

Girls screamed again, forming a wave of bodies pushing and shoving toward the front door. That exit was quickly blocked by a man with his pistol drawn. The girls screamed louder and backtracked to the center of the room, their eyes reflecting terror as the pistol threatened them.

"I want quiet," a gravelly voice bellowed. He waved his pistol at everyone in the room. "I mean it," he barked. Abruptly the screams died down to soft whimpering sounds. "I want my Mama..." one little girl hiccuped, crying.

"Shad-up!" Snapped Kannon.

Beth tried to say something but sick with fear, no words would come. Her face pinched white as she plastered herself against the slate board, smearing the chalk lessons.

Cotton's heart was in his throat when he heard boards creak. His head swiveled toward the sound. Two more men had walked through the fractured doorway, one holding a squirming Hanah and the other, Ben. Cotton's lips formed a tight line.

The men dropped the two kids. They landed with a thump, arms and legs tangling with each other. Scrambling up, they ran to Cotton. He wrapped protective arms around them both.

Realizing she still held the ruler, Beth struck the man closest to her, leaving a welt. Big Joe spun facing the schoolmarm, backhanding her hard and sending her to the floor. Staring at the sprawled woman

54

weeping and holding her bruised face, "That wuss the wrong thang ta do...sister," his gravelly voice threatened her.

Tears running down her face, shaking hands tried to brush them away. Beth turned slightly to stare at the gun then back to the man's angry face. "Who...who...What do you want?"

Big Joe roughly pulled her to her feet.

Beth struggled against his grip. "You're hurting me, let me go..."

"You sit...sister," he said, shoving Beth into her chair. "And not a peep outta ya...or I'll kill ya where ya sit."

Kannon looked around. "Wheat...you and Jake tie 'er up...and gag 'er good."

"Let's take her, too...I ain't had no fun in a good while," Jake said.

Beth's eyes grew round with fear at what Jake was implying. "No...you can't, the children...my husband..."

Jake laughed cockily. "Honey...I'd be a lot more fun than your husband." Hands found the base of her neck, making chills rattle down her back sending her body into tremors. Jake chuckled as he pulled her bun loose. Beth rose and Jake slammed her back in the chair. Grimy hands held her still. Beth tried to swallow but couldn't.

Muddy eyes roamed over the schoolmarm and then back to Jake. Finally saying, "Tie 'er and gag 'er."

"Awww...hell..."

"Shad-up, Jake!"

Kannon's eyes gazed over the frightened and still whimpering girls, the boys standing silently glaring at him. Absentmindedly he began totaling up the money he'd make off this haul. Fifty to a hundred per kid, except that bright redhead with the freckles standing next to the white-haired boy. Now that one he figured he could get at least two hundred for her.

Waggling his weapon at the kids, his gravelly voice ordered, "Ya'll kids line up now." The whimpering girls shuffled into a haphazard line. The boys remained where they were. "Quince, you and Dub, git that rope and tie 'em together."

The whimpers grew louder as Kannon's men began shoving the girls. Cotton's eyes settled on Thad, Chad and Dobie as he yelled, "Now!"

Thad and Chad lunged over the desks, toppling them in the process, arms stretched out as they attacked the men closest to them. Dropping them to their knees, the string of girls went down with the outlaws ending up in a tangle of rope, legs and arms. The girls screamed again. More desks clattered to the floor. Boots scuffled against the wood, umphs and grunts mingled with the swirling stench of week old elk carcasses in the heat of summer.

Dobie and Cotton dove after the tall, lanky man by the front door, knocking his feet out from under him. He yelled as both pounced on him, their fists landing blows. Ben Hudson didn't know what to do so he stayed hunkered down beside a desk, his brown eyes wild with fear. *Ned Buntline never said anything about stuff like this.*

Kannon shoved and stepped over the squirming bodies in the middle of the aisle. His gun barrel thumped the sides of Thad and Chad's heads, rendering them unconscious, they slumped into a pile. That same barrel thumped against the side of Cotton's and Dobie's heads. They too landed in a pile, unconscious.

Hanah became a miniature red tornado, yelling, "Don't you hurt my brother!" She plowed and pushed through the bodies in the aisle. Scrabbling up the side of Big Joe Kannon, her fingers like talons, she clawed onto his ratty coat. Her teeth latched on to his ear and she hung on.

"Ooowwwweee...git 'er offen me!" Kannon yelled. Whirling, he tried to shake off the little she-devil. Lenny scrambled, his pistol barrel landing across the top of Hanah's head. She slid unconscious to the floor with a thump.

Kannon's hand gingerly touched his ear. It was throbbing and hurt like hell. Pulling his hand away, he found blood drenching his hand. Looking down at the little firebrand, he dragged in air. He'd seen squirrels high-tail into trees, but he'd never had a human crawl up hi[m] like that kid did, latching onto his ear like a steel trap. The situatio[n] was not going according to his plan. He didn't expect the kids to figh[t] back. Air whistled as he sucked in more.

Beth sat tied securely to her chair, stinky rag stuffed into her mouth, bewilderment and fear flicking across her brown eyes.

As he sucked in more air his lungs whistled. "Awright...boys," he began. "We got them troublemakers under control. Finish tying 'em up and git them ta the wagon."

Someone grabbed Ben's arm pulling him up and over a desk, then shoved him toward the others. Rope lashed around his wrists.

Whimpers mingled with the quiet sound of boots and high-top shoes scuffling. Moments later, the other children were roped together, similar to a string of fresh caught fish. All were herded out the back door toward the brush. Two of his men carried the four unconscious kids, one under each arm like a sack of feed. Kannon slung the little redhead over his shoulder. As he walked to the door he cut a look at the schoolmarm, trussed up like a hog. Brushing dirt-crusted fingers across a hat as ratty as the buffalo hide he wore, he said, "Have a good day, Ma'am."

Beth Shemwell burst into tears.

ת
1

Chapter Twelve

Pulling the timepiece out of his britches' pocket, Ezra popped the cover open. He stared at the time, *5:15 PM.* Snapping the cover shut, he tucked the watch back into his pocket and wrinkled his brow thinking, *The kids must've done something really bad today for Beth to keep them this late.*

Lately it seemed their marriage had gone awry. Beth was constantly complaining about the dust, the chores, and even called the good folks of White River *animals*. She was always railing about something to him. Ezra wished now that he'd never asked her to marry him. More often than not, he didn't worry so much about himself as he did the boy Ben. No wonder the kid spent more and more time at the Lovetts' house, coming home only after darkness had settled and he knew his Mother had gone to bed. *If I had someplace else to go, I would too,* thought Ezra.

Standing on the steps of his store, Ezra squinted toward the direction of the schoolhouse. Hollering over his shoulder at Cody Brown inside he said, "I'm going ta the schoolhouse, see what's keepin' everyone."

Arriving in the school yard, Ezra Shemwell looked around and listened. The shadows of the schoolhouse and trees were longer now with the evening sun. *Nuthin',* he thought. *Nuthin', 'cept the evening doves and the quail callin' ta each other.* Quietly taking the steps, he stared at the door for a few moments, listening. *Too quiet,* he thought. Reaching for the knob and turning it, he pushed the door open. Ezra stopped short, staring at what once was a neat classroom, now turned disorderly. Desks over-turned, books and papers scattered across the floor, and not one child in evidence. Looking across the room, he spied Beth staring wild-eyed at him, bandana stuffed in her mouth and tied to her chair. Sprinting toward her, his hands quickly removed the bandana and began working the knots tying her to the chair, asking,

"Beth...what happened here? Where's the kids?"

"You bastard," were the first words out of Beth's mouth.

Ezra stepped back as if slapped.

Abruptly rising, she shook off the remaining lasso around her skirt and stepped over the coiled rope. Beth marched through the littered classroom toward the front door of the schoolhouse. She continued through the doors and down the steps. Ezra followed, asking again, "Beth...what happened? Where's the kids?"

She stopped in the middle of the school yard and whirled on him. Brown eyes wild with fear and anger, she screamed, "You bastard! You brought me to this God-forsaken wilderness, where people are animals. Those children, those hoodlums, are gone! They were taken by some wild men, stinking like they lived in the bottom of a privy!"

Taking her arm, Ezra steered her toward town. "We need to see Rawley."

Breaking Ezra's hold on her arm, Beth hissed at him like a rabid cat, "That sorry excuse for a peace officer? Ha!" Her voice came out guttural and bitter, "He can't even control his own daughter, she changed my sweet Ben into a miscreant just like her!"

Beth is losing it, she's finally cracked, Ezra thought. Taking her arm once again, he steered her toward the marshal's office.

Twisting out of his grasp, she shouted, "Don't you touch me...you bastard. This is all your fault," Beth sputtered.

Angry at Beth's continued use of the word *Bastard,* Ezra roughly took her arm and said, "We're talking to Rawley." His strength over-powering her, Ezra continued to drag Beth along toward the Marshal's office. But that didn't keep her mouth shut. Wild eyes gazed over the folks who had begun stopping and staring at Ezra and Beth. She shouted to them, "Your precious little angels...your children...your hoodlums..." Beth screeched, "...Are gone! Taken! It's all your fault for raising such animals...such hoodlums!"

Whispers began filtering through the bystanders with more coming out of their businesses and others stopping along the street to hear the shrieking going on.

Cody Brown came out of the mercantile and walked to the edge of the porch. His brown eyes squinted against the evening sun. Beth had become a little more crazy each day. But only he and Ezra knew about it. Cody didn't dare tell his wife Lydia as she would have spread it all over town. And he didn't want Ezra or Ben to have to put up with the pain of that. Still squinting against the glare, Cody watched Ezra drag Beth along, and he thought, *Beth must've snapped.*

Rawley and Bill heard Beth's ranting, too. Abruptly rising, they both exited the office and stood on the walkway. They watched Ezra drag Beth toward them, screeching and screaming unintelligible words.

Taking one look at Beth's wild appearance, Rawley told Bill, "Go get Doc."

Mike and Maddie, who were standing in front of the saloon, couldn't believe what their ears were hearing. "Taken?" Mike whispered. Maddie's cherubic cheeks abruptly turned the color of rice powder. Mike took Maddie's hand and they began running toward the Marshal's office.

Hearing the commotion, Luke came away from his bellows and walked to his stable door. He too, proceeded toward the crowd beginning to build in front of Rawley's office. Stopping abruptly, he returned to pick up his scatter gun in case it was needed.

Stepping aside, Rawley nudged his head, indicating that Ezra was to take Beth inside. Then turning back to the crowd encroaching on his office, Rawley held up his hand, stopping the incoming tide. "Wait here, folks. As soon as I figure out what this is all about, I'll come out and fill you in," he calmly stated. Rawley turned and shut the door on the rising voices of the growing crowd.

Ezra sat Beth in a chair at the table. She wrapped her arms around herself as if cold. Only a few quiet moments prevailed before she began rocking and caterwauling. Hearing the wailing rising reaching a crescendo, abruptly stopping and then beginning all over again, Rawley stepped closer to Ezra. Speaking over the wailing, he asked,

"What happened, Ezra?" Then his eyes refocused on Beth while he waited for Ezra to fill him in on Beth's distraught behavior. He continued to watch her rock back and forth, sending that high pitched wail echoing and bouncing off the log walls of his office. Rawley's gaze flicked to the store owner as he poked thumbs into his back pockets. As dark brows knitted together, he waited.

Ezra shrugged, his hands dropping from Beth's shoulders. He began, "The schoolhouse is a disaster...desks overturned...and no kids." Heaving air for his starved lungs, his stomach rolling like rocks in a barrel, he nodded at his wife, "Found her, trussed up and gagged...she said some men came in stinking like the bottom of a privy, and took the kids. That's all I know...Rawley."

Kannon! Sucking in air that seemed to have been siphoned from his lungs by Luke's bellows, Rawley's mind began churning with the fact that Kannon had taken the town's children. He was going to sell them as *trinkets* across the border into Mexico. He gagged, thinking of Hanah and the other little girls and of Lacy and what had happened to her as a young girl at the hands of a ruthless man. A weird thought flickered, *Skeletons...skeletons from the past,* thinking of Kannon and Justin Carrigan, Lacy's dead grandfather.

Refocusing on the hysterical woman sitting in his office, Rawley squatted in front of her and lightly touched her arm. "Beth?" Wild eyes stared back at him. Two hands shot out, gripping his throat, talon-like fingers dug into his skin, surprising Rawley that she was strong enough to choke off his air. She screamed at him, "You...you caused this!"

Rawley fell backwards, taking Beth with him.

Ezra quickly grabbed Beth as Rawley pried her fingers from his skin. Feet braced against the floor, Ezra pulled and pushed Beth back into the chair. He held her down.

Pulling his long frame upright, Rawley rubbed at the red marks he knew remained on his neck. "Doc 'll be here soon, to give her something."

Again, Beth began rocking and wailing in that sharp, piercing sound. It reminded Rawley of that ghostly wail one sometimes heard in the mountains when the wind picked up. That weird thought popped up again in his head, *Skeletons.*

Glancing up, Ezra saw the red fingerprints Beth had left on Rawley's throat. He spoke softly, "She's crazy, Rawley. She's been getting worser and worser here lately."

His eyes became sad, gazing at his friend. "I know, Ezra. I know," Rawley said softly. He'd overheard Hanah and Ben discussing the situation at Ben's house. He sighed inwardly: not everyone was as lucky in love as he and Lacy were.

A commotion outside had him dropping those thoughts. Doc's gruff voice came through the closed door. "Hear, now...you folks clear outta ma way...gotta 'mergency inside." Then a loud bellow, "I said...move!"

Rawley opened the door and standing aside said, "In here, Doc. Bill, get a rifle and stand guard at the door. I don't need this town coming unglued and storming in here." Bill nodded.

Mike hollered at Rawley, "What the hell is goin' on, Rawley? Is it true the kids have been kidnapped?"

Angry mummers rose, splashing against his ears resembling pounding surf. Rawley held up his hands, "As soon as I know something, you'll know."

The crowd pushed closer as more angry voices were raised. "We need to form a posse," one said. "C' mon, boys...let's git our harses!" Yells of agreement rose.

Bill came out the door. The rifle in his hands barked over the heads of the crowd. "You heard the Marshal...now ya'll jus' settle down," Bill yelled at the crowd. "As soon as we know something, we'll tell ya. Now settle down!"

* * *

Lifting the big kettle off the cook stove, Lacy sat it on the table. It took a lot of food to feed her growing family now that Ben preferred to eat his meals with them. Dark eyes grew sad as she thought about the situation with Ben and Ezra. Beth was seemingly coming unglued; even Cotton had begun complaining about her. And Cotton was not one to complain. Glancing at the clock in the dining room, a freckled brow furrowed. *5:30,* she thought, *where is everyone?*

Stepping out of her house, Lacy focused on the mixture of bright colored flowers dripping over the edge of the steps and their border. Pretty soon the colors would be no more. She smiled, skipping lightly past them and down the porch steps. Lacy headed toward town to find out where everyone was this evening. Hanah, she knew, had to be the best dawdler ever born. Stopping to check out or explore everything, not just once, but two or three times. Lacy smiled happily. Walking past Liv's house, she threw a wave at her old school teacher, now her best friend who was watering the flowers on her porch. *Won't have those much longer,* Lacy's mind said.

The sound of a rifle shot had Lacy stopping short. *That came from in town,* she thought. *Kannon!*

The water abruptly stopped pouring Liv turned toward the redhead. "Lacy..."

"Git back inside the house, Liv," Lacy ordered.

She took off running, her hand automatically reaching for the pistol nestled at her waist. Fingers just touched her shirt and leather belt. "Dammit," she hissed. It remained at the house. Lacy kept sprinting, slowing as she saw the crowd gathered in front of the Marshal's office. She slowed more when she saw Billy standing guard outside the door with a rifle in his hands negligently pointed at the crowd. Luke was standing alongside him, his scatter gun pointed at the crowd too. Her mouth dropped as her heart began thudding across her ribs, knocking the air out of her lungs. Picking up her pace, Lacy pushed her way through the crowd. "Billy...what is it?" She asked breathlessly, "Rawley..."

Bill nodded at the closed door, stepping back, "Better git

inside Mom...Dad 'll wanna talk to you." He opened the door for her, shutting it quickly when Lacy slipped inside. He faced the crowd using one of his Mom's best blistering glares that he'd learned from her, daring anyone to take one step closer.

Chapter Thirteen

Leaning against the door, Lacy stood in shock at what her eyes were witnessing. Her husband and Ezra had Beth pinned to the floor, while Doc tried to pour something down her throat. The table lay on its side. Chairs were scattered, a testament to the struggle that continued on the floor. Lacy moved quickly to sit on Beth's legs as she tried to keep them from thrashing. She felt like she was riding a bucking bronc.

Finally Beth succumbed to whatever Doc had managed to pour down her throat, relaxing and passing out. A loud whoosh of air escaped the four remaining people. Bewildered, Lacy canvassed three faces, "What...What...Is...Going...On?"

Trying to slow his own heart from just a thumping, Rawley said lamely, "Beth lost it...she went loco on us." He dreaded the moment when he had to tell Lacy about the children.

Lacy gave a very unladylike snort. "I can see that, with three of us sitting on her! Why? What made her go so crazy?"

The three men cut each other quick looks. Rawley stood, walked over, righting a chair as he stalled for time. He helped Doc to stand and then over to the chair. Finally he faced Lacy, "Sunshine...the children have been kidnapped."

Lacy's mouth dropped. "What?" She scrambled to her feet. Her eyes scoured her husband's face. Her husky voice whispered, "What do you mean...kidnapped?"

Tucking thumbs into his back pockets, Rawley braced himself for the outburst that was bound to come. "Jus' that...Sunshine." He nodded toward the store-keep. "From what Ezra here said. Couldn't get much from Beth, since she went loco on us." Rawley heaved in air. "The kids were taken out of the schoolhouse, all of them," he said quietly.

"Hanah and Cotton, too?" She asked, her eyes searching his for answers. Her voice thick with emotion, "It was Kannon wasn't it?"

Rawley nodded, watching the shimmer of tears spring forth in those dark eyes he loved.

Doc and Ezra kept cutting each other looks but kept quiet.

Taking a deep shaky breath, Lacy tried to think. She spoke so softly they could barely hear her. "You send a wire yet?"

Shaking his head, Rawley said, "No..."

Lacy sniffed, wiping her runny nose and the tears. "You gonna...?"

"...Yes."

She nodded and then spun. Lacy walked the few paces to the door and jerked it open passing through, she slammed it behind her. Lacy gazed over the townsfolk, feeling nauseated by what had happened to her children and the others. She tried to swallow the bile back down. It remained, burning her throat.

Mike piped up. "What the hell is goin' on, Lacy?"

Finding him in the crowd, she swallowed again, "You'll have to ask Marshal Lovett." Turning to Bill, she said, "Stay here. Luke, you come with me," then added softly, "Please."

Inside the office remained peppered with tension. Rawley stared at Doc and Ezra, offering, "You need help carrying Beth back to your place, Ezra?"

Ezra shook his head. "No," he said as he scooped Beth into his arms. Doc stood, picking up his medical bag, saying, "I'm comin' with ya."

Chapter Fourteen

Standing just inside the schoolhouse doors, Luke and Lacy remained mesmerized by the total chaos of the room. Desks were overturned, books and papers scattered hither and yon. The framework of the back door was shattered; the evening sun stretched through the trees shadows. Dust motes floated on the fingers of light that left a scattering of yellow upon the door resting quietly on the floor.

Glancing at Luke, Lacy heaved in air. As if reading her thoughts, Luke said, "I'll go out back, see what I can find." Boots thumped through the rubble. Stepping on the door, it cracked with his weight. Then Luke disappeared.

Moving her way through the debris, the room looking much like a war zone, Lacy looked for evidence. Lacy Watson, bounty hunter had returned.

Spotting dried brown splotches, her heart caught in her throat. Kneeling, one finger reached out to touch the drying blood, Lacy jerked her hand back. *Someone got hurt*, she thought. Lacy prayed it wasn't one of the kids.

Dark eyes filled with moisture. *Hanah's a scrabbler*, Lacy thought, wanting to fight at the drop of a hat. *Cotton is too.* But he preferred fighting with smooth talking words. Lacy also knew Cotton would use his fists if words didn't work. She sighed heavily. It felt as if Luke's anvil was resting in the pit of her stomach, making her body too heavy to move and she felt nauseated. Standing slowly, Lacy wiped the moisture from her eyes. The yellow patch of evening sun shining through the fractured doorway drew her in that direction.

Hearing rustling sounds coming from the patch of brush behind the schoolhouse, Lacy moved toward it. She called out, "Luke?"

"Over...here," Luke answered.

Lacy pushed her way through the brush until she stood beside him.

He gestured at the ground, "Plenty of footprints here, then they disappear. I reckon they's found a wagon ta haul off all them kids."

Freckles scrunched. "You hear 'bout any wagons missing?"

Luke shook his head. "Naw...Joe Jenkins...wagons, well...they's out back of my place. Got them before we burned the bodies and his barn, back a ways." Thinking again, "The only ones I knowed 'bout...might still be out at the Clancy's old place," Luke offered. He shifted uncomfortably then, cutting a short glance at Lacy before speaking. "The only thing I figure why's we ain't finding any sign, is they's put burlap or leather on their mounts' feet."

She just stared at Luke.

He continued to gaze off into the distance as he spoke again. "Them injuns I fought against during the Indian Wars...that was a fav'rite trick of their 'un." Luke brought his eyes back to Lacy's face. He squinted at her.

The only sounds were their quiet breathing and the soft chatter of birds and squirrels in the brush surrounding them.

Lacy's gaze drifted toward the tops of the trees overhead, colorful leaves hanging on for their last gasp before fluttering to the ground. *Gawd!* She thought, *Will the skeletons ever quit coming out of the past?* She remembered briefly how she and Rawley had found a little tow-headed boy, the only survivor of his family's gruesome murders. Now that little boy Cotton was their son. Or how she almost died from the bullets Lowell Taylor put in her and how he'd butchered and murdered Joe Jenkins.

She gazed back at Luke standing next to her. "Let's go back to town, I need to get supplies and pack."

Luke nodded, his face grim.

Chapter Fifteen

Piercing blue eyes followed Ezra and Doc as Ezra carried an unconscious Beth across the street to his store. Rawley focused on the crowd which was closing in on him demanding answers. Holding up his hands and patting the air with them, he quieted those folks in front of him.

Taking a deep breath, Rawley began speaking in his soothing calm baritone, belying the turmoil within. "Lacy and Luke have gone to check out the schoolhouse and when they get back, I'll have some answers for you," he said.

Loud rumblings continued from the crowd.

Cody Brown piped up, "What's the delay, Rawley? If the kids are missing...we need to saddle up and go rescue them." Murmurs of agreement washed over the crowd.

Holding up his hand, Rawley said, "You're right Cody. But we also don't need to go off half-cocked, either. Kannon is as smart as a grizzly bear, and as crafty as an old mountain cat. I'm not putting any of you in front of flying lead. It'll jus' be me and Lacy heading out after him."

"But yer gonna need backup," someone said.

"No. Lacy is all the backup I need," Rawley replied, thinking of how that fire-breathing dragon, now his wife, had pulled his neck out of the noose more than once in the past. And he had done the same with hers.

Catching movement out of the corner of his eye, Rawley looked directly at Luke and Lacy walking slowly toward them. They both gave a solid shake of their heads, *No*. Then he saw Lacy give a nod toward their house as Luke came up beside him. Rawley knew what that nod meant. Lacy would begin packing their gear.

71

Eyes flicked from Lacy back to the crowd. "Now...folks, you all jus' return to your homes and businesses. Lacy and I will be setting out here shortly." His eyes pierced the crowd of people. "I mean it...go home, try to relax." Rawley turned reaching for the door knob.

"Like hell!" someone returned. "You expect us to relax? When varmints got our kids? You expect us to go about our business like nuthin' happened? Yore loco...Rawley Lovett! Chust plain loco!" Voices rose in agreement, becoming louder. The crowd started edging closer.

Turning around, he took a stride to the edge of the planks. He felt Luke and Bill's presence move in beside him. Rawley held up his hands, "I'm making the citizens of White River a promise." A scene flickered through the dark recesses of Rawley's mind of a promise he made to a little tow-headed boy long ago by the name of Cotton. "Lacy and I will bring those kids back home, safe and sound...come hell or high water...no matter how long it takes us. I promise." As his eyes drifted over the crowd and found Mike with his arms wrapped around Maddie's shoulders, Rawley added, "Mike, take these folks over to your place. I'll settle up with you when I get back."

Mike nodded, "C' mon folks...I think we can all use a little something to settle 'r nerves."

Luke, Rawley and Bill kept watch as the crowd slowly dispersed, heading towards the saloon with the promise of free booze and to offer their opinions to anyone who would listen.

As Cody stepped closer placing a boot on the bottom step, he looked upward at the three. He said quietly, "I'm volunteering to go with you and Lacy...Rawley. Maybe having another set of eyes might be of help. And I'm a fair shot, too."

A faint smile peered out in a grim face. He was remembering the Cody Brown that hit town ten years ago, another vagabond from Lacy's past. His deputy had straightened the kid out mighty quick, producing the man who stood before him now. Rawley replied, "Thanks Cody. But I need you to get on the wires and send messages to every town between here and Mexico about this crime. Besides,

Ezra is gonna need you. Beth is sick...real sick. It'd be best you stick around to help him or Bill and Luke when they need it."

Cody nodded, saying, "Yeah...Beth is bad...real bad. Today may 'ave jus' pushed her over the edge." He turned and walked back to his and Ezra's store, not joining the others headed for Mike's.

Opening the door to the office, Rawley made a beeline for his Henry. Taking it out of the rack, he stepped toward the desk. A drawer scraped open in the aged, heavy piece of furniture. Rawley pulled out his well-used and worn saddlebags and they thumped the top of the scarred wood. His hand was reaching for the ammo drawer when he heard Luke clear his throat.

Rawley and Bill both looked across at the bowlegged livery owner.

"Rawley, hit jus' don't make sense ta take out after Kannon tonight, hit'll be dark soon. I know you wanna git after them...but hell they's not any sign...I s'pect they put burlap or leather on them mounts' hooves causing them to not leave any tracks."

Speaking quietly, Rawley leveled a steady gaze on both men. "He's heading to Mexico, Luke. Kannon is a slave runner. Those girls 'll be sold to a whorehouse and the boys to work the fields, mines or could even be sold to a whorehouse, too." He busied himself placing boxes of cartridges in one pouch.

Luke tore off his hat and threw it down. "Awww...hell!"

Rawley looked up from his task, automatically pulling the leather flap over the pouch and buckling it. "Kannon works for any sum-bitch he can make the most money from. And right now, slave trafficking fits the bill."

"I'm goin' wit ya," Luke said. "Wit three of us tracking, we's bound to find sometin' sooner."

Throwing the saddle bags over his shoulder, they thumped against his torso. Rawley picked up the Henry. "No. You stay here and cover Bill's back." Giving them both a long look, he said, "I trust you." And with that Rawley Lovett headed toward his house.

73

Luke sighed noisily.

Bill raised his eyebrows clear to his hairline.

Chapter Sixteen

Whimpers came from the wagon jostling, bumping and creaking along. The sound poked through Hanah's foggy brain. Her head hurt, but not as much as she had to go pee. Struggling, she finally sat up and cracked one eye open. Hanah's gaze pierced the darkness. She could just barely pick out the other kids in the wagon from the pin-pricks of stars above. As her eyes focused in the darkness, she could see Emily Harrison's eyes were swollen from crying. Emma Sue was quiet, and just staring into nothing. The other little girls were giving tiny hiccuping and mewling sounds. Everyone's hands were tied in front of them, the rope stringing them all together like fresh caught fish. Her eyes drifted to the boys - Thad and Chad, their backs resting against the wooden side with their eyes closed. Dobie Litchfield was doing the same.

Cotton sat next to her and their eyes met. Cotton had a dark welt along one eye. Leaning against him, Hanah whispered, "I gotta go pee."

Cotton rolled his eyes, making his head hurt worse. It felt like a drum beating a slow, heavy rhythm behind his eye. "Good luck, Punkin. They ain't gonna stop fer nuthin'. You'll jus' haft ta pee in yore britches," he whispered back.

"I will not," she whispered. Shifting against the wood, Hanah looked at the driver's back, sitting on the seat above her. Hanah called to him, "Mister...hey Mister...I gotta go pee...stop the wagon...please?"

The man glanced over his shoulder, "Pee in yore britches, kid."

A small freckled hand reached for the back of the seat as Hanah pulled herself up, stretching the rope that strung between the girls, pulling them toward her forcing louder mewling in response.

Bracing against the seat to keep her balance in the bouncing wagon, she tried again, "Mister...I really gotta go pee."

The man answered, "We ain't stopping...pee in yore britches."

Replying smartly, Hanah said, "I will not...it ain't polite; besides, then I'll stink." All the other kids in the wagon stared at Hanah in wild-eyed wonder. Ben Hudson couldn't believe what was happening to them, his eyes rounded like saucers in a pale face. In all those books he read, Ned Buntline never, ever talked about stuff like this. *This sure ain't 'the code of the west,'* he thought. *Where's the good guys that's 'sposed to rescue us?*

"Tuff shee-yut," the driver said.

Hanah didn't know how much longer she could hold the pee inside. Sucking in all the wind her lungs could hold, her freckles scrunched up as she bellowed, "Stop the wagon...I gotta go peeeeee!"

Big Joe Kannon yanked on his horse's reins, jerking the animal around. The wagon abruptly stopped. Kannon drew up alongside, gazing at the freckled firebrand standing behind his driver. Hanah stared boldly back. *Cute as a speckled pup, she is,* he thought. "Ya gotta go pee...sister?"

Her freckled face scrunched up again as a little girl's voice shouted, "My name is Hanah Marie Lovett...not sister!"

Surprise flickered through his muddy eyes, "You Rawley Lovett's kid?"

Hanah danced from one foot to the other.

Cotton spoke up disgustedly, "Yeah...she's Rawley Lovett's kid, and so am I."

Kannon grinned, "Hooweee, boys...how 'bout that! We's ended up wit both them Lovett kids."

Hanah interrupted Kannon's jubilee. "Mister...I gotta go pee...bad," she told him. Muddy eyes dissected the miniature firebrand. "Ohh...what the hell, harses need a break," Kannon said. "You kids pile outta there."

Twenty-eight legs scrambled like they'd been touched with a red-hot branding iron.

Leather creaked as Kannon eased himself out of the saddle. Hanah's nose wrinkled as she caught a whiff of Big Joe Kannon when he moved downwind of her.

Nodding toward the brush, his gravelly voice told them, "You kids go on, now. Go pee." Kannon threw an order toward his men, "Boys...follow 'em."

Pee had begun dribbling down the inside of Hanah's leg, but she wasn't gonna let some stranger watch as she pulled down her britches. Hanah yelled again, "Us girls ain't gonna let some man watch us pee...mister!" One tied hand raised as a finger thrust out, pointing. "You jus' stay right thar!"

Kannon reared back as a grin remained hidden under all that brush with the ferocity he found coming from the little redhead, that t'wernt no bigger than a grasshopper.

Hanah pushed out her hands and said, "Untie us. Us girls can't pee with our hands tied." Nodding at the boys, she announced the obvious, "The boys can..." She threw the big boulder-like man her best dirty look, trying to mimic her Mama.

Kannon raised a gristly eyebrow, listening to this miniature firebrand spouting off at him. He nodded toward his men allowing them to take the ropes off the girls. As soon as her hands were released, Hanah raced for the brush and the rest of the girls followed. The boys did the same, going toward another area but their hands were still tied.

Pulling her britches up and buttoning them, Hanah peeked through the bushes watching the men by the wagon. The sound of soft whimpering and mewling from the other girls made her head swivel. "Shad-up," she hissed. "Crying ain't gonna help none."

"I want my Mama," one little girl sniffled.

Tucking thumbs in her back pockets, mimicking her daddy, Hanah whispered loudly, "My Mama and Daddy will find us and take us back home. But right now, we gotta do what these men say." Her fingers felt the pocket knife her Mama had given her in secret. Her Mama had told her it might come in handy one day. Slipping the knife out of her back pocket, Hanah transferred it to a front one. Leaning in closer to the girls, she whispered again, "We gotta have us a plan...a plan to escape."

Emily Harrison stepped closer. "Like what?" Hanah was a daredevil. She always came up with something good.

Bright blue eyes gazed earnestly at the faces staring back at her. "Something..."

"You kids done in thar...we's got us a long haul."

Hanah's head swiveled toward the voice then back toward the girls. She whispered, "Me 'n Cotton 'll come up with something..." Turning, she shouted, her voice carrying out of the brush, "Yeah...we're done."

Ropes were retied around small wrists and bodies loaded back into the wagon, heading south, to 'the land that burns'.

Chapter Seventeen

Traveling until the stars were deep in the sky, Rawley and Lacy Lovett made a cold camp.

Wrapping his arms tightly around his wife, Rawley pulled Lacy closer within the folds of the blankets, her head resting into the concave of his shoulder. They were trying to get a few hours of sleep, if that was remotely possible after what had happened earlier in the small community of White River.

Lacy slept fitfully in Rawley's arms. Her restless mind flicked here and there over images: sitting on Beth Shemwell's legs, the empty schoolhouse, she and Luke not finding any definitive sign to follow. She shifted against Rawley and he tightened his arms around her. Lacy's leg draped itself over his muscular one.

Her mind kept darting in and out of the shadows, not allowing her body to rest. Abruptly a bright, white light appeared in one, dark cobwebby corner. A body seemed to materialize inside the light. The body transformed into a woman with bright copper-colored hair in a blue gown. It came closer. Lacy's Mother appeared before her mind's eye.

*Lacy...*her mother spoke softly.

Mama?

Yes...my darling.

Mama...what is it? The children...something's happened to the children.

No...Lacy, they are fine. I will continue to protect them until you reach them.

But...Mama...

Go south, little one, to 'the land that burns'. There you will find the children. A man Del Rio. God speed, little one.

A hand suddenly stuck itself into the darkness above him. The words surprised Rawley even more. "Mama...Mama...don't go..." Lacy mumbled still asleep. Her hand dropped abruptly when the light faded from within her mind's eye.

* * *

A brisk fall morning greeted Lacy and Rawley as they tied down their gear to the saddles. Fancy and Rawley's big bay waited patiently. Puffs of warm mist swirled above their heads and disappeared, only to return a few seconds later. Sunlight barely peeked through the fog-wrapped plains to the east.

Lacy spoke quietly as she continued to tie her raingear, ground cloth wrapped bedroll on back of the cantle. "Mama told me last night, we need to head south. Toward the 'land that burns'...do you know where that is?" She asked Rawley turning toward him.

Rawley's hands stilled. He gazed across the saddle at his wife. He'd heard Lacy say the word *Mama* in the wee hours of darkness. "Is that what she said?" he asked quietly as his hands finished tying the strings holding his outfit. His eyes darted back to Lacy.

Her fingers plucked at the pebbly wool of his bedroll. She nodded, "Mama said the kids were okay...and...and that she'd protect them 'til we found them." She turned and stuck a boot into a stirrup, slipping easily into the leather. Lacy gazed back at her husband, "She said, we were to look for a man by the name of Del Rio when we get to 'the land that burns'."

His mind drifted back to another time when Lacy's Mother had visited her. When Lowell Taylor had shot Lacy three times, almost killing her. That's when God allowed Lacy to see her Mother whole and not bloody and mangled from committing suicide. Her Mother told Lacy it was not her time to join her, that she had many more years here on earth. Now her Mother had come again, to reassure her

80

daughter that everything would be okay. He'd liked to have known the woman who had been Lacy's kin.

Leather creaked when Rawley stepped into his saddle. Puffs of fog accented his words, "That's a good thousand miles, Sunshine. Guess we better get started, huh?" He smiled reassuringly at her.

Lacy's lips clamped shut as she gave her short non-communicative nod.

Rawley signed inwardly. *Lacy Watson is back.*

Chapter Eighteen

Beth Shemwell stirred against the bedclothes. She felt foggy and disoriented, then it all came back to her. Moving to this God forsaken town, living with a bunch of heathens who called themselves people. Marrying a man she'd come to despise. Dust...the constant dust and blowing wind. Her disheveled mind grasped at other thoughts. Her son Ben, now gone, taken by some lawless bandits. Beth somehow knew she'd never see her precious angel again. *Ezra!* Her mind raged. *This is all his fault.*

Throwing the covers back, she sat up. Her spinning head had her hands pressing hard against her temples. When it had eased off, she opened her eyes and looked around her bedroom. Everything looked the same, orderly. A coal oil lamp glowed with a low flame on her bedside table. Beth glance at the curtained window; it was dark out. She didn't know for how long she'd slept or what day it might be.

Rage exploded as colorful sparks of red, yellow and white danced in her mind. *Ezra! This is all his fault!* Her hand reached out and the bedside table drawer silently slid open. Inside rested a loaded revolver, its shiny blue barrel glinting in the glow of the coal oil lamp. Beth picked it up and cradled the cool metal against her breast with both hands. She'd bought the gun in St. Joe after her husband Rod had been killed for cheating in a poker game. Wild eyes darted toward the closed bedroom door. She stood. Her bare feet silently padded toward the door, her nightgown swirling gently around her ankles and the revolver still clutched tightly against her breast.

Ezra felt a presence breaking into his restless sleep. He opened his eyes, startled to find Beth standing over him with a revolver pointed at his chest as he lay on the sofa. Slowly pushing himself up and resting against the arm of the couch, he continued to stare at Beth. The normally neat bun at the back of her neck was pulled apart and drooping tiredly over one shoulder. But it was her eyes that kept him mesmerized, that and the unholy snarl that graced once pretty lips. Right now Beth reminded him of a rabid dog, noting the dried spittle that had formed at the corners of her mouth. "Beth..." he began, pushing himself up straighter gaining leverage to jump her if he couldn't talk her out of dropping the revolver or giving it to him

At his movement, Beth backed out of his reach. Wild eyes glared at him. Spittle flew as harsh words were uttered, "You...you...took everything I loved away from me."

Ezra shifted again, placing himself in a better position, his bare feet touching the wood floor he worked so hard putting a shine to. His calf muscles tightened in anticipation. He rested his hands curled into fists at his side. Leaning forward, Ezra questioned, "What do you mean, Beth?"

She backed away another step when Ezra leaned forward. "My son," she said.

Ezra scooted his butt closer to the edge of the sofa. "Ben 'll be back, Beth. Same with all the rest of the kids," he tried to reassure her. "Rawley and Lacy know what they're doing. They've both been bounty hunters and lawmen before." He paused gazing at Beth's face. That wild look remained, his words having no effect. "Beth, give me the gun," he said, holding out his hand. His quiet voice belied the turmoil of his heart banging against his ribs, shoving the air out of his lungs. Leaning further toward her, his fingers stretched and gestured. He told her again, "Beth, give me the gun."

A once sweet smile twisted in a tortured face. Eyes flicked rapidly back and forth from the gun to Ezra's face and to the gun again. Stepping back further, her voice registering the hollow and tortured soul from within Beth announced, "I'll never see my son again," she said. Raising the revolver, she placed the muzzle flat against her temple. A finger pulled back the trigger.

Half rising, his hand reaching out, Ezra screamed, "Nooo..."

* * *

The constant wind blew, scattering and separating the grey layers of clouds hanging overhead. A few rays of sunlight poked through every now and then, highlighting the folks standing in the town's cemetery. The Reverend said a few peaceful words over the casket quietly waiting to be lowered into the ground. The Reverend walked over to Ezra Shemwell, whispered a few words and shook his hand.

Slowly the crowd began to disperse, stopping beside Ezra to offer words of sympathy and encouragement. Silently Ezra would nod his head and shake the hands offered, accept the hugs given.

Holding on to Ezra's hand, Mike volunteered softly, "We're holding a little wake in the saloon, Ezra." He looked earnestly into a face that seemed to have aged overnight. "Maddie's put together a mighty nice spread, and I'm bringing out ma best rye." He hoped that would convince Ezra to come along.

Gazing sadly back at Mike and Maddie, Ezra knew his friends meant well but right now he wanted to be alone. Brown eyes flicked from one kind face to the other. "Thanks...but I think I want to be alone for a while. Maybe later," he said.

Taking Maddie's hand Mike nodded, understanding. They began moving off the hillside.

After watching his friends leave, Ezra turned his back on them. He stood by Beth's final resting place and stared across the terrain he loved. His hands jammed themselves into his trouser pockets. The plains dotted with sporadic trees still held a few gems of color, along with the persistent and hardy flowers gracing the landscape. Grasses swayed in the constant breeze bending their blades to it's will, carrying a reddish-purple tint the way they always did as winter approached. The mostly flat terrain reached out like a blanket covering miles, coming to an abrupt halt when it reached the mountains, now with a dusting of snow covering their peaks. Ezra sighed heavily. His one and only venture into finding a woman to spend the rest of his life with had turned into a disaster that ended in Beth's suicide. She'd never become accustomed to the constant wind and dust that always swirled through the air. Instead she hated it, the town and its citizens. Beth's last words echoed in his mind...*I'll never see my son again.* He sighed wearily thinking, S*he's right, she'll never see Ben again. But I will, and I'll raise him as my own. That's the least I can do for Beth.*

Hearing dirt thump hollow on top of the wood box, Ezra turned. Silently he walked past Clay filling the hole in the ground.

Chapter Nineteen

Four metal-rimmed wheels clattered over scree and bounced over larger rocks in the wheel's path, waking Hanah and the others in the wagon bed.

Sleepy and tired whimpers accompanied the wagon's rattles and groans traveling across rough terrain. Shod hooves clicked against the loose shale, igniting sparks in the darkness.

Pushing herself off Cotton, Hanah's eyes tried to pierce the darkness that surrounded them. She could barely make out the faces sitting in the wagon with her. Glancing upward, all she saw were millions of stars that peppered the black expanse of sky. It seemed they'd been sitting in this wagon for months, but in reality maybe three weeks. The terrain had gradually changed from the flower dotted prairies of Wyoming and Colorado into a dry parched land. Hanah couldn't grasp the number of days, they seemed to all roll into one with her. She just knew she felt dirty and her butt was sore and she was tired. Her wrists were rubbed raw from the rope that always bound her hands together.

Her tummy growled. For the first time tears filled blue eyes, spilling over. She remembered how her Mama always fixed the best meals, ones that she could wash down with a cold glass of milk, tasting so good. Hanah angrily brushed the tears away. All they'd been given since they were captured had been some dried beef and beans, cold and most times burnt. Freckles scrunched, thinking of the awful food. Her tummy growled again, as Hanah realized that not only was she hungry, but cold and thirsty as well. Her elbow jabbed into Cotton's ribs.

"What?" He asked sourly.

"You cold?"

"Yeah...I'm cold." Cotton cut a look at his sister, "What of it? They ain't gonna stop...ta give us blankets...we're their prisoners...they don't care." He sighed. Closing his eyes again, Cotton's head drooped wearily onto his chest.

Hanah determinedly announced, whispering, "Well...I'm gonna do something about it."

"Hanah, don't..." Cotton pleaded. His wrists protested, rubbed raw from the weeks of being tied up as he tried to grab his sister's arm. "They could pistol-whip you and might even kill you."

Hanah whispered harshly, "So...if that happens...then I can go live with Gramma."

Cotton gasped. His eyes narrowed at his sister, "That ain't funny, Punkin."

Staring boldly back at her brother, Hanah insisted hotly, "Well...we gotta do something...besides sitting like a bunch of dumb rocks in the back of this wagon."

Cotton sighed inwardly. Sometimes his sister could be the devil when she set her mind to it; and this was probably one of those times. He licked dry lips before speaking, "What 'r ya gonna do?"

Flashing a smile in the darkness, Hanah whispered back, "I'll jus' set up such a roocuss," she exaggerated the word, the way she'd heard her Mama say it. "That they'd have to stop."

Cotton's eyes grew round in the dark.

Hanah grinned again, "Well...it worked last time...didn't it? Long time ago...when I had to go pee."

Cotton shrugged his shoulders, shaking his head. He stared at his daredevil sister.

Tucking her legs underneath her, Hanah struggled to her knees amid the bouncing and jerking of the wagon as it rolled along. Her tied hands reached for the seat-back above her and grasped the wood, pulling herself into a standing position. Tied together as they were pulled the girls forward causing them to awaken and whimper, laying across each other. Hanah's feet braced against the constant motion.

A voice whispered in the driver's ear making him jump. "Mister...Mister...we're cold, tired, hungry and thirsty...cain't we stop for a few minutes?" Hanah asked.

The driver glanced to his left. It was that freckle-faced redhead again, her face inches from his. "Shad-up...kid, and git back thar," he growled.

Hanah didn't budge. "Please...Mister?"

"Shad-up!"

Eyes narrowed beneath ridiculously long lashes. Sucking in enough air to fill a blacksmith's bellows, Hanah screamed in the driver's ear. "Stop...The...Wagon! We...Want...Food...And...Water!"

The whimpers grew louder in the ensuing silence.

Big Joe Kannon jerked his horse around when he heard a voice bellow. Looking he saw it belonged to that freckled kid *again.*

Cotton just buried his head in his tied hands, thinking, S*he's gonna git us killed. Hanah's gonna git us all killed.*

His ear ringing from that redhead bellowing into it, made his left arm jerk out, hard and fast. Hanah landed, sprawled against the other bodies in the wagon. The girls squealed. Chad shouted, "Hey...!"

Jerking hard on the reins, the driver halted the mules. Scrambling over the seat, his hand reached for the front of Hanah's shirt. Her eyes grew wide at the man's angry response. His fist pulled back as he shouted, "Ya damn...l'il shee-yut! That 'll be the last time ya yell in ma ear!"

Frightened by the gruff voice, the girls squealed loudly. The boys yelled, scuffling and scrambling against the wood, trying to gain leverage, the rope interfering with their progress.

Launching himself across the short space, Cotton rammed his head into the man's ribs. A yell and a whoosh of air suddenly exploded from the driver. He fell on top of Cotton, pinning brother and sister against the other girls. Hanah and Cotton tried to wriggle free. Thad and Chad moved as one, dragging Dobie and Ben with them, into the man sprawled against the girls creating one huge pile of squirming, screaming and yelling bodies. The boys' tied hands became battering rams across the man's neck and shoulders. Hanah kept throwing short jabs at the man's face even with her hands tied. Cotton slammed balled fists into the man's ears. Dobie added his blows, pummeling the man across his head. All this mingled with boots scuffling and thunking against wood as the sounds of umphs, screams and thuds filled the darkness.

Riding upon the pile of bodies flailing at each other in the wagon bed, Kannon yanked his pistol from his side and fired it over everyone's heads. The sound bounced and ricocheted across the landscape.

Silence, except for the harsh breathing and rustling sounds as bodies tried to reclaim their limbs.

A gravelly voice ordered, "Jake...git yore arse outta thar and back on tha seat. Ya ain't gonna harm tha merchandise."

Standing and rubbing the back of his neck and shoulders with one hand continuing to cup an ear, Jake heaved in air. "That damn kid blew ma eardrum out. She ain't got no cause fer that!"

A pistol calmly leveled at Jake's belt.

Fourteen pairs of eyes, round as saucers seem to blink in time to a silent rhythm.

"Jake..." Kannon's voice began, "Effen ya want yore share of thisss payout...ya climb back on tha seat."

His hand slid closer to his gun belt. It touched empty leather. Jake quickly looked around for his gun. "Whose got ma damn gun?" He aimed the words at fourteen kids. They remained quiet, scooting back against the sides of the wagon. Ben sat still as a church mouse on a hard metal lump.

A slight metallic click filled the air.

Head swiveling, Jake stared at the muzzle aimed at his gut from Kannon's hand. "Sumbuddy's got ma damn gun," he groused.

90

"Git yure arse back on tha seat, Jake," Kannon said.

"Aww...go 'head...shoot 'im. Be one less ta divide tha money over," Lenny chimed in.

"Shad-up...Lenny, 'r yore next," Kannon told him, directing his attention back to Jake standing in the middle of a passel of kids. "Well...Jake..." he began, letting the words trail off.

"Yeah...yeah, I heerd ya," Jake said, "But sumbuddy's got ma damn gun!" He muttered, stepping over limbs and climbing back into the seat. Jake picked up the reins again.

A pistol whispered back into it's leather. Leaning on his saddle horn, Big Joe's voice broke into the quiet, "Now...what's ya fussing 'bout thisss time, sister?"

Hanah opened her mouth to reply. Cotton punched her tiny arm. Her mouth slammed shut, but that didn't hide the dirty look she gave him.

Cotton piped up before his sister could cause more trouble, "We're cold, 'n tired, 'n hungry, 'n thirsty..." then added as an afterthought, "and we all gotta go pee again," he said. His mind thinking, *Maybe we can slip away in the dark.*

Pushing himself up off the saddle horn, Kannon narrowed eyes at the boy. A string of dark juice flew before he spoke. "That so..." he answered. Right about now, Big Joe Kannon wished he'd never hatched his so-called brilliant plan of getting back at Rawley Lovett. He'd hauled kids before; usually they were too scairt to give him a lick of trouble. But with this bunch...Kannon was gonna have to make a change of plans.

Fourteen kids held their breath in anticipation. They zeroed in on the boulder-like man sitting astride his horse.

"Aw right, ya kids pile outta thar," Kannon sighed heavily. Scrambling noises were heard as the kids climbed out of the wagon faster then chickens stampeding out of a hen house. In the darkness, Ben quickly stuffed the pistol into his britches under his coat. "Wheat, go untie the girls," Kannon ordered.

91

Holding up his tied hands, Cotton piped up, "Us...boys, too."

Kannon swung his head toward the voice.

"Our wrists have been rubbed raw...untie us too," Cotton said.

Finally sighing noisily, Kannon told Wheat, "The boys, too."

The girls ran toward some rocks and the boys followed them. Cotton's fingers plucked at Chad's shirt sleeve, slowing him as he whispered, "We're gonna try and make a break for it."

Chad nodded. Catching up to his brother Thad, he passed along what Cotton told him.

Pulling up her britches, Hanah jumped when Cotton touched her arm. "Punkin, we're gonna try and run," he whispered so softly Hanah could barely hear him.

"But we don't know where we are..." she whispered back.

"North star," he said, pointing to the sky. "We follow that."

Hanah nodded. Cotton was as sharp as a tack.

Cotton took off, running down the embankment. Thirteen others followed, slipping and sliding through loose shale and scree.

Chapter Twenty

His copperhead had clammed up on him again, just like she used to do when he first met her. Now Lacy Lovett, his wife had retreated into the dark recesses of her mind, only engaging in little snippets of conversation here and there. Rawley sighed inwardly; the little bounty hunter he'd found on the river bank years ago had returned.

"Sunshine...you've been awfully quiet the last few days."

Lacy's head swiveled around. He saw the shadows of worry that flickered through the depths of her eyes with dark circles like bruises under them. Rawley spoke softly, "We'll find them, Sunshine. We're both good at what we do...we'll bring them back."

Her eyes darted quickly away from soft blue ones. *I'm not gonna cry...crying won't find the kids,* Lacy scolded herself. She refocused between two black-edged grey ears that bobbed with each step Fancy took. Lifting her eyes, Lacy gazed around the Colorado plateau. The grasses carried a burnished golden color, like wheat. She could still see the bright spots of flowers bobbing within the waves of gold; flowers that remained reluctant to turn into dried stalks with the approaching colder weather. They'd bypassed the more rugged terrain of the mountains, their tops already white with early snows. The aspens shimmered with their gold coins in the constant breezes. White trunks of the stately trees stood in sharp contrast. They had stuck to the Old Cherokee Trail, now a route for the Overland Stage when she and Rawley had ridden out of Laramie, Wyoming and entered the state of Colorado. He'd said it would be quicker. *Nuthin' is quick enough,* she thought, *to finding those kids.* Lacy took in more air, hoping that it would settle her rolling stomach that she'd had the last few days. *Nerves,* her mind said. That snarling ball of barbed wire had returned, slicing her gut to shreds making her feel nauseated all the time.

Leather creaked as Rawley hitched around in his saddle to gaze back at his wife. Lacy looked awfully pale to him astride Fancy plodding after his bay. Her sprightly energy seemed to have vanished into thin air the last few days. He turned back around, leather creaking again. As long as they kept up a steady pace they might be able to catch Kannon before he crossed the border. He and Lacy had stopped in various towns along the way, asking questions and receiving no positive response about a wagon load of kids with a bunch of hide hunters. *Nuthin'*, he thought, *nuthin'*. He knew Kannon had animal instincts that made him shrewd and wily. But how he'd managed to disappear with fourteen kids in tow, Rawley didn't have a clue. Especially with Hanah Marie Lovett along. A faint smile flickered as he thought of Hanah. That daughter of his was as bold and brassy as her Mama - not afraid of anyone or anything. She probably had Kannon wishing he'd never laid eyes on her right about now. Rawley's smile deepened as he whispered softly, "Give him hell, Punkin."

Hearing a thud behind him, Rawley threw a glance over his shoulder. Fancy had stopped and Lacy lay sprawled on the ground, not moving. Jerking the reins, he whirled the big bay around. He rode back to Lacy, dismounting on the fly. He knelt and gathered his unconscious wife into his arms. Rawley gazed at a face that looked as pale as death. Dark circles under closed eyes stood out like bright banners. *This ain't good,* he thought.

Placing her hat under her head, Rawley stood and walked over to Fancy, pulling Lacy's canteen off the horn. Taking his bandana out of his back pocket, he knelt again. Twisting the cap off, he poured water on the piece of material and began wiping her face, trying to bring Lacy around.

With the sun beginning to hang low in the western skies, sending reds, oranges, pinks and purples across the edge of land, Rawley knew they'd have to make camp right here. Lacy still hadn't woken up and that worried him. But being miles from any settlement or even a town, he decided it would be best if they just made camp. There remained plenty of grass for the horses and since streams crisscrossed the landscape frequently, they'd also have plenty of water.

* * *

94

Lacy flew up from under the blanket, jerking Rawley awake. Running a few yards, her hands gripped her knees as she bent forward and began puking. Her stomach continued to roll and heave even after it had been emptied, creating a wet gagging sound.

Black brows fused together as shadows of concern flitted through Rawley's eyes. Flinging the pebbly wool blanket from his legs, he rose. Walking over to the canteens, he picked one up and continued toward Lacy. Resting a hand on her back, he bent down and gazed tenderly into her face which was red-blotched from vomiting so hard. "Sunshine..." he began.

"Leave me be, Lovett." Bitter bile made her voice thick and hoarse.

Straightening, Rawley continued to wait still holding the canteen. Something in his gut told him they had another baby on the way. He sighed inwardly, *This is not the time for Lacy to be expecting with the traveling we still have to do.* Rawley exhaled noisily.

Hearing that, Lacy finally straightened, cutting him a crooked look. Wiping her mouth on the sleeve of her shirt, she reached for the canteen. Unscrewing the cap, she let the tepid water flow into her mouth and down her throat.

Out of the blue Rawley asked, "When did you have your last monthly?"

Lacy's head swiveled. The word came out scratchy, "What?"

He tilted his head, "You heard me." He knew she'd never been regular. Rawley always felt it had something to do with her grandfather raping her at such a young age. "Well..." he prompted.

Thin shoulders shrugged as Lacy turned away from him and began walking back to their bedroll. Collapsing down on the blanket with the canteen cradled against her chest, Lacy closed her eyes.

Wandering behind his wife, Rawley came to stand beside her. It kind of surprised him that Lacy was expecting their second child, but then it didn't. They had a very active love-life. His knees cracked when he squatted next to Lacy. Her eyes flew open at the sound. A big palm caressed the face he'd fallen in love with. Lacy closed her eyes at his tender gesture, snuggling her cheek into his cool, calloused hand. His soft caramel baritone washed over her, "Well...Sunshine..." he began. "Reckon Hanah, Cotton and Bill are going to have a little brother or sister."

With her eyes still closed Lacy gave that short nod so characteristic of her. Her soft throaty voice whispered, "I know...I just never thought after all this time..." she swallowed. Opening her eyes, her hand reached out lightly touching his chest. She whispered hoarsely, "I love you, Rawley Lovett."

A smile eased out. He loved hearing those five little words. "I know you do...Sunshine," he replied.

"Let me rest some...then we'll get back on the trail," Lacy said.

Rawley nodded. Taking the pebbly wool blanket he covered his copperhead. Standing, he moved toward the coals, stirring and adding more wood and set about making a fresh pot of joe. Waiting on the coffee to brew, a dark thought slammed into his brain. The reason God was blessing them with another child after this length of time. Hanah, Cotton and the others were dead. *Nooo...*he thought, *no...don't even go there,* he scolded himself. *Kannon wouldn't do that, he wants the money too bad,* Rawley reassured himself.

Glancing over at his sleeping wife, Rawley decided they'd take a detour into Gunnison. Have Lacy see a doctor there, make sure she was okay. Then he'd get her some place to stay in town. He knew he'd have to put his foot down, *hard,* for Lacy to stay put. She'd argue with him, big time. Then he'd get back on the trail after the kids. *Besides,* he sat thinking, *I can move faster by myself.* Nodding, Rawley decided that's exactly what they'd do. Pouring himself a cup of fresh brewed coffee, he nodded again taking a sip. His mind echoed, *Yep...that's exactly what I'll do.*

Chapter Twenty-One

"Like...hell...Rawley Lovett," his wife snapped. "I ain't seein' no doctor...we ain't got the time." Her eyes gazed heatedly at her husband. "'Sides the sickness will wear off soon, just like it did before with Hanah," she said heaving in air, her mouth ready to fling more heat.

Rawley stopped his wife's next words, "Sunshine...I don't want you losin' this baby...and I don't want to lose you, either." Gazing at Lacy, he reminded her, "I almost did once. I won't let that happen again."

Lacy's mouth snapped shut, remembering how she almost died from taking three bullets from Lowell Taylor. A thought invaded her mind. *Skeletons.*

Warm eyes became more direct as they looked at snapping ones, "Like...I said, Sunshine. I don't want you losing this baby...and maybe you. Both of you mean too much to me," he said trying to reason with his hard-headed wife.

Lacy's mouth spit out a "Pffftt" into the air.

Ignoring Lacy's reply, Rawley continued, "It's gonna be a long hard trail...I'll be able to move much faster...I want you to stay here and rest." He watched Lacy's head snap toward him, her eyes popping with anger. *Oops...* he thought.

She hissed at him like a mad cat, "Damn...you, Lovett. You ain't gonna git rid of me that quick." Her words ground out between tightly clenched teeth, "I ain't gonna let you go after those kids by yourself!" Her eyes swung toward the shingle announcing *Dr. Al Goodfellow, MD.* Giving a very unladylike snort, Lacy said, "And I ain't letting some quack by the name of *Goodfellow* examine me neither!" She slanted a blistering look at her husband, the one that would make a skunk roll over and play dead. Rawley didn't even flinch. She added,

"We've wasted too much time as it is." Lacy backed Fancy away from the rail in front of the doctor's office. Turning the grey mare she nudged her into a fast trot, then a ground eating lope. Lacy headed south back through town and toward a nonexistent trail.

Pursing his lips Rawley blew hot air between them as he gazed after the stiff back of his wife astride the grey. Whipping off his hat, he slapped the bay's rump making the horse jump into a trot, then a lope. Jamming the hat back on his head Rawley took off after his copperhead.

* * *

Waking suddenly, Rawley lifted his head, gazing around. The sun barely peeked over the eastern horizon. He let his head flop back against his saddle. They'd stopped here last night after putting a week's distance between them and the last town, taking a bit more westerly turn into Arizona territory where parts of it truly remained, 'The land that burns.'

Feeling his movement in her sleep, Lacy snuggled in closer. Lifting his head again, he kissed the mass of copper curls. Slowly he eased his arm from under Lacy's head as he slid from beneath the blankets. Standing, he stretched, then reached first for his rig, buckling it on. Old habits die hard. Then slipping his shirt on as he strode to the fire, stoking the coals. Adding more mesquite, he set about making fresh coffee.

As he waited on the coffee, his mind hashed over the last few weeks. Still no kids, nothing. Kannon continued to be the wily old cougar he knew. Looking up at the few remaining stars left in the new day blossoming that was promising a hot one, Rawley sent a silent prayer to the heavens. *Keep your arms wrapped around those kids protecting them, Lord.* Thinking again, *But...Lord, I gotta favor to ask...throw us some kinda bone...some kinda lead...so we can find them, bring them home.* Rawley sighed heavily and then added. "But...thankee, anyhow. I know you're protecting the kids," he

98

whispered. *Or...at least Lacy's Mama is,* his mind echoed.

Rawley stirred the coals with a stick, sending orange and yellow sparks into the early morning air. They'd been making good time here lately. Lacy's sickness had been easing up as the days passed, causing her to become her feisty old self. He smiled, they'd made love again last night. It's a wonder she'd never had twins as much as they made love. He rakishly smiled again.

Lacy stirred and then stretched. Hearing the rustling, Rawley looked up and said, "Coffee's 'bout ready, Sunshine."

Sitting up, she nodded. That's when she heard the agitated rattle coming from somewhere near her. Rawley heard it too. Rising he ordered crisply, "Don't move, Sunshine." He advanced toward her, his pistol drawn.

Her husky voice whispered, "Where is it?"

His finger made a motion toward his lips, telling her to be quiet. He crept slowly and silently toward her feet like a cat stalking its prey. His eyes pierced the ground around Lacy and the bed. Spotting something moving under Lacy's britches where she'd thrown them prior to their lovemaking, his left finger pointed. Her eyes trailed down a long arm and then dropped off the end of that finger to land on her britches. Her mouth formed a wide 'O'.

Flames spit from Rawley's pistol. Lacy's britches jumped when the bullets tore through the canvas material.

Lacy rolled in the opposite direction and then scrambled up. "Sheesh...Lovett. Just blow my eardrum out...will ya!" Her finger stuck itself into one ear jiggling it, trying to bring her hearing back.

Giving one of his own dirty looks at his wife's comment, Rawley stood staring at his redhead. Then a smile busted out as he continued gazing at his wife. Standing there in her pantaloons, brown socks dripping around her ankles with a green-checkered shirt unbuttoned exposing pink-ribbon underclothes. Disheveled copper curls framing her face just made him want to make love to her *again*. He cleared his throat.

Tilting her head, she gazed at this handsome man who'd made love to her last night. Dark hairs dusting his chest were still exposed through his open shirt. *Oh...how I love running my fingers...*throwing that thought out of her head, Lacy placed her hands on her hips. She asked instead, "What?"

Quickly dropping his own thoughts, Rawley bent down. Picking up Lacy's britches, he tossed them to her, "Nuthin'." Bending again, he picked up the dead rattler. Walking past her he shook the snake in her face. Lacy reared back. "Breakfast?" He asked her.

"Ickkk..." she said disgustedly. Narrowing her eyes Lacy sent him another dirty look, "You know how many of those dad-blasted things I've eaten over the years on the trail?"

Rawley turned and waggled the snake again as he grinned, teasing, "Tastes...like chicken..."

Copper curls shook silently. "To you maybe...but to me it's just eatin' a snake."

A smile broadened beneath his eyes.

Looking over the canvas material before sliding her legs into her pants Lacy exploded, "Sheesh...Lovett! You blew two holes in my britches..."

Looking up from skinning their breakfast, Rawley waggled his hunting knife at her saying, "Be thankful...I'm not using this knife to bleed the poison out of you."

Lacy rolled her eyes as she stepped into her britches.

He grinned; things were back to normal between them again. Hearing Lacy plop down on the blanket with a grunt then picking up a boot to put on, he warned her, "Make sure you check your boots for scorpions...they're worse than a snake bite."

She gave him a cock-eyed look, "Sheesh...Lovett. You act like I'm some kinda greenhorn or a shave-tail."

He grinned.

Refocusing on the one boot, Lacy turned it upside down and

slapped the sole several times with her hand. Satisfied when nothing fell out, she slid that boot on. The same process was repeated with the second boot. Standing, Lacy walked over and took the cup of coffee that Rawley offered her. She then walked to a little ridge twenty feet away from camp.

Sipping coffee, Lacy gazed over the terrain. It kinda sorta reminded her of a wrinkled quilt with its valleys, rough and tumbled peaks and rounded hills covered with mesquite scrub, brittlebush, cacti, ocotillo, tumbleweeds and sand. Thinking *lots of sand.* She sighed wistfully, already homesick for her mountains and colorful flower filled plains. Rawley knew this territory from his drover days, driving cattle to the rail heads up north; she didn't. It persuaded her to allow him to be their pathfinder. A dark thought slammed into her brain. *The kids!* Whirling, Lacy's pace picked up. She tossed the left-over coffee from the cup. Running back to camp she dropped the cup next to Rawley, causing him to glance up. Lacy hurriedly began rolling up the bedrolls and ground cloths gathering their gear.

Sensing an urgency, he laid the snake in the pan to fry. Rawley then picked up the two saddles and blankets and began saddling the bay and Fancy.

Tying their outfits behind the cantles, Lacy looked across at her husband. She asked in her soft throaty voice, "Where could they be...Rawley?"

Tightening the cinch around Fancy's girth, he looked up at the question. "Do' no...Sunshine." Looking around at the parched landscape, he added, "We may already be ahead of them...lotta lonesome ground around here." Refocusing on her face and eyes shadowed with worry. "We'll find 'em...Sunshine." Resting his forearms on the saddle, Rawley lightly clasped his hands together. He gave Lacy another reassuring gaze. "We've just gotta be smarter than Kannon," he said.

Lacy just nodded, fingers plucking at the pebbled wool of the bedroll.

Stepping around the mare he pulled Lacy to him. She went

willingly into his strong arms. "We'll find them...Sunshine." Lacy nodded against his chest, her eyes squeezed shut to keep the tears from escaping.

"C' mon...you need to eat something," he said laying an arm across her shoulders and leading the way toward a sizzling breakfast of fresh kilt rattler.

Lacy pulled out of his arms. "I ain't eatin' damn snake for breakfast...it'll just make me start throwing up again," she said adamantly. "I'll just have some dried beef."

Rawley grinned.

Chapter Twenty-Two

Twenty-eight legs continued to pump and weave through sand, mesquite scrub, cacti, ocotillo and desert ironwood. Shale and loose scree clattered under their feet on their way to freedom. *They hoped.* Winding their way through the darkness, stumbling, falling frequently and whimpering as they pushed on, Cotton, Dobie and Ben led the pack with Thad and Chad bringing up the rear. Corralling the girls in the middle, picking up the ones that fell, urging them to keep up the pace that Cotton set.

Slowing then abruptly stopping, Cotton tried to draw air into his starved lungs. Hanah, who was running with her head down, plowed into Cotton's back sending them both sprawling to the ground, sand sprinkling them amidst a tangle of arms and legs.

"Dammit...Punkin," Cotton hissed. "What'd the hell...ya go and do that for?"

"You jus' shad-up...Cotton Clancy Lovett," Hanah hissed right back. "I didn't do it on purpose."

Shoving his sister off him, Cotton rose and spoke quietly to the others, his voice breaking into the heavy breathing that permeated the air as they all tried to gain their wind back. "We'll rest here a few minutes," he said. Looking back the way they'd come, he added, "We've not even run a mile yet." His eyes traveled eastward where a slight lightening of the sky had begun. Heaving in more air Cotton said, "We're gonna have to find some cover for the daylight hours and only travel at night." He crossed his toes and fingers for good luck. It was going to take him and his band of brothers and sisters everything they had and all of the smarts they could muster to keep out of Kannon's grip. "C' mon...let's move," Cotton whispered curtly.

* * *

A black string of juice flew through the air, landing six feet away. A grimy paw swiped at the leftover dribbles sliding into a matted and dirty beard.

"Quince...go see what's takin' them kids so long," Kannon's grainy voice ordered another of his men.

Looking eastward, a slim line of color had begun breaking between the edge of land and the darker star studded sky. Kannon sighed noisily as he thought. *Them damn kids is eatin' away at any lead time me 'n the boys 'ave.* Big Joe also knew, Rawley Lovett was one of the best trackers he'd ever know'd. Tying brush onto the back of the wagon to cover their tracks, putting burlap on their horses feet and then sticking to shale, scree and rocky terrain not only slowed Kannon down, but would slow Lovett down as well, but not for long. Muddy eyes pierced the slip of dawn. *Nope...*he continued thinking, *We's gotta abandon the wagon...* A voice hollered, breaking into his thoughts.

Quince came running back. He panted out the words, "Them kids is gone...ain't no trace of 'em nowhere's."

His eyes narrowed hearing Quince's news. *Dammit,* Kannon thought. *Them kids is smarter and more feisty than I figured on.*

Lenny stepped closer, that crossed eye squinting, "That wuz one dumb move you made Kannon, untying them damn kids."

A head swung on a thick bull elk neck. Kannon's eyes grew ugly.

Lenny stood his ground. "I know'd I should'a kilt you sometime back. Now we's gonna lose more time chasing 'em down."

"Shad-up, Lenny," Kannon growled. "You git on yore harse and head on down that-a-way," he said pointing where the kids had headed. "Tha rest of you men, mount up...set up a perimeter...we can corral them kids in the middle...they's ain't got far...they're afoot."

Leather creaked as eight men stepped into their saddles, then hooves clattered against the scree.

* * *

Spotting a dry wash in the slim light, Cotton headed toward it. Noting the scrub bushes that hung to the sandy sides, it would give them some cover as they rested. Sliding down the dry bank creating a slight rustling sound, he dove for the cover the spindly bushes provided. Thirteen others followed.

Rolling over on his back, Cotton drew air into his lungs as he gazed at the brightening sky. His nose wrinkled, smelling something like tar. He realized then that the smell came from the bushes they rested under. His thoughts turned elsewhere. They had no food or water. And in this landscape he knew they would need water most of all.

Something flickered in his tired mind...something Luke had told him. 'When's ya in dry country wit no warder...cut open a cacti, it don't taste the best...but hit's warder. It'll keep ya goin'.'

He sat up and gazed at his classmates sprawled against the sandy bank, everyone too tuckered out to be whimpering. The girls were going to be the problem. Those dresses they wore hampered their running. Also, they didn't have the stamina the boys had. Cotton's gaze landed on Hanah. *Except for her,* he thought. For once he was thankful Hanah always dressed in britches mimicking their Mama and had more energy than a fish trying to rid it's mouth of a hook.

Sighing heavily, his mind reflected on home, food, water and a nice soft bed. Tossing it quickly out of his mind, Cotton rose. They'd rested long enough. "C' mon...we gotta move," he said. Bending low, he took off in a running crouch hanging close to the brush in the sandy bank.

A few groans mingled with rustling sounds as tired legs pushed bodies up; they followed Cotton down the wash, hugging the bank like their leader.

* * *

105

Riding close to a dry wash, Lenny kept his eyes peeled, looking right, then left and back again. His eyes followed the line of black scrub in the dim light. He reined up and sat listening. The scent of tar wafted across his nose. His eyes shifted, grazing the terrain. His horse shook its head jangling the bit in its mouth disturbing the predawn quiet.

Looking through the scrub, Chad saw the lone rider a scant thirty yards away, silhouetted against the grey dawn. A chill ran down his backbone. Picking up his pace, Chad grabbed Cotton's arm pulling him down under the brush. The others seeing that movement followed and hunkered down under the scrub bunched up in a pile.

"They're here," Chad whispered hoarsely. "We got a rider...behind us."

Cotton peeked through the black-barked spindly growth, the smell of tar heavy. He saw the lone rider on his horse just on the other side of their cover.

"What 'da we gonna do, now?" Chad whispered.

Thoughts wildly ricocheted off the inside wall of his skull. Cotton had to come up with a plan. Then it dawned on him. *The horse...if they could somehow jump the man...grab the horse...* Cotton looked over the band of brothers and sisters. Thad was the best rider of them all; coming in second most times in the Fourth of July races. *If they could get the horse and have Thad ride for help...* Motioning the kids closer Cotton issued orders briskly, "We're gonna jump 'im," he began; the pile of girls gasped while the boys' nodded in agreement. "Ben...when us other boys jump him, you grab that horse's reins...you got that? Don't let it git away...or we're sunk."

Ben nodded as his heart clattered around in his chest knocking the air out of his lungs. He inhaled more. This adventure sure was a lot better then reading Ned Buntline's dime novels. Then he remembered the pistol sticking in the waistband of his britches cutting into his ribs. He'd shucked the weapon from Jake's holster during the tussle in the wagon. He pulled it out from under his coat. "Here," he said.

106

Chad, Cotton and Thad just stared at the pistol Ben held in his hand. Chad asked, "Where'd you get that?"

Ben grinned. "While you were punching Jake back there, I stole it."

The three nodded. Chad praised the younger boy, "Smart move, Ben."

Ben's smile grew wider.

Cotton said, "Thad, you take it."

Relieving Ben of the gun, Thad tucked it into the waistband of his britches.

Refocusing his thoughts, Cotton turned to Dobie, "Dobie...you help Ben." Then he thought of something else, "Get the rifle and the canteen."

Dobie nodded.

Grabbing and pulling Hanah in closer, Cotton whispered, "I want you to create a diversion..."

Hanah piped up, "What's a der...version?"

Rolling his eyes Cotton said, "I want you to run out there, make him chase you..."

"But...he'll catch me..."

"No he won't..." Cotton interrupted. "If you do like I say...run in a tight...small circle. Stay behind his horse...so he has ta keep whirling it around. Then take off running back here...run past us...so's we can jump him." He gazed hard at his sister. Red curls bobbed, *yes*. A lungful of hot air escaped Cotton's mouth. His eyes settled on Thad's face. "You're the best rider we got...oncet we git the man offen his horse...you git on it, and ride like there's no tomorrow," Cotton whispered.

"Ta where? We don't even know where's we at?" Thad asked.

Cotton looked at the grey dawn spreading, lightening the parched landscape. "Ride east," he said. "There's bound to be a homestead or

107

town somewhere's out here...find the sheriff and git us some help." Then he added truthfully, "We won't be able to hold Kannon off."

Thad nodded.

Looking at his band of brothers and sisters sprawled around him, Cotton said, "You girls git up under this brush...and stay there. Keep outta us boys way." He added, "And keep quiet."

The girls made slight rustling noises as they did what they were told, huddling together again. Fear registered across innocent tired and dirt smudged faces.

His eyes landed on his sister. "Punkin...you ready?" Cotton asked.

Copper curls bounced.

Cotton realized at that moment he was glad that his little sister was such a daredevil, always ready for anything. He grabbed her thin arm and shoved her through the brush. "Go...Punkin," he ordered harshly, pushing her through the undergrowth. Lenny saw the kid pop out of the scrub, running right slam-damn across the nose of his horse, startling it, then cut behind him. It was that freckled pip squeak. He whirled the animal around. The girl cut back; then he did, too. She ran a few yards in front of him, spun and poked thumbs in her ears as a tongue stuck out while fingers wiggled at him, taunting him.

Seeing that, Cotton rolled his eyes and groaned inwardly.

Lenny spurred his horse trying to run over the kid. The small body danced out of the way, wheeling behind him again. Jerking hard on the reins Lenny spun the horse around as the kid ran for the dry wash. Aiming his mount in that direction, he spurred the animal again.

Hanah ran down the embankment, her short legs pumped past the boys hidden in the scrub. The boys' muscles bunched in anticipation as they waited.

Hooves pounded the sandy loam. Cotton yelled, "Now..." Five bodies flew out of the brush, the horse reared in surprise, dumping its rider. Ben and Dobie grabbed the startled animal's reins. Suddenly Hanah was there helping. Dobie reached for the rifle butt and missed as his legs danced out of the way of the mount side-stepping and

108

whirling. Hanah and Ben continued to hang hard onto the reins that were dragging them across the sandy floor of the wash as the horse kept dodging and shuffling, trying to get away. Finally Dobie was able to jerk the rifle out of it's boot, while the other hand lifted the canteen, tossing both aside. Thad jerked the reins out of Ben and Hanah's hands. He stepped into the stirrup and slid into the seat quickly, then banged his heels into the horse's ribs, making it grunt. Thad began riding hard, pushing the animal toward the rising sun.

Chad and Cotton were scrabbling with the man on the ground, landing as many blows as possible, the man returning them. Grunts and umphs accompanied thudding fists landing into bodies. Sand continued to fly sprinkling them like rain. Ben jumped into the pile, adding his fists to the tangle of arms and legs flailing about causing more sand to fly. Dobie waited for the right moment. He saw it, pushing his way into the fray, his hand gripped the man's pistol butt and yanked it out of it's leather boot. Backing off, he aimed the muzzle at the pile of squirming bodies. His other hand slammed down the hammer, cocking the pistol. The cylinder rolled stopping with a slight metallic click, ready to fire.

The squirming bodies abruptly lay still. Heads swiveled, all eyes on Dobie Litchfield. Ben, Cotton and Chad slowly pushed themselves off the man and put some distance between them and their captured prey. Heaving in air, they came to stand next to Dobie. Thirteen pairs of eyes, round as wagon wheels, and about as big continued to stare at the man lying there in the sand.

"Ya...damn...l'il shee-yuts," Lenny yelled. Scrambling up, he lunged at the boy holding the pistol.

A finger convulsively pulled back on the trigger. *Crack...*the sound reverberated across the dawning landscape.

Kannon jerked his horse to a standstill hearing the sound of a pistol firing. A mile...half-mile away maybe. His ears continued listening, hard.

The piece of lead entered flesh, driving to its final resting place in Lenny's chest. He flew back, landing hard in the sand. Rising slowly he staggered toward the boy, reaching for him. Dobie's hand slammed hard on the hammer again.

A shot blistered the air, reaching Kannon's ears for the second time.

Flames spit, catching Lenny's shirt on fire; the second bullet entering at point blank range. Lenny fell into Dobie, his dead weight shoving the boy back into the sandy loam. A grunt exploded from Dobie when he landed.

Thirteen pairs of eyes continued to stare in amazement. Then six hands jumped into action, roughly shoving the man off their hero. Dobie scrambled up, his shirt moist with the blood from their prey, the pistol still gripped tightly in his hand.

Amazement tainted his words. "I kilt 'im...I kilt him..." Stunned eyes flowed over Cotton, Chad and Ben. "I really kilt 'im..." he repeated.

Silence echoed like a tomb around the youngsters.

Chad reached over and removed the weapon from Dobie's hand.

Quickly Dobie snatched it back, raising his voice, "It's mine! I kilt 'em fair and square...the gun's mine!" tucking it into his britches.

Stepping in front of Dobie, Cotton said calmly, "Give the weapon to Chad...Dobie."

"No!"

"Litchfield, we ain't got time to stand here fighting! Kannon is gonna come blasting in here...give Chad the gun.

Puffing out like a prairie chicken, Dobie bragged, "Then I'll jus' kill him too!"

The others remained quiet as they watched Cotton's leadership being threatened.

Hanah was about to say something when she saw Chad ball his fist and swing. Her eyes grew round. The lick caught Dobie on the chin sending him spiraling and landing with a thud.

110

Ben, being the closest, whipped the pistol out of Dobie's britches and handed it to Chad.

Chad nodded his thanks as he flexed the hand that threw the punch.

Cotton broke into the deathly silence, "C' mon...we wasted enough time...Kannon was bound to have heard those shots." He ran, stopping only long enough to pick up the tossed rifle and canteen before picking up his pace again.

Dobie rose slowly, brushing the sand off his backside. He spat disgustedly at the way things had turned out, he had wanted that pistol. He began following the others bringing up the rear.

Tired legs had renewed energy as they followed Cotton. Their feet dug into the sand leaving numerous prints. The kids knew they just might have a chance with the two weapons and a canteen of water.

Chapter Twenty-Three

Riding into Arizona territory Rawley remembered he had a good friend in a dusty, dry-parched town not too far from where they were now. He spoke to Lacy over his shoulder, "We're gonna stop and pay a visit to friend of mine. He may know something."

Lacy glanced up, "What?"

Glancing behind him he knew Lacy had been a million miles away; she'd barely spoken the last few days. Rawley repeated, "Buckshot Kelley...we're gonna stop...see if he knows anything." His gaze continued to roam her features. Even with her hat Lacy's face had blistered; dried scabs now covered her nose and cheeks. He made a mental note to himself to get some salve for her when they reached Top Notch and Buckshot Kelly.

Choosing to ignore him, Lacy's mind continued to tumble with worry. A sunburned hand swiped at the moisture running from her scalp down the side of her face. Her shirt, wet from sweat, plastered her back as did Rawley's. She wiped the remains of moisture on dusty canvas britches, the ones with two bullet holes in them.

Her heavy sigh pierced the air as Lacy watched waves of heat shimmer across the land, dancing across sand like water from the unrelenting sun. *I'm beginning to hate this country,* she thought. Right about now she would give anything for a hot bath and fresh clothes; they had become so stiff with dust and the salt that poured out of her skin. The dry air would lick at the moisture, whisking it away quickly, leaving a white powder-like residue marking their shirts like starch.

Here lately that snarling ball of barbed wire had returned, not from her expecting their second child, but from worry. She and Rawley had been heading south for three, maybe four weeks and still no evidence of the kids had been found. And that worried on her like a hound dog loaded with fleas, scratching constantly.

Lacy couldn't understand it. How could fourteen kids disappear into thin air like that? She and Rawley were good at tracking and flushing fugitives out of the brush. Her mind suddenly jumped back in time...when she had disappeared into the nether lands of the territories, becoming Lacy Watson...the bounty hunter. Her grandfather had never been able to find her during those nine long years she spent on the trail. The west still remained a large and unpopulated area, enabling folks to hide themselves out here. She exhaled noisily again.

Hearing that, Rawley reined up waiting for Lacy to pull alongside. When he spoke, his smooth baritone washed over her.

Lacy stiffened; she wasn't in the mood for that warmhearted voice to turn her insides to mush.

"We'll find them, Sunshine. We'll find them," he said.

Her head swiveled toward Rawley. Her eyes sizzled as hot as the air that surrounded them. "You've been saying that for weeks..." she announced angrily. "...And you with your Cheyenne blood...ain't been worth a damn...Mr. Pathfinder," she said sarcastically.

Rawley's eyes turned just a tad bit frosty.

Seeing the coolness, Lacy's head turned as she resumed gazing over Fancy's ears. Abruptly, she gouged the grey's ribs, making the horse grunt. Spurring the mare into a ground eating lope, she put distance between herself and Rawley.

Licking his own sunburnt cracked lips, Rawley reined up the bay and sat watching his wife ride off. *We're both frustrated and angry, but that ain't gonna find the kids,* he sat thinking and watching the distance between them grow. Lifting the canteen, he unscrewed the top and poured a few tepid swallows into his mouth. He let the water sit on his tongue for a few moments before swallowing. *Think...think, you damn fool. Put yourself in Kannon's place...think like him,* Rawley scolded himself as he replaced the top on the canteen and rehung it on the horn. He looked up at the sky sending a mental message, *Lord...ya gotta help us out here...throw us a bone...a sign...anything.* He whispered out loud, "Please..."

114

Fatigued eyes dissected the hot dusty street. Lacy noted the shoddy one story primitive adobe huts that lined the perimeter of the town. Abandoned roofs had caved in, tumbleweeds and mud plaster laid in piles against 'dobe brick walls. Rawley had told her this town carried the name of Top Notch. *Dumb...*her mind said sourly. *Don't look much like it's in Top Notch shape now.* Rawley also said this used to be a Top Notched, right active little cattle town. Her mind *pffted* into the air. *From the looks of it, that happened a mighty long time ago,* she thought.

Rawley's eyes shifted over the sundried washed-out buildings and sporadic signs littering adobe walls, announcing what lay inside. A few loaded wooden two-wheeled carts squeaked along guided by crusty men were the only activity he saw. Finally spying what he was looking for, Rawley urge the bay in that direction. Pulling up in front of the water trough, he slid tiredly out of the leather. The bay's nose dove into the tepid water and began sucking the moisture back into its body. Fancy followed suit as Lacy slid off her saddle. Standing next to Fancy's head, Lacy bent over and began splashing the warm water on herself washing the caked trail soil and salt off.

Rawley whisked his hat off and plunged his whole head under the water for a few seconds. Rising he continued to allow the river of water to cascade down soaking his shirt, cooling him. Long fingers raked back his hair, droplets flew.

Resettling his hat Rawley strode toward the adobe building some twenty feet away, it's walls glaring back at him in the afternoon sun.

Two barred windows stared blankly at the street. The open door between them reminded Rawley of a mouth. He stepped through and then stopped, allowing his eyes to adjust to the gloom and his body to savor the coolness from within the thick walls.

Two worn boots with rounded heels clunked to the floor as a figure sat up, making the chair squeak.

Eyes adjusting to the dark interior, Rawley glanced briefly at the figure sitting behind a desk. Dust motes floated in the streaks of filtered sunlight poking through slits in the mud and grass walls.

Buckshot Kelly leaned forward, gauging the man who'd stepped through his door. He was a good six inches taller then six feet and had powerful shoulders that tapered to a lean waist. His shirt sleeves rolled to his elbows and exposed tan, muscular forearms. His pistol boot was tied to his thigh and rode low enough for his long arms.

Fuzzy white brows drew together above an angular deeply-lined face as the man squinted and eyeballed the tall stranger who stood in his office. One arm rested casually on the dusty, scarred top of his desk, fingers inching closer to the barrel of a shotgun loaded with buckshot. His eyes were still cautious as the other hand edged toward the wooden stock, ready to pick it up and fire quickly if the need arose.

A soft, deep baritone spoke. "Hallo...Kelly," the stranger said.

* * *

The heels of Lacy's palms pressed into the edge of the trough as she bent over staring into the dingy water. Her mind reflected on the clear cold streams of Wyoming. How she wished she was washing in one of those instead of what laid before her. Lacy sighed again as fingers flicked the water sending little sprays upward into the air. She looked up and scrutinized the landscape within this hole-in-the-wall town called Top Notch. A snort escaped, *I'd take White River any day of the week over this place,* she thought. Lacy knew they had to be close to the border now. She sighed heavily again, thinking about the kids. Glancing at the mare, her hand reached and smoothed the sweaty neck. Lacy thought, *I outta climb back on Fancy and set out myself. It'd be quicker...*she sighed again, knowing she wouldn't. Her energy levels hadn't been the best here lately. Worrying over the kids and now carrying Rawley's baby had drained what reserves she normally had.

Bending closer to the water, Lacy proceeded to splash the tepid

116

liquid over herself again. Wiping the droplets from her eyes, she straightened looking for Rawley. Spying the sign above a door announcing Sheriff's office behind her, Lacy wandered in that direction.

* * *

It had taken Kelly a few moments to register the tall man with the soft baritone standing on the other side of his desk. When it did, he rose quickly, a smile flashing brightly as he gripped the hand extended. "Lovett...ya old dog...how's ye been?" Kelly's smoky voice asked.

Eyes smiled in return. "Can't complain," Rawley returned.

Hearing the light cadence of boots, Rawley turned; Lacy stood in the doorway. He gestured for her to come stand next to him. She did. The cooler, dark interior washed over her parched skin like the cooling effects of a waterfall. A small sigh escaped her blistered lips as she glanced around the office, looking much like any other law enforcement office she'd seen throughout the dusty years. Her eyes finally landed on the man standing in front of his desk. She gasped, her body tensing immediately at the sight.

Rawley threw a brief look toward his wife when he'd heard the light gasp.

Lacy recoiled inwardly at the sight of of the man standing in front of her. He was almost the spitting image of her deceased grandfather. *Skeletons,* she immediately thought. But this man was lean and hard with rounded shoulders. Lacy knew a lot of miles had been tacked onto his weathered hide over the years. But what startled her most was the shock of unruly greyish-white hair that sat atop his angular face. His fluffy sideburns and horseshoe mustache were drooping down the corners of his mouth hiding his lips. That affect reminded her of her grandfather. Lacy swallowed air, thinking again of the *Skeletons* that continued to pop out of her past.

Recovering, she scanned the man's face further, settling on his own brown eyes flecked with gold and green. These eyes registered a softness, a warmth her grandfather never had. The brown eyes filled with a hint of amusement as he'd watched her giving him the once over. Embarrassed, Lacy's eyes darted quickly to the dirty floor, then glanced shyly at her husband. Her neck was becoming warm, and that warmth spread upward to the roots of her red hair.

Kelly grinned. He'd seen freckles on folks before over the years. But never in his born days had he seen as many as this girl had, and with that copper hair and those black eyes...well...he'd just best leave that thought set right there, not let it go any further.

Kelly cleared his throat, "Lovett...where the hell ya been...youse still chasing them cows' arses up the trail?"

Rawley grinned, shaking his head, "Naw...got me a marshaling job in a little town in Wyoming now."

Kelly sat down on the edge of his desk and folded arms across his chest as he said, "Ya don't say..." His eyes flicked at the redhead again, carrying a question.

Noting that, Rawley reached for Lacy's arm, pulling her in closer. "Kelly...I'd like you to meet my wife, Lacy."

Kelly's eyes popped. "Well...I'll be damned..." he said softly. "Never thought you were the type ta settle down Lovett," Kelly grinned. He glanced at the redhead as he teased, "This young buck sowed enough wild oats way back yonder...ta set up population booms in several towns..." he chuckled, shaking his head at the memories.

Rawley turned redder than a beet under his browned skin as he flicked a glance at Lacy.

Her mouth dropped at this new revelation. She slanted a dirty look at Rawley but her husband didn't even flinch. *He never told me about that,* her mind buzzed.

As Kelly was grinning he stood and offered his hand to the woman.

Lacy's head swiveled at Kelly's movement. Her eyes first glanced at his face, then traveled down his arm to his hand. She hesitated, then shrugged as she stepped forward and clasped his cool, dry calloused

118

hand in hers.

"Welcome to the 'land that burns'," he said.

Lacy jumped hearing those words. She quickly withdrew her hand and wiped it down her dusty britches.

Questions flitted across Kelly's face at the girl's reaction. He cut a swift glance at Lovett.

Speaking as if on cue, Rawley began, "Kelly...we need your help," he said. "We're looking for some hide hunters...eight of 'em all total...probably got ah wagon with them. Their leader is a big man...boulder shaped...little shorter then me. Stinks like rotting elk carcasses. Goes by the name of Big Joe Kannon..." he tilted his head. "You know of him?"

Kelly's eyes narrowed shrewdly before he backed up a step and leaned on the edge of his desk. "I've heerd of 'im...never had the pleasure of loading his ugly carcass full of buckshot." He asked, "Why? You on his trail?"

Lacy kept quiet, eyes flicking from one man to the other. Her fingertips found their way into her britches' hip pockets as she waited on Rawley to answer.

"He stole all of our kids out of the schoolhouse one day..."

"He did what?" Kelly asked in surprise.

Giving Kelly a businesslike look, Rawley continued, "He's slave trafficking mostly...nowadays."

"I'll be...damned..." Kelly said.

"He has some kinda gripe with me 'n Lacy," Rawley stopped and nodded toward his wife. "So...to get back at us...he took the children...to sell across the border..." He gazed intently at Kelly. "You know of anything...seen or heard anything..." he let his words trail off.

Canvas britches made a slight rustling sound as his butt scooted further onto the desk and Kelly folded his arms across his chest. Lips went into a tight line under the brushy overhang. He shook his head as his mind tried to dredge up any pieces of information he might have picked up the last few weeks. There was none.

Noting the deep silence Rawley added, "They would be traveling with a wagon...and...fourteen kids and eight men."

Kelly's head popped up at that, "Fourteen kids?"

Lacy spoke in her husky voice.

Kelly's eyes flicked toward her.

"Two of the kids are ours...Hanah and Cotton," she said. "We're getting desperate," she admitted. Lacy darted another look at her husband. "Rawley and I are both good trackers but Kannon is wily enough to somehow disappear into thin air...any help you might could offer would be greatly appreciated," she finished.

Enjoying the feel of her warm throaty voice floating over him Kelly thought, *No wonder Lovett married her, along with a million freckles.* His thoughts added, *The redhead don't look old enough to have birthed two kids.* Clearing his throat and shifting on the desk again, Kelly tossed those thoughts out of his head. "I don't know how much help I can be...kinda quiet 'round these parts," he began, "Cattle drives don't much come through here nowadays, what with the rails crossing the land...further ta the north."

*Hellfire...no...fooling...*Lacy thought, sourly. *Ya got damn buildings falling down.*

Glancing at Rawley he added, "Not like hit wuz when youse wuz driving them scraggly cows' arses...Lovett," he grinned. "Place is almost a ghost town compared ta back then." Squinting at the lawman and his wife, Kelly changed tactics and issued an invite. "How 'bout we head over ta the Cantina and grab a beer...it ain't cold...but hits wet?"

Rawley remained silent, thinking. Lacy waited on him to say something. *He always does...jabber-mouth,* she though not too nicely, rolling impatient eyes.

Noting the silence, "Someone's bound ta know sometin' in thar..." Kelly offered up.

120

Finally, Rawley answered, "As long as you're buying, Kelly."

"Hell...yeah...I'm buying," he replied.

Both men proceeded to walk through the door of the jail, leaving Lacy standing alone. Her jaw dropped, her eyes narrowed venomously. *Damn men,* she thought, *Ain't good for nuthin'... 'cept target practice!* Following them, her eyes darted arrows into their backs as they walked toward the open air saloon. *Damn men,* her mind repeated sourly. She heard Rawley ask Kelly, "You heard of a man by the name of Del Rio?"

"Del Rio?" Lacy heard Kelly repeat disgustedly. "That side-winding Mexican...I heerd tell he likes busting them young girls...hisself, afore he sells 'em."

A chill ran down Lacy's spine hearing Kelly's words. Even though the memories had faded somewhat, she still remembered the first time her grandfather had raped her. Lacy gagged. Standing by the trough she plunged her head into the dingy water, hoping that might help wash away the sudden return of those painful memories. *Skeletons,* she thought, *again.* Rising and taking a deep breath, she flicked the water from her eyes. Gazing around at the nondescript town of Top Notch, Lacy spied what might be a livery. Taking the reins of both horses, she headed in that direction.

Chapter Twenty-Four

A lathered sorrel continued through parched rolling terrain that resembled a wrinkled quilt with its soft hills and shallow sandy valleys, littered with outcroppings of boulders, brittlebush, ocotillo and cacti. Sand swirled and flew beneath four hooves. The boy rode low over the neck of his horse, saddle horn gouging into his stomach with each stride the animal took. Riding as Miz Lacy had taught him; becoming one with his mount.

Topping a slight ridge in that wrinkled landscape, Thad pulled up the flea-bitten sorrel for a breather. It wouldn't due to run his mount to ground, killing the gelding and leaving him afoot out here; that's the last thing Thad wanted. He skimmed the landscape, squinting against the harsh glare. Nothing greeted him except the shimmering waves of heat, cacti and scant spindly brush. Thad wished he knew where he was...he could be traveling in circles for all he knew. Licking his lips, he tried to stir up some moisture; there was none. His mouth remained as parched as the land around him. Thad tried swallowing...there was nothing to swallow except grit.

Slipping out of the saddle, Thad took the reins and began walking, his boots and the gelding's hooves sinking hock deep into the sandy ridge.

* * *

Digging spurs into his mount's ribs, Kannon tore off in the direction he'd heard the pistol crack; half-mile to a mile, northwest. Reaching a dry wash bed, he plunged the horse down the bank. Hooves dug into the sandy loam sounding like muffled thunder. He jerked hard on the reins when he saw a body lying in the sand fifteen feet from him. The horse protested, half rearing and whinnying shrilly.

Thirteen heads turned briefly at the sound echoing up the wash. Cotton's eyes narrowed when he saw the amount of tracks they were leaving on the surface. He whispered harshly, "Chad...break off some of that brush and start wiping out our tracks...a blind man could follow us." Chad nodded dutifully. Dobie and Ben went to help, knowing time remained of the essence.

Cotton was glad now that he had paid attention listening to old Luke tell his stories. The tidbits he'd gleaned from the old man just might give them some time to find a place to fend off Kannon and his men. He took off again, the girls following him all bunched up together. The three boys hurriedly swiped away tell-tale remains of their presence.

* * *

Leather creaked as Kannon's bulky form slid from the back of his horse. Cracked worn boots landed softly in the wash. Holding on to the reins, Kannon and the horse walked quietly toward the body; the light scent of spent black powder wafted across his nose as he drew closer. His eyes squinted, drawing in dirt crusted crows feet as he gazed at the two holes in Lenny's body. Black flies had already circled and descended in the early morning light, buzzing in the holes decorating his shirt, lapping up and laying eggs in the drying blood.

His eyes lifted and scanned the churned sand around the dead man. Walking past the body, he continued following the roiled ground that broke up the windswept smoothness. Coming to the edge of the agitated sand, he continued to follow the tracks left by the kids. Picking out shod prints, his eyes followed them climbing the bank through the scrub heading east. *Damn*...he thought. *One of 'em got away.* Full lips buried under all the brush on his face, tightened into a thin line.

Turning quickly at the sound of his men riding up the wash, Kannon waited. Yanking on their mounts' reins, nostrils snorted, bits jangled and leather creaked as six men pulled up, surrounding their

124

boss.

Kannon pointed, "Jake...you and Quince...follow them shod prints." He squinted, his eyes sending them a warning, "You bring that kid back alive...ya hear me?"

Jake and Quince glanced briefly at each other and then nodded. Urging their horses forward, they plowed through the brush and over the bank.

"Tha rest of ya boys...follow me," said Kannon as he stepped into the stirrup. Creaking leather responded as his bulk settled onto the worn seat. Five men and their horses fanned out riding the wash, looking for thirteen kids bound and determined on escaping.

Chapter Twenty-Five

The lathered sorrel gave one last weak gasping whinny then collapsed, it's nose diving into the sand, dead. Caught unawares, Thad lay pinned under 1200 pounds of horse meat. Gathering air into his lungs, he lifted his head and stared at the mound of leather and foamy sweat drenched hide. His head flopped back into the sand as a small groan escaped his cracked lips. Trying to gather strength, Thad took in another big drought of air. He began wiggling back and forth scooping out a hole in the sand with his butt and back so he could slide his body out from under the animal. Using his elbows for leverage, he finally managed to pull his legs out. The exertion left him gasping for air, his body worn down to nubbins, he passed out.

* * *

Spotting the buzzards circling in the air, Lemony Jones spoke to his burro, "Lookie thar...Becky...looks like we's got company."

Becky answered with a sharp bleat.

Lemony grinned, tugging on her halter he pulled her along. "Let's go see what we find this time...sweetheart," he said.

Lemony Jones was a short scrappy fella with a leathery skin-draped buzzard neck. The head under the dusty hat sported some salt and pepper hair, although not much as what covered his skinny jaws. The hair reminded one of pulled apart and well used dirty, steel wool. He was a prospector, tempered by the abrasive land; a survivor, now turned desert scavenger.

If one was not strong, one became strong or one did not survive out here. Only hardy souls lived to see another sunrise; it was the harsh reality of the west. When folks from the east began converging on the new and open territories, they'd pack everything under the sun in those prairie schooners to begin their new life on the other side of the great river. When their mules and horses began dying due to pulling the heavy wagons thousands of miles, folks began pitching their belongings out the back of the schooners to lighten the load. Those belongings left a trail of their own - now bleached and scratched from the blowing sands and scattered across the miles. Over the years, Lemony Jones had found family heirlooms, bureaus, beds, dishes, books, clothes, good silver and even a piano once.

Leftovers of the days when gold disease and the promise of new and fresh land afflicted many a soul, families traveled looking through rose-colored glasses at the promise of excitement, adventure and new dreams. A lot of those rose-colored glasses became scratched, cracked and then shattered. More than one family turned tail and headed back to civilization; their stomachs no match for the harsh realities. Others died from those afflictions, their bones now bleached white by the harsh sun. But ones like Lemony Jones had lived, surviving to scavenge and glean the pickings from those many pilgrims.

Fifty yards ahead two dark mounds lay against the buff colored ground dancing in the shimmering sun. It was hot; hot enough to fry an egg. Lemony couldn't remember the last time he had an egg.

He looked up. The vultures were circling tighter, dropping a little lower with each pass, eyeballing the ground below. Lemony smiled, he knew them beaks had to be dripping with anticipation, waiting to dig into their fresh prey. But he was gonna have first pickings and when he was through, he'd let them ugly sum-beches have at it.

Stopping ten feet or so from the carcasses, rheumy sunburnt eyes gazed over the bodies. Eyes darted toward the saddle on the horse. One gnarled hand scratched the thatch of grey sprouts growing from his weathered cheek. *Might could git me a few dollers fer that saddle,* he thought.

A turkey vulture settled on the sand four feet from the horse. Glimpsing the ugly skin-head, Lemony dropped Becky's rope and jumped toward the bird, flapping stringy arms like wings shouting, "Not 'til I'm done...ya neked haided...sum-bech."

128

As a moan whispered from the sand, Lemony's head swiveled. He saw fingers twitch against the sand and a boot move. Eyes grew wide in that strip of dried hide as he moved toward the body.

Kneeling next to the boy, his eyes grazed across the still form. It's chest continued to slowly rise and fall. Lemony's gnarled knees protested as he pushed himself up and wandered back to Becky. Reaching for his sheep's gut water canteen he said, "Looks like we's jus' might 'ave us a live one this time, Becky."

Gnarled knees protested again as he knelt next to the boy. Removing the wooden stopper, Jones poured some of his precious water over the boy's face and into his mouth. The boy stirred. A tongue snaked out and licked at the drops of moisture. His mouth opened like a hungry baby bird. Lemony poured a little more into the boy's mouth. Swallowing, the mouth hungrily opened for more. The old prospector complied, then replaced the wooden stopper. The mouth opened for more. Lemony spoke, "Jus' a li'l at a time, sonny."

Hearing the voice, Thad cracked open swollen blistered eyes. He stared at the form blocking the sun's rays. His savior appeared to be surrounded by a halo. Thad struggled to sit up. The old prospector slid an arm under Thad's shoulders helping. At first the words wouldn't push past his dry throat. Finally he was able to speak, and the words emitted sounded like a new rope rasping across a wooden beam. "Where am I...I need ta git help," Thad croaked out.

Lemony looked around as he answered, "Somewhere's between hell and purgatory," his own voice rusty from lack of use.

Thad pushed himself into a sitting position. His eyes landed on the skin bag holding the water. They gazed hungrily at it. Lemony handed the bag over, saying, "Easy now, sonny...it'll make ya sick...ya drink ta much."

Lowering the bag after a few swallows, wiping at the dribbles,Thad nodded. Then the words seemed to pour out of the boy's mouth, "I need to find a sheriff...a town. Us...kids...we wuz kidnapped from..." he swallowed and pulled in more air before continuing. "From Wyoming...they's taking us across the border to sell us...as slaves...We

129

got away...jumped one of 'em fer his horse..." Thad nodded at the dead animal. "The rest of my friends...is still back there...waiting on me to git help." He looked hopefully at the old man.

Rheumy eyes narrowed in a time-worn face. Lemony said, "That's some tale...youse be a spinning, boy."

Thad pushed himself into a standing position, planting wobbly legs to stay upright. He dropped the water bag by the man's cracked boots, glaring at the grizzled old coot. "It's tha truth, old man." Thad's look hardened, "And iffen ya ain't in the mind ta help me...jus' point me in the right direction." His eyes took in the harsh landscape with heat waves shimmering like water across the scrabby ground. Thad refocused on the prospector again; sighing he spoke softly, "I need to save my friends."

"Youse a fiter, ain't cha...boy," Lemony said.

Thad nodded asking, "You gonna help me...Mister...or not?" He held his breath waiting on the old man's answer.

Lemony Jones inched up, his creaky old bones protesting all the way until he stood to his full height, which was just a few inches shorter than the boy.

Thad continued to hold his breath.

Rheumy eyes dissected the hopefulness he saw in the boy's face. "I reckon...but first..." Lemony heard the explosion of air from the boy, he smiled faintly,

"But...first...hep me git tha saddle an' bridle offen that nag...it'll bring me a right few purty dollers," he said.

Chapter Twenty-Six

Raising his eyes from the ground, Kannon scanned further ahead. Nothing odd popped out of the wavering landscape. Reining up his bay, Kannon whistled in wind thinking, *Damn kids causing me more trouble then a pound of pennies.* He never expected the kids to fight back or be as cunning as they were. *They's makin' me earn every doller,* he told himself. *I otter jus' let them kids shrivel into nuthin'.* But Kannon wanted that money from Del Rio in his empty pockets.

He glanced over his shoulder; his men waited silently behind him. Those kids putting down Lenny didn't bother him so much; they had actually done him a favor. Now he didn't have to listen to Lenny's mouth all the time.

Muddy eyes flicked back to what lay ahead. The terrain remained the same with its sandy rolling hills and broken bluffs with rocky outcroppings, dotted with scraggly ocotillo, mesquite and cacti. Scanning the far distance, he settled on the largest monument of burnt rusty colored rock. *I don't see them kids goin' that far...that's a good fifteen miles,* he thought. Hitching around in his saddle, Kannon told his men, "Fan out...them kids is got to be 'round here somewheres'." The worn heels of his boots nudged his mount forward as the men behind him did the same.

* * *

The band of brothers and sisters kept up the speed Cotton set. Glancing over his shoulder and seeing the straggly string of classmates, he knew they couldn't stay at this pace much longer. With Kannon and his men on horseback, they could easily overtake them at any moment. As he ran Cotton's eyes scavenged the area looking for a place to briefly hide and rest. Spotting a low ridge, he veered off to his right towards it; the others followed. Rounding the top, he slid a short way down then waited on the others. As they came over the top and toward him, Cotton motioned with his palms for them to lay flat. "Not a peep...you hear me? Not a sound!" he whispered harshly. The only sound he heard was the gasping of air.

Chad, Ben and Dobie arrived continuing to brush out their sign.

Something nudged Cotton in his brain...something Luke told him...about leaving a fake trail that veered off into nothing. He closed his eyes momentarily, trying to dredge and sort through Luke's many tales in his brain and find the one he needed. *There!*

Opening his eyes, he focused on Chad. "Chad...you 'member Luke telling us about how to make a fake trail that goes nowhere?"

Chad's forehead scrunched, trying to figure out what Cotton was talking about.

"You know...." Cotton began, "...about walking so far and then stepping backwards in your same tracks...so it looks like you just vanished into thin air? Remember Luke telling us about that?"

"Yeah, he said the Indians did that a lot, leading you right into an ambush."

"Right," exclaimed Cotton. "So we are going to lay a fake trail for Kannon to follow then it leads to nowhere."

"That's stupid, Lovett," Dobie said tiredly from where he had collapsed. "It ain't gonna work."

Spinning on Dobie Cotton challenged him, "You got a better idea?

"Too late..." Chad said, pulling Cotton down alongside of him. "They're here."

Two sets of eyes peered over the sand watching five men slowly ride past looking for some sort of sign from thirteen kids.

"How far do you think those bluffs are?" Cotton quietly asked Chad.

Shrugging his shoulders, Chad answered, " Do' no....the air makes them seem closer, but could be ten...fifteen miles away...do'no."

Ben scooted in next to Cotton and peered over the ridge and whispered, "What are we gonna do now?"

Chad piped up, "Pray?"

"We're gonna need more then prayers...we need a miracle," Cotton added.

Three sets of eyes continued watching the men on horseback fifty yards away. Three lungs held air as the men stopped, gazing at the buff colored ground around them. Three hearts stopped when Kannon looked up and toward the little rise where they lay hidden. Only when they saw Kannon silently speak to his men and move on did they let the air escape.

"That was close," whispered Chad.

Ben and Cotton nodded.

Cotton passed the canteen around. "One sip...that's all ya git," he said. "Its gotta last us," he looked around, "Til we find some water..." *which ain't looking so good right now,* his mind finished. He sighed heavily. His bloodshot eyes raised to the sky above, Cotton sent a plea, *Lord, we need a miracle right about, now...*his mind said. Another voice seemed to enter his mind, a female voice. *Do not fret...little one, I will protect you.* Cotton jumped. His heart began a rapid tattoo in his chest, banging the air out of his lungs. His body swiveled in a 360 degree circle. No one was there except his band of brothers and sisters sprawled in the sand.

Tilting his head, his eyes cast upward. The same female voice added as if reading his mind, *I'm your grandmother.*

Cotton's heart really thudded against the walls of his chest. His Mom often told Hanah and him stories of her Mother, saying how much they would have loved her. And now he was hearing her voice for the first time. It scared the bejeezus outta him. The voice entered his mind again. *Go...run...I'll delay the men chasing you...*his grandmother said.

He exhaled heartedly. *It's jus' the lack of water...heat...exhaustion,*

133

his mind tried to reason from hearing the voice. *Illusions, like some magician.* Washed-out eyes scanned the distance between them and the bluffs watching the trail of dusty haze as Kannon and his men headed toward them. *Lotta open ground,* he thought. *We'd jus' look like a string of ants on a picnic, crossing that open space. We gotta change directions.* The voice broke into his frenzied thoughts. *Hurry...little one...hurry...*He pushed the voice out of his head.

A thin breeze began lifting cotton-colored hair that had turned almost transparent with sweat on the boy's forehead. Cotton spoke harshly to the little band of brothers and sisters, "C' mon, we gotta move." Voices protested as twenty-four tired legs pushed themselves into a standing position. Cotton's look grazed over his comrades, "Let's go," he urged the others as exhausted bodies began following the white-haired youth.

Twelve tired kids stumbled behind their leader as they headed towards the blistering sun in the east and away from the rusty colored bluffs and Kannon.

* * *

Increasing winds had them side-winding, heads down and plowing through the wind, bitter dust and sand. Tumbleweeds slammed into them, tripping short legs. The wind tore the whimpers and cries from their little mouths. The little band struggled on, pushing through the winds and sailing sand. The sun turned into a red ball and then totally disappeared.

Turning his back to take the brunt of the wind and sand, Cotton felt like he was choking, the fine dust clogging his nose and lungs. Cupping his hands around blistered eyes, they squinted against the pain of swirling grains scratching at them like slivers of ice. He looked for shelter from the storm but he couldn't see a thing within the dust-caked air.

Something jiggled in his brain. 'Whens ye in dry country...and ya gots a storm bearing down on ya and no cover...hunker down, lay flat on yer belly...cover yer face and haid wit yer arms and wait it out.' Cotton remembered Luke saying.

Bracing tired legs against the force of the wind, Cotton yelled as the wind whipped the words out of his mouth, sending them sailing along with the wind and sand. His mouth was spitting grit as much as the words. The others didn't hear him. Cotton ran the few yards toward the others, picking a hand or two from the swirling dust and dragging the little girls. Chad came up behind him with Emily, Emma Sue, and Julie pushing them toward the other girls followed by Dobie and Ben. Cotton forced words through the wind, "Lay flat and cover your heads!" He then motioned for the rest of them to do as he did, pressing himself into the ground. Hanah landed next to him. Shoving her down, Cotton laid his body over hers, then buried his head in his arms. The last thing he remembered was the stinging sand hitting him all over his body.

* * *

Kannon and his men hunkered down, waiting out the blasting storm. *Damn it,* he thought, his face buried within the folds of his ratty buffalo hide. *Them kids is gittin' to be mighty expensive cargo.*

* * *

An extreme silence and cold seem to invade his tired mind. Cotton didn't want to wake up. He wanted to stay in his nice soft bed and sleep forever. He rolled over as sand spilled from his back; then reality struck hard. Cotton groaned.

Cracking open his dust laden eyes, he stared at a star-filled sky. His finger swiped at his sand crusted lashes. Pushing himself up, more sand fell away as his elbows rested on the sand beneath him. He gazed around. The kids lay sprawled against the ground, half-buried in sand;

sleeping deeply, exhaustion claiming their bodies. Cotton's tongue moved behind his teeth. It felt like gritty mud as he tried to spit but couldn't; his mouth too dry.

He searched for the canteen, finally digging it out of the sand and he picked it up, Cotton shook it, water sloshed inside. *Not much left,* he thought. More sand fell from his torso and legs as he sat further upright. Fine sand built up underneath the metal cap made a protest as he unscrewed it. Opening his mouth he started to pour a short swallow, then stopped himself. The water needed to be saved not wasted. Cotton replaced the cap and refocused, thinking of something else besides being thirsty. Rising, more sand fell as he stood. Cotton gingerly walked away from his friends and stood scanning the darkness. He wrapped his arms around himself to ward off the chill. *How can a place be so hot in the daylight and so cold at night,* his mind wondered. So far since escaping, they had been able to keep out of Kannon's clutches. But the odds of that continuing were slim to none, Cotton knew. He had no clue as to where they were. His eyes rose, traveling across the velvety sky. A memory popped into his brain of his Mom telling him and Hanah stories of how she always thought of the night sky as a big, black piece of felt. And the stars, pin-pricks in all that black, allowing folks up there to watch protectively down on those below. Right now Cotton wanted to believe that story...he needed to believe that story. Right now he and his band of brothers and sisters needed a miracle.

Chapter Twenty-Seven

Brazos' eyes squinted within a face as bronze as worn saddle leather. Lightweight homespun clothing draped his medium frame, not much taller than the girl. His sleeves cut at the shoulders exposed a quarter moon scar on the upper limb of one arm. He continued watching her as she took care of the big grey and the bay, her hands sliding over their sweaty backs checking for sores. He took a few steps closer, "You stay long?" His eyes continued to travel across her thin frame with a sun blistered face topped off with a slouch hat covering her hair.

Lacy's head swiveled at the sound of his voice. She took in the scar on his arm and her eyes rose. In a tired voice she answered, "A few hours...maybe." Her hand remained on Fancy's neck, fingers playing with the grey's mane as she turned toward him. "I'm looking for someone..."

A leathery face contorted. Brazos blurted out, "Who?"

Lacy shrugged tiredly. "Hide hunters...you know of any...come through?"

Taking a few steps closer he gazed into the darkest eyes he'd ever seen, 'specially for a white girl. "'Round...here...?"

Lacy sighed noisily, dropping her hand from Fancy's neck she said, "Grain 'em good." She headed back into the bright sun toward the open air saloon.

His eyes followed the girl walking toward the stick and 'dobe building. *Interesting...,* he thought. There was an edge to the girl unlike most women who were soft and voluptuous with curves in all the right places. This one had no curves, just a stick for a body. Plus that side arm resting butt forward in its boot under her left elbow made one wary, giving the impression you didn't mess with her. Sighing, he turned toward the bay and the grey.

* * *

Fingers of sunlight filtered through a make-shift roof of dried foliage and the poles supporting it, knocking the brunt of the sun off a dirt-floored patio area. A few roughshod cottonwood tables and chairs were scattered about. Yellow heat wilted candles stuck into bottles sat lopsided on irregular branches lashed together forming the top of each table with rickety chairs around.

Moving toward a window, Lacy placed the 'dobe wall between her and the patrons inside. She peered around the edge of the thick wall, noting the layout and who was sitting where. Even though Lacy knew Rawley was with Kelly, her bounty hunting cautiousness returned.

Inside she saw Rawley and Kelly, their elbows and forearms resting on planks laying across the top of three wooden barrels, hands wrapped around earthen mugs. Their arses were sticking out like they was airing wind stuck in their britches. Lacy rolled her eyes at the thought. As the barkeep held the same position on the other side of the planks, their muted conversation reached her ears.

Her eyes flicked toward the few patrons. In the far back corner, one body lay sprawled across a rickety table, sombrero covering everything but his back encased in light-weight homespun. *Drunk...passed out or asleep,* her mind said. *Probably all three.* She continued to scan the area. Three others played cards; two of the players faced her direction. Lacy searched their leathery faces for recognition but her mind came up empty. The third man sat with his back catty-cornered to the bar and door. She couldn't see his face, but his position enabled him to keep tabs on the rest of the room. Smoke from his cheroot wove its way into the air above sandy brown hair that curled and dipped over his shirt collar. Eyes roaming over the rest of his body, she noted the suit clothes. Red eyebrows inched up, *Traveling...through...decided to milk the locals,* she thought. Lacy pulled away from the window, resting her back against the dried mud.

She sighed, closing her eyes against the harsh glare bouncing off the street. *We'll never find Kannon at this rate,* her mind said. Her hand slid south, resting just below her gun belt, where the baby nestled inside her womb would blossom and grow. Lacy was tired; she needed to rest for her sake and the baby's but she couldn't. Other childrens' lives were at stake. She and Rawley needed to cross that border and find them before they became permanently damaged goods, especially the girls. She sighed heavily again. Pushing herself away from the wall, she walked inside.

A hand lightly touched Rawley's shoulder. He turned and saw tired eyes beckoning him with a message. *We need to move,* Lacy's eyes said.

Buckshot Kelly also turned toward the girl. Intuition honed over decades picked up on the silent messages being slipped between the two next to him as well as the girl's exhaustion.

Chairs scraped back. The other men at the table quickly stood, knocking over the table. *Kerpow! Kerpow!*

The barkeep ducked behind a barrel. Spinning toward the sound, Kelly and Rawley crouched and pulled their weapons. Lacy pulled out hers and hit the dirt floor.

The sandy-haired one looked over his shoulder at the three, their weapons pointed in his direction. He grinned offering a simple explanation, "Caught him cheating, he drew first."

The acrid scent of black powder mingled with the puffs of grey smoke hanging above the overturned table and chairs. Three sets of eyes stared at the two standing and the body lying between them. Weapons whispered slightly as they were re-tucked inside their leather.

Lacy rose with the help of Rawley's hand, but her eyes remained downcast. She would love to stay on that dirt floor and sleep for twenty years, like Rip Van Winkle did in a book she'd read once.

Carson Beckett blinked and then blinked again. There stood Rawley Lovett and Lacy Watson. He blinked again.

"Lacy?" Pronouncing it *Lay Cee.*

Her head bounced up at the soft familiar lilt. Rawley spun back around.

Lacy swallowed cautiously asking, "Beckett?" While her brain interjected, *Skeletons, again.*

The familiar soft huskiness of her voice washed over him. He covered the space between them. "Well...I'll be damned...Lacy Watson," he grinned.

"Used to be," came her soft reply.

"Huh?"

Feeling that Beckett still wanted to mark his territory, even after all this time, Rawley said curtly, "Lacy Lovett...now, Beckett. We've been married almost ten years," he informed the man. *Damn it...Skeletons!* He thought.

Hazel eyes flicked to the tall man beside the petite redhead. His mind conjured up their last meeting with Rawley's statement. He'd been let out of prison early by the Wells Fargo boys. The deal? To find Lacy Watson, his old partner and they work a special mission for them. Beckett finally found Lacy in the small hamlet of White River, deputy marshal to Rawley Lovett. But he had to work the mission himself, Lacy stayed behind. Beckett had missed working with the freckled venom-packed copperhead. He refocused on the two standing quietly against the planked bar. "What are you doing way out here, 'in the land that burns'?" he asked.

Leaning his spine against the makeshift bar, Rawley folded his arms across his chest. His eyes narrowed, "Could ask you the same question?" Carson Beckett posed no threat despite the fact he felt Beckett would have liked otherwise. "Beckett...?" He prodded.

"Huh...oh..." he dragged his eyes away from Lacy, aiming a direct gaze at Rawley, "Finished a job down this-a-way."

Kelly rested an elbow on the planks watching the awkwardness pass between the three. He hadn't seen Lovett in a long time and from the looks of things, he'd been missing out on quite a bit.

Rawley open his mouth to speak, but Lacy beat him to it. He

glanced at her.

"We're looking for someone," she began. "Eight hide-hunters...with a wagon load of kids. You run across that?"

"Hide-hunters...with kids...way out here?"

Her eyes took on a venomous look. She snapped, "Damn you...Beckett." Tugging on her husband's shirt she added, "Lovett...we gotta move..." Dropping her hand she began walking toward the blistering sun.

Straightening, Kelly said, "No, you don't..."

Lacy whirled as her eyes narrowed, sending a black look toward Kelly. "What?"

"I said...no...you don't."

Lacy's eyes sent Kelly a warning, "Mister...you don't tell me what to do..." She sent that same look toward her husband, Rawley didn't flinch either. "Lovett...you comin' or not?"

Beckett continued to watch with mild interest.

Leaning back against the planks, Kelly offered up, "Us...boys got some figurin' ta do."

Rawley's eyebrow shot up, wondering what Kelly had up his sleeve.

"Them harses of your 'ns needs a break..." Kelly cocked a brow at Lacy. "...And from the looks of it, you do too. You jus' go back ta the office and hit one of them bunks," he ordered.

Lacy didn't move. Another blistering look landed on Rawley, trying to singe his eyebrows. She snapped, "You comin'...Lovett? Or do I have to find those kids myself?"

Rawley knew Lacy had been hanging on by a thread the last few weeks; Kelly was right. "Sunshine...a few hours won't make that much difference. The harses...us...could use the rest," he said.

Lacy just stood staring at him, her mouth hanging open wide enough to catch flies.

141

"Go...on, Sunshine." he urged softly. "When we have things figured out, I'll come get you...okay?"

Lacy's mouth snapped shut.

Rawley watched her exhale noisily and her body wither from exhaustion. She nodded, turning and walked toward the door, her tiredness evident in her footsteps.

When she'd tracked out of earshot, Kelly folded his arms across his chest saying, "Lovett...how 'bout ya filling us in...then we can make some plans on how ta git yore kids back."

Dragging his eyes away from Lacy's disappearing back, Rawley turned toward the bar and nodded.

"Pedro...gimme a bottle," Kelly cut a look over his shoulder at Beckett, "An' ah 'nother glass." His eyes returned to the barkeep and hardened, "And not that snake-tail whiskey...n'ither...the good stuff."

Chapter Twenty-Eight

Cotton knew they needed to move...now while it was still dark. The storm had moved on leaving the night sky crisp clear and the air chilly. Cotton's ears pricked up listening, he only heard the thick silence.

His eyes squinted, trying to peel away the layers of darkness that laid upon the landscape like a blanket. *Nuthin'..cain't see nuthin',* he thought. His mind suddenly began forming a plan. *What if...* The plan took further shape in his mind. Their previous tracks had been covered by the blowing sand. He scrambled, waking the others. "C' mon...let's go...we're goin' back," he announced.

Chad scraped crust off his lashes. "Back? We can't go back...you know what they'd do ta us, if we went back," he exclaimed.

Picking up the rifle and the canteen, Cotton shook the sand from them as he explained, "We've been able ta avoid Kannon this long. He won't be expectin' us to turn back. Hopefully we'll by-pass him, reach the wagon and mules first. We'll have food and water then. Make another run fer it."

Dobie piped up, "Yore loco, Cotton Lovett...jus' plain crazy loco!"

Cotton spun at Dobie's remarks. He sent a blistering look through the dark like he'd seen his Mom do...his Mom could throw the nastiest looks he'd ever seen; make a skunk roll over and play dead. "Ya got a better idea?" He snapped.

Dobie shrugged.

Air escaped Cotton's lungs; reaching down he pulled Hanah to her feet. "Since ya ain't got a better idea...move...we're goin' back."

* * *

Sand poured off the brim of his ratty hat like rain when Kannon stirred. Ears picking up the silence, he glanced around. Kannon remained hunched into his buffalo hide. It was still dark out. Moving, he stood and shook himself like a wet dog. The sand flew from the moth-eaten hide creating a shushing sound as it poured from the folds of the tatty fur. He rolled his tongue around in his mouth and spat a string of gritty juice. He moved then, the toe of his boot kicking at limbs, rousing his men. More sand shushed away from bodies as his men began stirring. A few coughs broke into the stillness. "Mount up...boys," Kannon's gravelly voice said. "We's got a passel of kids to catch."

Chapter Twenty-Nine

Stepping into the cool semi-darkness of Lemony Jones' cave-like home, Thad's eyes grew round in wonder. It was decked out with all the comforts of a real wood-framed house. The floor was fine sand, like it had been filtered through a tightly woven screen. The sandstone walls were a beautiful picture in itself with soft streaks of pink, buff, rust, and white emblazoned across the interior. A fancy flowered chintz sofa was pushed up against one sandstone wall with a matching wing-backed chair alongside. To his left, a cupboard held various items along with dishes. Make-shift shelves held books, and humped-back and square topped trunks were scattered about. Scroll-back upholstered chairs pushed around a table with brass candlesticks sitting on it's dusty surface in the center. His eyes continued to roam, not believing what he saw. They landed on the wall across the cavern-like room where a large colorful blanket was tacked into the sandstone. Thad walked over to it, noticing that it seemed to cover an opening. He pulled the blanket back and gazed into a sun-dappled, narrow channel that had been carved into the rock. His hand reached out touching the smooth sides. Throwing the words over his shoulder at Lemony, he asked, "Where does this go?"

Lemony looked up and came to stand next to the boy. Peering over Thad's back, he answered simply, "My escape route."

Eyebrows shot up. "You carve this outta this rock?"

Lemony chuckled, "Naw...this wus done way afore 'r time, sonny. Mebe...thousand year 'go." The old man took a step into the channel, his hand caressed the multicolored sides. "Tha wind and rain did this." He gazed at Thad, "Purty hain't it."

Thad nodded stepping back to let Lemony pass, "So...where does it go?"

The old man said, "Comes out above, so's ya kin look down on anyone snooping afore theys git you."

Slowly turning, Thad refocused on the items in the rest of the room. The large head and foot board half his height had another bright coverlet on the bed. Thad moved, plopping himself down on the sofa, exploding a fine film of dust into the air. He heaved a sigh leaning back against it's comfort. His hand roaming across the rich colors, he looked up. "Where in the world did you find this stuff?"

Blowing out the match, Lemony placed a coal oil lamp on the table, it's light picking up the dusty film. "Them easterners..." he began, "...Wuz traveling cross country. They wuz ambitious but none too bright." Lemony walked over to Becky and began removing the saddle he'd scavenged and her pack. "They's thought they could haul all the comforts of home in the back of them schooners...nev'r givin' thought ta all tha weight them poor mules and harses had ta haul."

Thad closed his eyes listening to Lemony drone on.

Lemony set Becky's pack on the ground. A raspy sound filled the room as he pulled the brush across her coat. "A thousand miles later, when their stock began dying is when theys finally got some smarts and started pitching their belongin's to lighten the load."

As he turned ready to say more, a smiled cracked his leathery skin. The boy had fallen asleep. Lemony wandered over and lifted the boy's legs, straightening them across the length of the sofa, gently removing the pistol still tucked into the waistband of the boy's britches. He spoke softly, "Sonny...we'll git hep fer yore friends...Top Notch is only one, mebe haft day from here. Ole Buckshot...he'll know what ta do." Laying the weapon on the dusty surface of the table, he let the boy be.

Chapter Thirty

At first Cotton headed the little band east away from the bluffs. Then he turned south, back the way they'd come. By then a slim line of color had begun edging the strip of land, making a definitive space between sky and earth.

Twenty-six short legs pushed and scrambled, weaving their way through sand; white sand, red sand, buff sand. Rocks of all sizes and shapes were patterned with pink, yellow, white and rust colored stripes embedded in the shallow ridges. Cacti, mesquite, ocotillo and loose tumbleweeds further embellished the land. Cotton's legs gave out sliding down a little embankment. He laid back trying to catch his breath. Soft rustling noises filled the quiet morning air as the others did the same. Now the only sound that remained was the heavy breathing. Half sitting up, his elbows resting behind him Cotton gazed around. His eyes landed on a clump of barrel cacti. *Water,* he thought, *we need some water.* Luke's stories came to mind once again. 'That round cacti...minds one of a small keg...hits got the most water. Cut it up like ye wuz cutting a big juicy hunk of warder-melon,' Cotton remembered Luke saying. He pushed himself upright and began searching for a sharp rock to cut off the spines. Once he got them spines off he could reach the meat.

Hanah watched her brother wondering what he was up to.

Slicing at the spines, some broke off, others pierced his hand. He would jerk back at the sharpness, then resume.

Sitting and watching Cotton's attempts to break off the spines, Hanah's hand found its way into her front pocket. She pulled out her pocketknife, staring at it for a few seconds before she rose and walked over to him. "Here," she offered, thrusting the knife toward him "Maybe this will help."

Glancing at the knife and then up at his sister, Cotton took it,

147

asking, "Where'd you get this?"

Tucking hands in her dusty britches' pockets, Hanah replied, "Mama gave it to me."

His face pulled a frown, "How come she didn't give me one?"

Shrugging, Hanah said, "Maybe, 'cause ya ain't a girl..."

Cotton gave his sister a dirty look.

Catching that look, Hanah continued, "Mama jus' tol' me it might come in handy one day and ta never leave the house without it."

Cocking a blonde brow, Cotton opened the knife and resumed his work on the cacti. Hanah stood over him, watching.

Walking over Chad knelt next to Cotton. Digging out his own knife, opening it and saying, "I got one, too." He began slicing through another keg-like cacti.

Eying his sister and Chad, Cotton said, "How come everyone's got a knife 'cept me?"

Chad and Hanah cut each other a glance and then shrugged.

Cotton just shook his head. He sliced into the meat, cutting out a chunk and handed it to Hanah. "Pass this around...Luke said it don't taste so good, but it's water."

The moisture dripping through her fingers, Hanah nodded and walked back to the others.

Later when they'd all had their fill of the life giving liquid, Cotton had them on the move again. Topping another short, multicolored rock strewn rise, he called a halt. Sunburnt eyes grazed the distance, looking for tell-tale pockets of dust from Kannon and his men. The land remained barren and rugged. Eyes swinging around to the west, he spotted the thin string of brown powder moving toward the rusty bluffs. He quickly dropped against the ground. "Awww...hell..." he muttered.

Hearing that, Chad crawled next to his friend. His eyes too, found the string of haze in the distance. He echoed Cotton's sentiments exactly, "Awww...hell... they're still looking." He flopped over, on his back with his eyes closed, "Why can't they go kidnap someone else..."

Cotton shook his head, "It won't take 'em long ta figure out they're on a dead trail and swing back around. They's got horses...we ain't," Cotton reminded Chad.

Pushing off the ground, Chad kept his crouch as he moved toward the others. His voice carried an urgency, "C' mon...let's move!" He grabbed two little girls' hands as they struggled to stand on wobbly legs. He was running too fast for the girls to keep up and they fell to the ground, whimpering. Pulling them up, Chad continued as fast as he could, towing the two little girls. The others crowded in close behind.

Chapter Thirty-One

Kelly walked out of his office and piled his gear in the chair next to the open door of the 'dobe jail. Resting his Henry 44/40 against the dried mud, he waited. Beckett walked up the street toward Kelly, towing Lovett's bay, Kelly's black-lined dun colored mule and his chestnut. He stopped at the hitch rail.

Taking his gear off the chair, Kelly began tying it behind the saddle on his mule.

"Where's Lovett?" Beckett asked.

Nodding toward the door, Kelly answered, "Inside...saying goodbye ta his wife."

Beckett's eyes popped; he knew what kind of temper Lacy had. "She awake?"

"Naw...don't look like she'd moved a lick since she hit that bunk."

Walking through the doorway, Rawley stepped up to Beckett relieving him of the bay's reins. Stepping into the stirrup, he swung himself lightly onto the leather. He grinned at the other two men as he swung the bay around, "Ya know what's gonna happen when she finally wakes up and finds us gone...don' cha?"

Beckett snorted, "Madder 'n a wet hornet!"

Climbing into the saddle and swinging his dun mule around, Kelly pulled it in next to the bay. "Now...Lovett, we's awready been over this. No 'spectant muther needs ta be a goin' where we's a goin'."

Pulling alongside the other two, Beckett piped up, "Yeah...but you don't know Lacy..." Thumbing between he and Rawley, "We do...and I...for one, am glad we're leaving town."

Rawley's grin broadened, "Yeah...first she'll track us down, then she'll shoot me dead and *then* ask for a divorce."

"Pshaw..." Kelly returned. "She ain't gonna do that."

Two voices chimed in unison, "Wanna bet?"

Grins appeared on three faces as they nudged their mounts into a lope. They hoped to find the fourteen kids quickly and without Lacy busting in and screwing things up.

Chapter Thirty-Two

Julie Parks stumbled and cried out, her hand slipping from Chad's. She whimpered, "I can't...my feet..." Moisture rose in her grey eyes and spilled over, mingling with the dust leaving a muddy trail. "My feet...hurt too bad."

Hanah plopped to her knees and began untying Julie's shoe strings.

"Prob'ly filled wit sand," Dobie interjected sourly.

Easing the shoe off, Hanah's hands stilled as she glanced over her shoulder. "Cotton...her foot is all bloody." She gently removed the other shoe, "This one, too. No wonder she cain't walk no more."

Cotton landed on the ground next to his sister. Picking up one foot, he examined it. The flimsy cotton hose had rubbed away, allowing bare feet to rub against sand and inside the leather of the shoe. It had created blisters that had popped then rubbed her tender feet into bloody pulp. Looking up, he asked, "Anyone got a bandana?"

Twelve heads said no.

"We need something to wrap her feet in."

Emily Harrison scooted in closer as she pulled up her skirt exposing her petticoat. She tried ripping the material. "It ain't very clean...but it might help."

Pulling his knife out, Chad dropped next to Emily and cut her petticoat into strips, handing them to Cotton as he did so.

Glancing at Julie, Chad praised the little girl, "You never complained Julie, and I knowed it hurt like fire. You're a brave little girl."

Julie sniffled, "But...I'm slowing us down."

"Now...you don't worry 'bout that...we'll make it," Chad

153

reassured her. The others remained silent as they watched Cotton gently wrap the petticoat strips into tight bandages around Julie's feet.

When he'd finished, Cotton glanced at each of the twelve faces staring at him. "Anyone else got the same problem?"

Twelve heads said no, again.

Pushing himself up, Cotton spoke to Chad, "Put 'er on my back...we'll take turns carrying her."

Ben Hudson spoke for the second time since they'd slipped away from Kannon. "I'm thirsty again...and hungry."

Dobie whirled on him, fist ready to fly. Ben flinched, his arms going up to ward off potential blows. "Well..." Dobie pronounced it, *way-ell.* "Ya is jus' gonna haft ta stay thirsty, 'til we find some more cactus," he chewed out. "An' we ain't got no food, ya dum-ass!"

All eyes traveled back and forth from one kid to the other, waiting.

Hanah bounced up. Placing her hands on her hips, she gave Dobie her sternest expression. "You jus' mind yore manners Dobie Litchfield. It ain't his fault, he's thirsty...we're all thirsty an' hungry." She took a step closer, Dobie backed off. "But it still don't give you cause ta fite. We's gotta stick ta-gether, help each other...ya got that, Dobie Litchfield?" Hanah continued with her evil eye.

Dobie ducked his head and backed away, his hand giving a dismissive wave. "I heerd ya...I heerd." He walked off by himself.

Her ridiculously long red-gold lashes drew closer, pinching freckles surrounding her eyes as she watched him pace off a few feet. Satisfied, she landed next to Julie again asking softly, "Can you get on your knees so's one of the boys can put you on Cotton's back easier?"

Chad stepped forward. "I'll carry her."

Heads swiveled and eyes stared.

Chad gave them all a squirrely look. "What? Julie ain't nuthin' ta what I'm used ta hauling." Still gazing at their surprised looks he added, "Don't worry...I'll share," he grinned.

154

Smiles popped out all around, lightening the mood and adding a little energy to thirteen very tired kids. Pretty soon the little band of brothers and sisters continued south back the way they'd come, still hoping to stay out of Big Joe's clutches until help arrived.

* * *

A hand raised, slowing the men behind him as Kannon reined up. Yellow-brown dust swirled around them like thrown flour. Kannon hitched his bulk around in his saddle as he squinted back at the four men. There were only five of them now. Lenny dead, Jake and Quince never returned. If he ever found them, they would be dead, too...offering up a nice fresh kill for buzzards.

"Biff...you 'n Dub, head west see if ya can find any sign," Kannon gestured. "Pac...you 'n Wheat, go east...I'll head straight." He shifted the wad of chaw in his cheek to the other and spat. He watched the string of juice fly before he brought his eyes back to the four, packing the wad firmer in his cheek with his tongue. "'Member now...no harming tha merchandise," he warned. "Them kids 'ill still bring us a right purty penny." Picking up on the looks garnered by his boys, muddy eyes tightened. Kannon ordered, "Go on now...git. Youse a-wasting daylight."

The four reined their mounts around, heading off in the direction their boss said.

Kannon spat another string of brown juice. Worn heels tapped ribs, forcing his horse to move forward.

Loping east, Pac and Wheat slowed their mounts down to a walk. Exhaling heatedly, Wheat looked over his shoulder at Kannon moving toward the bottom of the rusty bluffs. "Damn arse hole," he exclaimed. "Don't know why he's so hell-bent on finding these kids...we could 'a already had money in 'r pockets wit others."

Pac hitched around in his saddle as his gaze followed Wheat's, then hitched himself back around. "Kannon's got somtin's caught

155

deep in hisss craw 'bout them kids. I's overheerd him sezs 'it wuss payback time' way back yonder sev'ral times."

"Damn...arse hole," Wheat muttered, his eyes traveling the ground as they rode. Several hours later they came upon a small swell naturally formed in the landscape; Pac saw the sign the same time Wheat did. Both reined up in unison. "Well...well," Pac said. The men sat quietly for a few moments studying the many footprints marking the sandy, rusty and buff colored ground and now heading southwest instead of due east.

"Damn...kids," Wheat muttered again looking up. He squinted against the glare following the prints leading off into the distance.

Wheat nudged his horse forward, but he reined up quickly when Pac said, "Wheat...what iffen we's ketch them kids an' head off down ta Del Rio...us selves..." He nodded over his shoulder, "Leave Kannon an' tha others out of this..." Pac watched Wheat's expression. "Keep tha money fer us selves," he finished.

Wheat swung his eyes over his shoulder, then back to Pac. "Kannon 'd skin us 'live iffen he caught us."

Pac nodded. "True...but I ain't lettin' him ketch me."

Wheat threw Pac a grin. "What 'd we wastin' daylight fer, then?"

Chapter Thirty-Three

The storm had wiped out the tracks of the boy and Lenny's sorrel, but Jake and Quince kept moving knowing they'd be carcasses if they didn't return with the kid.

The sky, a brassy blue that seemed to go on and on along with the sun, was broken only by scrabby vegetation and multihued sandstone crumbling into the landscape. They'd been trackin' the kid for a day and half, keeping on in the same direction the tracks had been heading before the storm.

They spotted the skin-heads circling the sky at the same time. Cutting each other a short glance, Jake and Quince nudged their mounts toward the birds. The stench arrived first. The two men pulled up five feet away and watched the skin-heads fly off and then return, beaks plucking and tearing the flesh of the already bloated carcass.

"That's Lenny's harse...sur'nuff," Quince said. "Run tha damn thang ta ground...that boy did."

Jake barely heard Quince, his eyes studying the ground. Lifting his eyes, they followed the scuffled sandy layer. Two sets of boot prints, one set deeper then the other, indicating one person was heavier. Unshod hooves spaced close together. *Probably a burro*, Jake thought. He nudged the ribs of his mount to follow the prints. Every now and then they seemed to stop then continue on. Quince joined him.

The two followed the sign, slipping into a narrow arroyo. A sandstone face bit into the sky with numerous cavities within the formation hollowed out from frequent rains and winds from millions of years ago. The tracks headed in that direction so they followed.

Outside, Lemony sat in a rocker he'd salvaged, waiting on the coffee to boil from the small fire he'd built. Becky's head turned and she bleated. Lemony stiffened, halting the rocker's back and forth motion. Rising, he disappeared and then returned with his loaded scatter gun resting comfortably in the crook of his arm. He waited.

Ears dulled by age finally picked up shod hooves clicking against scree and sand. The scatter gun slid lower on his forearm, double barrel pointing toward the soft sound. Becky bleated again. Lemony squinted into the glare outside the shade of the formation behind him.

Two men, haggard and dusty, astride a blood-colored bay and a paint came around the slight bend.

Quince and Jake reined up about fifteen feet from the scraggly man holding a scatter gun on them. Their eyes shifted, taking in the scene. There was a rocking chair by a small fire, a burro standing quietly watching them behind the man with the scatter gun.

Suspicion clouded Lemony's old eyes. No one spoke, continuing to size each other up.

Quince broke the silence first with a "Howdy...ole timer."

Lemony nodded as his eyes flicked toward four hands where they continued to rest on their saddle horns. He knew the breed. Rough and mean, made cruel and hard by nature, without a care toward other folks 'cept their selves. Gun belt leather tied to their legs gave the old prospector another indication of their intent. Except one's gun boot was empty but his rifle remained in it's scabbard next to his knee. Lemony had tangled with that sort of breed in the past but now he had a kid to protect and he figured these two was after the boy.

Jones spoke, "Looks as iffen your harses could use some warder," nodding at the nags whose heads drooped to their knees. "Theys good warder further up," Lemony nodded over his right shoulder. "'Bout thirty yards...nice l'il spring." The two didn't budge, causing his gut to tense even more. Lemony allowed the sensation to travel, preparing himself. His hand slipped closer to the double triggers, finger itching to reach around the metal half-moons within the guard.

Tension filled the air, making it crackle as if a waiting thunderstorm hung in the skies. Silence stretched as the three continued to eyeball each other. Lemony waited patiently. Over the years, he'd learned to let others show their hand first. He waited some more.

Something stirred Thad, rousing him from an exhaustive sleep. He came fully awake. Opening his eyes, they flitted over the dim interior looking for the old man. Half sitting, he focused past the small circle of light from the coal oil lamp on the table toward the entrance. Glancing briefly at Becky, he saw her watching Lemony's movement. His focus jumped to the old man pointing his scatter gun at something. His stomach lurched sending a warning.

Thad quietly eased himself off the sofa onto his knees. He didn't see his pistol. His eyes bounced around the interior looking for another gun. There against the sandstone wall next to the bed leaned a rifle. He crawled toward it.

Quince spoke breaking the thick silence. "Looks right homey 'round here..." he began.

Lemony ignored him, saying instead, "Better warder them harses afore they leave ya afoot."

Reaching the rifle, Thad listened to the voices outside. He only heard Lemony's and one other. He pushed down the cocking lever to check if the chamber was loaded. The sharp click seemed to echo within the cavern-like walls. Thad glanced over his shoulder, Becky wasn't paying him any mind munching on some grain. The rifle had a shell in the chamber; he let a small sigh escape. Easing the lever closed, Thad began crawling toward Lemony as he heard the man speak once again, "Lookin' fer a boy..." Thad heard Lemony answer, "That so..."

"Killed our friend," Quince said. "Stole hiss harse...we found it daid back yonder ways." Quince fell silent. His hand slipped to his thigh, closer to his weapon on his hip. He waited.

Catching the subtle movement of the man's hand, Lemony's old eyes turned shrewd. "That so..." he repeated. "Ya say, ya found a daid harse back yonder way? Anythang...worth scavenging offen it?"

Jake leaned forward, his hand settling on the rifle butt. "Old

159

timer...I's 'bout ready ta make ya 'nother meal fer them skin-heads. Where's the boy?"

"Ain't seen...no boy."

"Like...hell, old man!" Quince snapped. "They's two sets of boot sign...leading rite back here."

Lemony kept a hard gaze on the two men. His game-playing poker face in place covered his grizzled mug, his finger now on the two metal half-moon triggers of the scatter gun, it rose slightly. He lied, "Lak...I said...I ain't seen no boy."

Thad continued crawling toward the opening. He peeked around the buff colored stone. He still couldn't see who Lemony was talking to. Thad scooted backwards, and then stood. Pulling the length of the rifle close to his chest, he sidled in closer so he could peek around the edge of the opening. When he did, Thad's eyes popped. He jerked back, hauling in air for his suddenly deflated lungs. Two of Kannon's men, Quince and Jake, had found him. His adam's apple bobbed as he swallowed. Glancing left over his shoulder at Lemony, he thought, *Now...what.* His eyes flicked back inside the cavern as they landed on the blanket covered escape route. Fine sand cushioned his steps as he ran. Pushing aside the blanket, Thad disappeared into the narrow pass.

"Ol'...man, I's awaitin,'" Jake snarled.

Eyes dimmed by age got ugly. Lemony held his ground, not bothering to answer. *If I die, I die,* he thought. The finger wrapped tighter around the two half-moon triggers. He remained silent, watching...waiting.

Reaching the top, Thad peeked over the formation. Only one showed up in his sight, except for Lemony. Slipping further out until he had both men in his sight, he brought the rifle up. Squinting down the barrel, he brought the stock closer to his cheek, readjusting his sight. Thad waited.

Pulling the rifle from its boot, Jake threatened. "Mebe...ya need sometin' ta jog yer m'rey." The noise fired over the head of Jake's horse startling it. Lead bit the ground in front of Lemony's cracked

160

boots. Dust and grains of sand peppered his britches. Becky bleated, wheeling her rear around, dancing against the sudden noise.

Lemony let loose with both barrels. Horses squealed and reared. Becky hee-hawed, kicking air. Two men howled and danced in their saddles as hot lead pelted them from the double-load of buckshot.

Thad pulled back on the rifle's trigger. Jake flopped forward like a rag doll from Thad's bullet. He slithered out of the saddle leaving a blood trail on his horse's shoulder as he ended in a heap on the sand. The horse shied off.

Quince tried to control his mount wheeling and rearing from taking some buckshot.

The rifle above quickly ejected the spent cartridge and Thad loaded another and aimed.

Flames blistered the front end of Quince's gun hitting Lemony a glancing blow to the shoulder, spinning him against Becky's rump. She squealed, whirling against the rope that held her, kicking again and barely missing the old man's head as he slid down her haunch.

Quince aimed again, ready to finish off the old man. Something seared his back, drilling through his chest and shoving him forward causing his breath to catch. The pistol slid through his fingers to land in the swirling dust. He pulled himself upright again just as hot lead bit the back of his neck, exploding blood, bone and flesh across the neck and ears of his horse. Quince's eyes rolled back in his head; dead before he fell out of the saddle to lay near Jake.

Thad stood and worked the cocking lever, ejecting the empty brass shell and loading another into the chamber. He waited; nothing moved.

Lemony looked up and then called out, "Sonny...come hep me."

At the voice, Thad left his position arriving at Lemony's side. The rifle clattered against rock as both of his hands slid under the old man's skinny arms and hauled him to his feet. Walking and settling him in the rocker, Thad then focused on the two men he'd killed. He sucked in air hoping it would calm his sloshing insides. His adam's

161

apple bobbed trying to swallow the bile rising.

A pain filled smile poked from a time worn face, "Boy...wherein the hell did cha learn ta shoot like that?" Lemony asked.

Thad's head swiveled. "Prairie chickens," he replied simply and then added, "I ain't never killed nobody...before." He quickly swallowed again.

Lemony nodded. "Thankee, son...I's be buzzard bait, iffen it twern't for you."

It was Thad's turn to nod in response.

Chapter Thirty-Four

Thirteen tummies growled with increasing frequency as they continued to push south. Their last meal had been almost two days ago before they escaped. The only thing they'd had since was the tasteless watery pulp from the barrel cacti and dust. Lack of food and water had begun taking it's toll on the little band. They stopped more frequently, trying to dredge up what reserves of strength they had to keep going. That energy was dwindling by the second with the continued blast of the sun heating the air and ground like a furnace.

Chad tripped, causing Julie to roll from his back to land a few feet away. She whimpered. Rolling over, Chad's chest heaved from exhaustion. The others followed suit, hitting the buff colored sand gasping for air.

Ben Hudson laid there, breathing heavily from his cotton filled mouth or so it felt. He was beginning to get mad; mad at Ned Buntline and his lies about the west. He decided when he grew up, he'd track Ned Buntline down and give him a piece of his mind. Maybe even a few punches thrown in for good measure, too.

Dobie Litchfield voiced what everyone had been thinking, "I quit! I'm jus' gonna die right here...let tha buzzards have me."

Cotton pushed himself up, resting on his elbows that were dug into the hot sand. He squinted against the sun's blazing reflection. "That don't s'prise me none...ya always wuz one ta avoid any kind of work. Oh...well, one less ta worry 'bout," Cotton said drily.

Dobie's eyes turned mean as his head swiveled, "You jus' shad-up, Lovett!"

Ignoring him, Cotton gazed over the other kids. There was only one he remained truly worried about: Emma Sue. She'd been in a trance-like state with her eyes carrying a glassy-look ever since they'd been herded out of the schoolhouse. Emily Harrison had to force the cacti water through her lips. Emma Sue clung to Emily's skirt like she was blind. *Maybe she is in a way,* Cotton thought. Pushing himself into a standing position, his legs wobbled. He grimaced at how that slight movement highlighted his ever growing weakness. He told Dobie, "Your turn to carry Julie."

Springing up making the sand fly, Dobie spat, "Like hell...let 'er walk like the rest of us!"

Cotton walked a few paces and let his fist slam into Dobie's jaw taking him by surprise. Dobie flew back against the ground, his eyes watering from Cotton's sudden attack.

Chad rose as did Ben, both stepping closer to Cotton.

Hanah's eyebrows shot clear into her hairline. She'd never seen Cotton swing before. She was usually the one swinging and getting into scrapes. The other girls had bunched up again, huddled together with Julie in the middle.

Eyes of polished flint continued to send a warning. Cotton's fists remained along his sides ready in case Dobie came up swinging. That swing left him even weaker, only his anger at Dobie Litchfield kept him standing. Cotton spoke softly, "You'll carry...Julie." Wheeling, he bumped into Chad and Ben. An unspoken understanding seemed to pass between the three. Cotton nodded. Ben and Chad separated, allowing Cotton through.

Chad refocused on Dobie. "Move it...Litchfield...like Cotton said...your turn to carry Julie."

Dobie climbed sourly to his feet, his hands angrily swatting at the sand on his backside.

The little band struggled to their feet, exhausted. With Dobie carrying Julie, they formed a string behind Cotton.

Emily Harrison heard the sound first. She stopped and Emma Sue bumped into her knocking her down. Ben bent to help her up. Emily stopped his hand saying, "Listen...you hear that?" Her heart began a rapid beat in her chest, making it hard to breathe, afraid of who or what might be on the other side of the natural wind blown divide.

"Hear...what? Ben asked.

"Shush...listen!"

He heard it then; grunting, snuffling and snorting noises. His heart jumped into his throat, cutting into his air supply. Dobie walked past carrying Julie paying them no mind. Chad who was following Dobie to keep him moving, stopped alongside wide-eyed Ben and Emily.

"What?" He asked.

Fingers signaled Chad to be quiet. They pointed to their left toward the ridge line.

Ben whispered kind of loud, "Over there, something's...over there."

Chad heard the snuffling and grunting as he told Ben, "You kids git on up ta the front. You tell Cotton to move faster and find some cover. I'll catch up later," he ordered. Fingers pulled the pistol from his britches. He cocked it and blew the sand from under the firing pin easing the hammer back down. Waving the pistol he instructed, "Go on...move!" He watched them scramble, running, passing Dobie and Julie. Catching up to Cotton, Ben spoke to him. Cotton whirled. Chad waved him on with the pistol. Cotton turned and picked up his pace with the others sensing an urgency.

Crouching, Chad ran lightly toward the ridge and the few pieces of brush that seemed to survive in this God forsaken place. He dropped to his belly, inching along. The grunting, snuffling and snorting was becoming louder. *Some kind of wild animal,* he thought. Slowly, he peeked through the spindly stalks. His mouth dropped open at what greeted his eyes. He blinked. *A hog?* Then, *Food!* By the time his brain landed him back in the present he was becoming confused. *Out here?* He'd never seen this kind of creature before. Looking like a hog but with furry, black brown coloring with tusks like the elephants he'd seen in picture books curled toward his snout. His mind repeated itself. *Out here?* Eyes flicked over his shoulder; he didn't know where Kannon might be, whether he remained on their trail or had given up. His shooting the hog would give away their location to Kannon - but could they continue without food? He knew the girls were on their last

165

legs; they all were.

Unbeknownst to Chad as he looked over his shoulder for tell-tale dust in the distance, the boar had picked up the boy's scent. Suddenly it charged.

Chad's attention snapped back when he heard the boar ripping through the spindly brush. He tried to roll out of the way but the boar's snout and tusk cuffed his shoulder, ripping shirt and slicing skin. The pistol flew out of reach. The boar raced past him, wheeled and charged again. He'd never run into such a vicious animal. Chad rolled again unable to get his feet under him fast enough. The beast spun around and charged again, tearing a deep gash in his thigh. He hollered in pain.

Whirling, Cotton dropped the canteen. He ordered the others, "Keep running...Chad's in trouble." The cocking lever of the rifle snapped down, loading a brass cartridge into the chamber as he ran back to Chad, stopping twenty feet from the brute attacking his friend. Cotton raised the weapon to his shoulder, placing the stock against his cheek as his finger latched around the trigger he then pulled. The vicious animal squealed, then whirled charging Cotton. The rifle quickly ejected the empty cartridge, loading another. The animal had it's head down, attacking him like a raging bull. Aiming at the head, Cotton pulled the trigger. Blue and orange flames spit from the muzzle. The animal dropped in it's tracks a mere foot from the toes of Cotton's boots as he stared at it. The sharp scent of burnt hair and black powder surrounded him. Just as quickly as it began, it was over, silence once again permeating the landscape with the constantly beating sun. A low wind continued to blow lifting blonde hair from a sunburned face. Cotton breathed deeply.

Ben and Hanah ran toward her brother, stopping alongside him.

"What *is* that?" she asked of no one in particular.

"A wild boar," Ben answered

"Huh?"

Tucking hands in his pockets Ben shrugged, "Mom made me read

166

a lot."

Freckles scrunched making Hanah's sunburned nose hurt. She followed her brother, squatting next to Chad where he was examining the boy's wounds.

Finding the half buried pistol, Ben picked it up and shook the sand from it. He began to pace right next to where Hanah stood.

Doc's words popped into Cotton's mind. 'Sometimes, ya jus' gotta let the wound bleed a little. Washes the impurities out.' Cotton sighed inwardly, *Maybe we are meant to die out here.* He quickly kicked that thought out of his head. *Chad is badly hurt, Julie still can't walk...what else is gonna go wrong...no water...no foo...wait!* He slipped an arm around Chad's shoulders. "Can you make it down to that little draw?" he asked. Against his better judgment Cotton continued, "We'll set up camp for the night," he nodded over his shoulder at the wild boar. "Build a fire and cook that...*whatever*...over there?"

Chad nodded.

Cotton issued orders, "Hanah...you and Ben git the others. Tell them we're settin' up camp. Then find something to build a fire with."

"Matches..." Hanah piped up. "...We ain't got no matches."

Ben grinned. "Yeah...we do," he said, pulling two out of his back pocket.

Hanah blinked.

Ben's grin grew, "I like smoking Pop's ceegars sometimes."

Chapter Thirty-Five

The urgency in Thad's voice had Lemony moving a little faster than he'd like, but then the kid had saved his life. Lemony's wound turned out to be just a scrape with a lot of blood. He had Thad apply his medicinal herbs and bandage his shoulder. It was a little stiff, but he'd live to see another sun.

After watering the horses and Becky, they set out. The boy, an old man, a bay, a paint and the burro loaded with the rigging from the dead horse, headed for Top Notch and Buckshot Kelly.

Arriving while some coolness remained and knowing it would be replaced soon by the blistering sun and heat, Thad squinted at the ruins of Top Notch. Tumbleweeds rolled by the adobe skeletons of huts with their roofs caved in. Pole beams resting against interior walls reached toward the sky like black fingers in that space before dawn would burst upon the land. He and Lemony continued riding quietly through the town.

* * *

Lacy stirred and rolled over, stretching her limbs. She opened her eyes and gazed around noticing the early morning light filtering through the cracks in the walls of the cell. A piece of paper floated to the dirty floor alongside the bunk. She half rolled as she reached out to retrieve the paper. She read Rawley's familiar scrawl.

Sunshine,

Beckett, Kelley and me have gone to rescue the kids. You stay put!!! Don't know how long it will take. Will pick you up on the way home.

Love you, Rawley

Sitting up abruptly, white sparks danced in dark eyes. *Why, that low-down...,* her thoughts began. Lacy remained sitting as anger changed from a slow boil into a hot rage. Rising swiftly, she moved to the open cell door, stopped and read and reread the note from Rawley. Her disbelief in the fact that they had left her behind continued to travel across her face.

Lemony and Thad pulled up in front of the squat building. The sign overhead said *Sheriff.* Slipping stiffly off the leather, Lemony said, "Sonny...iffen Buckshot ain't here," Lemony nodded behind Thad at the open-air Cantina. "He'd be thar."

Thad looked over his shoulder then back at the old man and nodded. He swung off the leather and wrapped the reins around a weathered hitch rail.

Boot heels clumping across dusty scarred planks had Lacy glancing and moving toward the sound. She stopped when two men ambled through the door. Weak light from outside left the men's faces in shadow. But she could discern that one was taller then the other and both so scrawny and covered in dust it was hard to determine what color they were. White, Indian, Mexican...she didn't know which.

The shorter one cleared his throat, "Uh...Ma'am...ya knows where we's might find Buckshot?"

Taking a step forward, she angrily waved the piece of paper still in her hand. "That's what I'd like to know too!" She snapped. "Seems I've been left behind!"

When the woman's husky voice washed over him, Thad's heart jumped.

"Miz Lacy?"

Dark eyes zeroed in on the taller one. When he'd spoken her name, Lacy didn't want to believe it, couldn't believe it. "Chad? Thad?" She could never keep the two straight.

"Thad," he replied.

Lacy rushed across the floor, wrapping her arms around Thad's neck in a death grip, covering his face in kisses.

170

Lemony coughed, just as embarrassed as the boy at the display of affection from this woman.

Thad tried to pry those locked arms apart. "Miz Lacy...pu-leeze..."

Stepping back, she refused to let go of his arms. Her fingers remained clutched like talons pinching into his skin. Her eyes searched his face looking for answers. Lacy's heart was just a thumping against her ribs knocking the air out. She hauled in more, her words tumbling, "The others...are they with you? Are they okay? Hanah...Cotton, the others..." Lacy glanced out the door, "Where are the others?"

Thad glanced briefly at Lemony, then back at Lacy. "We got separated, couple a days ago..."

Her question interrupted him, "Where...where did you get separated?" Her heart picked up it's pace to stampede level.

Shrugging Thad replied, "Do' no...we jumped one of Kannon's men fer his horse...I took off riding fer help...that's the last I seen of any of 'em."

Lacy released the biting grip she had on his arms. Breathing deeply, she tried to settle her whirling mind, regrouping her thoughts she asked, "Anyone...anyone hurt when you last saw them?"

"No Ma'am, they wuz all scrabbling wit Lenny...uh...one of Kannon's men when I jumped that horse and took off for help."

Thad nodded at Lemony. "Lemony...uh...Mr. Jones...here...saved my life...when the horse died."

"Jus' lak he did mine...yesterdey," Lemony piped up.

Lacy's piercing gaze left Thad's face to zero in on the old man.

Lemony flinched from the penetrating gaze.

"Much obliged, Mr...Jones." Swinging her eyes back and forth between the two Lacy asked, "What happened yesterday?"

"Two of Kannon's men showed up at Lem...uh...Mr. Jones' place looking fer me," Thad said looking at Lemony. The old man nodded in agreement.

Noticing the look between the old timer and Thad, her brow crinkled. "What? What...tell me..."

A sad and serious face flicked back to Lacy. Finally Thad blurted out, "I kilt two men...Miz Lacy...I kilt two men. I shot 'em in tha back...ya ain't nev'r s'posed ta kill a man in tha back!" He fell silent again.

Seeing the tears well up in the boy's eyes, Lacy's heart melted. She knew how he felt. She'd cried too after killing her first man. Gently she laid a hand on his shoulder. "It's okay, Thad...you did what you had to...to survive."

Thad's eyes dropped. He blinked, tears splattering the dusty floor.

Her hand lifted his face making him look at her. The boy seemed to have grown several inches in a month, now standing several inches above her five foot two inch frame. Not only that, Thad had become a man. Pride swelled in Lacy's breast. "Remember? In the past I've had to do that too...to survive." Glancing at his hair, Lacy tenderly smoothed the dingy brown locks from his forehead exposing white streaks where the sun had not reddened it. "You grew up Thad...and I'm proud of you," Lacy said softly.

Thad nodded. A grimy hand swiped at his nose and cheeks.

Lemony piped up, "Youse hiss muther?"

Smiling faintly, Lacy shook her head. "No. Just a good friend." as she moved and sat on the edge of the desk crossing her arms, Lacy became all business. Her eyes once again settled on the old man giving him a hard look.

Lemony flinched again.

"What do you know about this country...Mr. Jones?"

*Damn...*Lemony thought. *Them eyes could burn a hole right through ya.* He took several steps closer. Open curiosity filled old eyes noticing for the first time all the freckles that dotted a face topped with copper hair. His eyes shifted to the hardware cinched around her waist, holding a Colt in it's boot for a quick cross draw. The walnut grip he noted was smooth and shiny, attesting to its frequent use. *Not someone* *ya want ta mess wit neither,* he concluded.

Lacy tilted her head as one brow cocked up. She smiled faintly, knowing he was examining her as much as she was him. "Well...Mr. Jones?"

A dingy smile popped out amongst the brush growing from leathery skin. "What 'd 'cha say yer name wuz...uh...Ma'am?"

Continuing to smile Lacy dropped her arms, palms resting on the edge of the dusty desk. "I didn't...but it's Lacy Lovett, deputy marshal for the town of White River, Wyoming." She nodded at Thad, "Thad was one of fourteen kids kidnapped from our schoolhouse who is heading toward the border to be sold into the slave trade. Rawley and I...I mean my husband, the Marshal and I have been trying to find them before that happens." Lacy tilted her head again, "You might be able to help us...Mr. Jones."

"Lemony...Ma'am," he offered. He looked at the boy standing quietly next to him. *Their stories matched.* "What's 'cha offerin' ta pay...iffen I wuz ta join up wit ya?"

Lifting her palms, Lacy stared at the imprints her hands left on the desk. Rubbing the dust from her palms she glanced at Lemony. "Nuthin'...Mr. Jones," she stated firmly. "You'll do it because you want to help Thad find his friends." Lacy paused, then her soft voice added, "And I think you would...Mr. Jones."

Aged eyes tapered. *Damn...*Lemony thought. *Females!* He flicked a look at the boy. Thad stared back, his eyes pleading with the old prospector. Lemony sighed deeply, he'd been took. "Aw...right."

Two dimples emerged when Lacy threw a smile. "Thanks...Mr. Jones." She stood, redirecting her smile toward the boy as she said, "Go down to the livery Thad, and saddle up Fancy. Mr. Jones and I need to get supplies."

Thad nodded and disappeared.

"Ma'am...iffen we's ta be ridin' ta 'gither...ye kin drop the Mr. Jones and jus' call me Lemony."

"Deal...Lemony. And you can call me Lacy instead of Ma'am."

173

Old Lemony just nodded. He smiled - he hadn't been suckered by a pretty redhead in a long time. Lemony followed her into the bright sunshine.

Chapter Thirty-Six

Two riders continued across the cold rugged terrain with the stars being the only guiding light poking through a velvety backdrop.

Noses twitched recognizing the smell, Pac and Wheat swung glances at each other. Pungent mesquite smoke and roasting meat permeated the night air.

"Think it might be them...kids?" Wheat asked.

"Ya got yure damn arse 'rapped 'round yer damn haid...What tha hell ya thinks we's been trackin' all day...Ya numbskull!"

Wheat shrugged.

Worn boot heels tapped ribs moving their horses forward following the scent. When they could see the faint glow pinpointing their destination, Pac and Wheat eased out of the leather and walked their horses the last thirty yards. Their scrawny necks stretched like chickens peered over brittlebush and creosote that hung on to a wall of sand. In the short draw, dying flames sent flickers of light across thirteen kids sprawled sleeping. A makeshift spit with a hunk of meat hanging from it, dropped grease into the flames causing them to pop and sizzle every now and then.

Faint fingers of light reached out, bouncing and flickering across the two kidnappers. Sleeves rolled up on their arms exposed the grimy pink long-handles they wore. Dust cracked when they grinned at each other. "Piece of cake," Pac whispered, tying his horse to the brush.

Quietly stepping over legs, Pac and Wheat looked around. Four boys lay scattered amongst the girls' as if protecting them. Once pretty dresses were dirty and tattered. Traces of stockings still clung to the girls' legs above worn high-top shoes, except for one little girl whose feet were bandaged. One child slept still clutching a piece of meat in her hand. Barrel cacti rinds scattered the sand as if a watermelon feast had taken place. The men made a beeline toward the meat. Squatting, Pac's knees cracked; he stilled as did Wheat who was looking around. The kids hadn't budged, sleeping the sleep of exhaustion and finally full tummies.

Pulling out his bowie knife, Pac cut two hunks of meat off the spit and handed one to Wheat, who bounced it around in his hands blowing on it before taking a bite. The knife drove into the sand next to Pac's leg. Gnawing on the meat, two sets of eyes continued to roam over the scraggly bunch of kids looking mighty worse for wear.

Wheat spoke quietly, "We's gonna haft ta git them kids cleaned up wit new duds...ta even git close ta a hundr't fer each," he said. "An' pack some meat on 'em."

Mumbling around the pork in his mouth, grease shinning in the glow of low embers dribbling over his lower lip into his beard, Pac said, "Mebe..."

Pain reaching into his mind, Chad stirred. Laying on his side the pistol remained tucked under his armpit while his hand continued to grip the butt. Unable to fall into the deep exhaustive sleep as the others, the throbbing pain from his shoulder and leg kept him teetering on the edge of consciousness. His ears pricked up hearing unfamiliar voices. His gut instinct told him to lie still like a possum. He listened hard, barely breathing. His hand gripped the butt of the weapon tighter. A finger digging through sand found the half-moon trigger and wrapped around it. Cracking an eye open, he couldn't see the figures conversing quietly. Closing the eye, Chad scooted around issuing a groan as he did so. Then he settled back into the sand, pistol still hidden and pretending to be asleep. He cracked an eye. His breath caught. *Kannon's men!* Chad held back the groan that wanted to slip out.

Pac and Wheat stiffened, glancing at the boy who'd moved then became quiet again. Wheat walked over to the boy and stood staring, taking in the bloody, bandaged thigh and the gash on the kid's shoulder. Chad held his breath feeling the presence. Walking back, Wheat settled next to Pac again saying, "Kid's been busted up some, he'll slow us down." Looking around he spotted the girl with bandaged

176

feet. He nodded, "That one, too."

Pac shrugged.

Listening to the men's voices, Chad's mind began whirring, tumbling like rocks in a barrel down a steep hill. The constant throbbing pain in his thigh and shoulder added to his anxiety. He tried to remember how many bullets he had left in the pistol. *Two went to Lenny,* thinking, *I've got four left.* For some reason his mind picked a scene out of the past, of he and other boys sitting and listening to Luke spin tales. The older Luke got, the more tales he told. The one Chad remembered at that moment was how you never put a sixth cartridge in the cylinder always resting the firing pin on an empty chamber, 'Else ya jus' might blow a hole in yer leg,' Luke had warned them. And if Kannon's men followed that rule...there would have been five cartridges in the cylinder. *So...three, I've got three.* Chad didn't want to make any moves to double check. He prayed his guess was correct. His mind continued to whirr under the premise of sleeping. He knew he could get off one shot but not two. He'd be dead before he could get that accomplished and he wasn't quite ready to die, *yet.* He knew Cotton had the rifle, knew a few rounds remained in it. Apparently the men didn't think they had any weapons, else that would 'ave been the first thing they'd check. *Nope,* he thought, *I gotta wait.* Chad laid there working out a plan for when the right moment appeared. And it would present itself; he knew that without a doubt.

Despite his heart throbbing in time with his leg, Chad dozed. Dim voices broke into his mind again. He came instantly awake but his eyes remained closed, still playing possum, Chad listened. He heard sand scrunch coming closer. A boot abruptly kicked his bad leg sending the pain ricocheting through the limb. Chad bit his tongue to keep from crying out and rolled surprising his opponent. He palmed the pistol shooting blindly. The sudden noise woke every one. Pac was standing a mere four feet away when the lead drilled into his gut. He screamed in pain, clutching his belly and dropped to his knees. Dobie saw the man reach for his gun ready to fire on Chad. Scrambling and running, he kicked the pistol out of the man's hand. Pac yelled and watched the gun fly through the air to land out of reach as he brought his eyes back to Dobie and mouthed, "Ya damn...l'il shee-yut." Then his skin turned the color of ashes from an old fire. Suddenly his eyes rolled back in his head and he slid into the sand, dead. Crimson continued to run from his gut, staining and soaking the buff colored earth.

The girls were screaming as confusion and fear marked their faces. Disoriented, they wanted to escape from the gunfire but didn't know which direction to turn. They bunched up clutching each other, focusing on the second man as he wheeled around and brandished his gun at them.

Eyes wild, Wheat kept spinning. He couldn't figure out what just happened, 'cept Pac was down, gut shot. He and Pac never figured on the kids having guns. He didn't want to kill any of them...too much money sitting in the sand staring back at him. Spinning again, Wheat thought wildly, *Tha hell wit tha money...I'm outta here...* He began backing away moving toward the horses.

A hand quickly pulled the cocking lever down then rapidly clicked closed. Cotton's finger closed around the trigger.

Wheat spun toward the sound.

Seeing his chance, Dobie charged.

Something slammed into Wheat's back, he went down weapon flying from his fingers.

Hanah moved quickly, plucking the gun from the sand. Both hands held the butt of the pistol as two short legs splayed just like she'd seen her Mama do. Two thumbs struggled to push the hammer down. She pointed it at the man and yelled, "You jus' stop right thar...Mister!"

Wheat stared at the little firebrand.

His finger leaving the half-moon trigger as he sprang up, Cotton relieved his sister of the pistol aiming it at the man's head. Right about now he didn't care if the man lived or died. Dobie slowly rose off the man's back and stepped away.

Cotton tossed the rifle to Dobie.

178

Wheat just laid there, sprawled like he was staked for the skin-heads, scrawny neck bent backwards staring at the kids who now held him hostage.

Cotton's gaze never left the man in the sand. He called out, "Everybody okay..." Not receiving an answer, he ordered, "Dobie get that rig off the other one and check on Chad."

"I'm...okay," Chad answered.

With eyes still glued to the man sprawled in the sand, Cotton nodded in response to Chad's reply.

"Take your gun belt off, Mister," Cotton jiggled the weapon in the air. "One false move and you're buzzard bait," he threatened.

Wheat slowly pushed to his knees as his hands unbuckled the belt. He held it in the air.

Hanah moved forward to take the belt.

"No!" Cotton yelled. "Stay away from him."

She stopped mid-stride.

Nodding to the side Cotton continued, "Over there, throw the belt...over there." Wheat did.

"Now...back on yer belly," he ordered. Wheat slid back into the sand. Hanah picked up the belt, walked over and gave it to Dobie.

Heads swiveled when they saw Ben Hudson walk into the circle of dying embers towing two horses. Noticing the silence, he grinned, "Figured they had to have horses. Figured too, we could use a ride for a change," he said.

Blue eyes creased, cracking the dust surrounding them. "Dobie...," Cotton began, "...Git tha rope off a saddle and tie this bastard up." Dobie quickly jumped at the chance. Cotton aimed his next words at the outlaw lying in the sand, "You give him any trouble...I'll make sure you n'ver see 'nother sun...you sum-bitch!"

Wheat's adam's apple bobbed when he swallowed.

Red-gold eyebrows soared. Hanah had never heard Cotton cuss

179

before.

"Wait..." Cotton's words stopped Dobie. "Hanah...stir those coals," he said. "An' add some more brush."

Wheat's eyes got ugly when he heard those words. The white-haired boy's eyes mimicked a polished gun barrel, just eyeballing him.

Cotton's pistol threatened the man in the sand. "Take your boots and socks off..."

Slowly Wheat began to sit up. "Like hell..."

Lead splattered sand into Wheat's face. The huddle of girls screamed. Two horses snorted, half rearing. Ben hung on to the reins, sliding through the sand pulled by their force. Weighing not much more then a thimble herself, Hanah added her weight to the reins trying to help.

He rose to a half crouch, "Why...ya l'il shee-yut!" Hearing the click of hammers pulling back, Wheat stopped and swiveled his dirt-creased neck. Eyes narrowed when he spotted the other two boys, Chad and Dobie palming pistols, meaning business. Their fingers were more than ready to pull triggers should he jump their friend. Wheat's face turned grim as white traced a line around his lips.

Cotton spoke, "Mister...I'm gittin' awfully sick and tired of you arse-holes chasing a bunch of innocent kids through this Gawd forsaken territory. Coming after us...like we wuz criminals with bounty on 'r heads!"

Hanah's head swiveled, listening. She'd never seen Cotton get mad much, 'cept at Miz Shemwell. But she knew this; when he got mad it was as good or better then when her Mama did! She waited anxiously.

A weapon waggled, "Off with the boots and socks...Mister," Cotton repeated. In the silence, his ears picked up the muted whimpering of the girls huddled together. He heard the grease sizzling every now and then dripping into the fire. He listened to the quiet sound of breathing, the horses shuffling through the sand while he waited for an answer. Cotton spoke again, "Mister...I'm past the point

180

of caring whether you live or die," he said tiredly. The hammer cocked back, it's metallic sound loud.

Wheat shifted around, sitting. "Ya...damn...kids," he mumbled, "More trouble then a pound of pennies." Pulling one boot off, a grimy sock followed. He tossed both aside.

"In the fire," Cotton ordered.

Eyes narrowed at the boy.

"I said, in the fire."

As Wheat reached out, his hand filled with sand flinging it into Cotton's face. He scrambled up making a beeline for his horse.

Surprised, Cotton's finger convulsively pulled. Flames burst from the muzzle of the gun he held sending the bullet spattering sand five feet away. The girls screamed again. Cotton staggered back as he tried to dig the sand out of his eyes.

Sharp retorts responded as two pieces of lead from Dobie and Chad's weapons dug into Wheat making him spin. He grunted, crumpling to the sand.

Horses jerked and whinnied. Ben and Hanah hung on to the reins, sliding through the sand as the horses reared and backed away from the noise.

Recovering, Cotton ran to Wheat's side and kicked his ribs. Wheat grunted when he rolled over. Cocking the hammer back once more and pointing the muzzle at the man, Cotton inhaled a deep breath trying to calm his pounding heart. The acrid scent of fresh black powder stung his nose and tainted the tense atmosphere. *Finish the bastard...*his mind said, but his finger wouldn't pull the trigger.

Wheat's voice pierced the quiet, "Ya...sum-bitch..."

Cotton's lips formed a hard line. His finger tightened on the trigger.

Wheat's voice, weakened from his wounds, taunted Cotton, "What's sa' matter...boy...ain't got tha guts ta finish me?"

181

Cotton's finger tightened even more around the metal half-moon. "I'm thinking 'bout it," he said through clenched teeth.

Dobie appeared next to Cotton. He aimed his weapon at Wheat's chest; the hammer clicked back. "I already kilt me one man. Now...two? That'd be a nice prize. I could put me two notches on this here gun then," Dobie said.

Cotton eased his finger pressure off the trigger and his thumb slowly lowered the hammer of his gun as he lightly touched Dobie's arm. He shook his head stating quietly, "No. He took two bullets...he can't last much longer." He looked around at the others, their silence echoed in the night air waiting expectantly for him to say or do something.

"Leave 'im be, Dobie," he said tiredly. "We need to pack and ride." Cotton turned and paced toward the dwindling coals. He pulled the bowie knife from the sand, bouncing the hilt in his hand, thinking.

Garbled wet words came from Wheat, "You sum-bitch...finish me off!"

Cotton wheeled, his eyes cold. "No. You die on yer own." He tore his eyes away from the man bleeding out, turning the sand dark red beneath him, Cotton refocused on the horses. Not everyone would be able to ride at the same time. It was a fluke, two of Kannon's men following them and riding horses. As he lifted eyes to the sky, it surprised Cotton that it remained dark and still shrouded in stars. He felt as if hours had gone by. He thanked the heavens for the small miracle of the horses.

You're welcome, a voice seemed to answer in his mind. Cotton jumped. His nerves already ratty from exhaustion, strung a little tighter when he heard the voice. He kicked it out of his head.

Ben had been rummaging around in the saddlebags and speaking to no one in particular, "There's some dried beef and cartridges in the bags." Lifting one canteen, he shook it, "'Bout half full." He walked around to the other horse and shook that one too. "Both, 'bout half full."

182

Cotton came back to earth with the sound of Ben's voice, "That water is gotta be for the horses."

Dobie looked around at the others announcing proudly, "Two more rifles and two more pistols and ammo...we got us some fire-power now."

Raising his head, Wheat hoarsely ground out, "You sum-bitch...ya jus' gonna let me die..." his head flopped back against the sand.

Cotton walked over, blue flint gazing at the man dying. "It's pay-back time," he said and turned and walked away.

Wheat's cough sounded weak. He tried to breathe through the blood filling his lungs, wet gargle tainted his words, "That's what Kannon said too, when he hatched his all-fire brill'ant plan...to...to kidnap you kids...to sell..." his voice trailed off. Cotton's hands stilled hearing the man's words, then he resumed cutting the pork with the bowie knife to take with them. Silence surrounded them once again. Only the dying embers that sizzled every now and then broke into the deep quiet.

Eight kids packed the backs of two horses resembling squished sardines in a roll-top can. Five walked, all heading south back to the wagon they'd left almost three days ago.

Chapter Thirty-Seven

Three distinct riders sat astride hidden behind some brush staring straight ahead observing the seemingly dead village of *Las Culebras* below. Kelly, a six-foot wiry built man, wore a homespun shirt on his rounded shoulders that tucked into buckskin britches. Knee high, well-worn military boots completed his attire along with a bowie knife strapped to his waist. His head was covered by a fawn colored, wide brimmed, short crowned hat. Rawley Lovett sat long in the saddle above the other two. His grimy, sweat soaked shirt fit across strong shoulders. A man whose iron was tied to his thigh the way a gunfighter would. Carson Beckett remained down in the mouth. He would much rather have a pretty girl in his lap, teasing him with her kisses and a glass of good rye by his hand. He sighed inwardly, his mouth watering at the thought of some rye. He squinted at his two silent partners.

Cottonwoods, juniper and mesquite made a green, bark and charcoal colored line off in the distance indicating water. A bay, a black-striped dun mule and a chestnut shuffled restlessly smelling the water.

Eyes squinted before Kelly spoke, "Down there is where we might find some word on Del Rio," he said. Shifting the wad in his cheek, he spat, "If...not, I got me 'nother idee where we could look."

Rawley tensed. "Where?"

Spitting again, this time out the corner of his mouth, Kelly watched the juice sizzle against a hot rock before he answered, "Not jus' yet...Lovett. Yore pretty wife wouldn't want you packing extra lead betwix them shoulder blades. 'Sides from what youse and Beckett said 'bout her, I ain't really anxious ta tangle wit no copperhead if she wuz ta blame me for your death," he grinned.

The dun mule shuffled when Kelly leaned forward, resting his wrists on the horn, reins lightly clasped between fingers. "Naw...we'll jus' take it nice and slow, thinking smart..." he eyeballed Lovett. "Not goin' off, half-cocked..." a brow raised emphasizing his point. "Del Rio is pow'rful in these parts...way more pow'rful than us three," his voice intoned. With that he nudged the dun mule toward shade and water. Beckett and Lovett followed.

* * *

At the first opportunity, Rawley backed Kelly into a tree away from Beckett's ears.

Instead of being surprised, Kelly's eyes turned shrewd. He waited.

His hand gripping a fist-full of homespun twisted as Rawley pushed Kelly harder into the bark. Blue eyes flashed with anger as they bored into hazel ones, "I want to know what you know...ya slick bastard."

Face remaining deadpan, Kelly continued to gaze back. He knew Rawley was slow to temper, but he wasn't a man you'd want to tangle with when he did get riled. Years ago he'd seen Rawley bare-knuckle men twice his size almost to a pulp. Lovett had an uncanny natural grace about him, especially in a bare-knuckle fight, winning more than losing and Kelly knew he didn't want to go there. Chances were, if it came to that, Lovett would probably kill him.

"If you'd quit twisting my brand new shirt into shreds...I might tell you," Kelly said.

Beckett had built a fire and set the coffee to boiling but that didn't keep him from continuing to glance over where he'd seen Lovett shove Kelly into a tree. He couldn't hear the words, but by the gestures it could get ugly. He busied himself but kept a watchful eye.

Kelly's eyes remained steadfast on Rawley's. Finally, he felt the grip on his shirt loosen as Rawley pulled back a step. Kelly allowed himself to relax. Rawley still had shards of flint showing in his eyes, but the main threat had passed. Keeping eyes on the big man, Kelly spoke, throwing the words toward Beckett, "Beckett...that coffee 'bout

186

ready?"

Looking up, Beckett answered, "Soon."

Kelly nodded and began walking toward the fire. Rawley caught his arm, stopping him.

Speaking roughly Rawley said, "I mean it...Kelly. Two of those kids are mine. But I intend to bring them all back...alive."

Kelly just said, "Let's get some coffee," and continued walking. Rawley stared after him hauling in air trying to quell his anger. In a moment, he too headed for fresh coffee.

* * *

"Del Rio ain't somebody ya want ta mess with," Kelly began, slurping his hot coffee. "Unless ya got a full-proof plan."

Rawley's face remained grim, staring and swirling the dark liquid around in his cup, cooling it.

"So...you know him," Beckett said, lounging against the ground, making the words into more of a statement then a question.

"Aye...I know him," Kelly answered. "But ain't n'ver had no reason ta involve myself in his affairs...'til now," he glanced at Lovett as he added, "After he and some of his men bust the girls and women..."

Knuckles turned white around the cup Rawley held.

"...They take them to sell in Mexico City. Some of Del Rio's men...got a taste fer boys..."

Rawley quickly swilled some coffee down his throat; it burnt while shoving the bile inching up back down.

"...After that, them boys is sent to work Del Rio's mines."

Rawley's head jerked up. "Mines?"

Beckett's skin had begun crawling sometime ago, he tried to shake

187

the feeling. It stayed.

"Yup, silver mines," Kelly nodded. "Lotta them kids don't make it. Heerd tell...they's got a mass grave dug, jus' ta chunk the dead ones in it all the time. Heerd tell, it fills up mighty quick too."

Kelly reached for the pot, black brew splashed into his cup, the only sound besides water whispering over rocks in the creek and the fire spitting and sizzling eating at mesquite and cottonwood. He threw a look at Lovett again. "That's why we's gotta have a darn good plan to rescue yore kids, Lovett."

Rawley couldn't seem to shake the black gloom that covered his shoulders like a heavy cloak. His stomach wanted to puke with Buckshot's information. His insides strained to keep that from happening. Kelly interrupted his thoughts saying, "Del Rio's got some real bad boys in his employ. Worsen then Comanch an' 'Patch. We's jus' a sight outnumbered, that's why we's gotta work smart."

Nodding toward the town in the distance, Beckett asked, "What about those folks, think they'd help?"

Kelly shook his head. "Naw...Del Rio's got them so scared, they'd pee in their britches if they could. 'Sides they ain't got no weapons, 'cept them farm tools. They can't fight over a hundr't men when they's come swooping down on 'em wit farm tools."

Rawley and Beckett glanced at each other. "How'd you get to be so knowledgeable about his operation?" Rawley asked.

Tilting his head, Kelly gave the two men a square look. "Been keeping my eye on 'im fer a long time. Been wantin' ta shut 'im down in the worst way an' bury 'im six foot under. Turn tha mine back over to its rightful owners." Buckshot drained his cup and nodded toward the little village, "Them. But like I said, ain't had no 'cause to interfere 'til now."

Kelly zeroed back in on two faces. Beckett continued studying the bottom of the cottonwood leaves above that shaded them. Lovett's face grim, his eyes darting and piercing whatever he'd found to focus on in the distance, thinking.

Rising, Kelly ambled over to his saddle. His Henry 44/40 whispered out of the scabbard. "Let's take us a little walk boys," he said.

Chapter Thirty-Eight

Ben Hudson refused to ride when it came his turn. Hanah was next to him with her skinny arms folded; she stood her ground too. Ben pointed out, "There's others in worse shape and they need to ride." Gesturing at Hanah, he said firmly, "Me and her will walk."

Cotton looked at his sister - dingy copper curls bounced in agreement with Ben. For all the trouble these two had caused in White River just being kids, it seemed Ben and Hanah had growed up some during this ordeal. Cotton just nodded tiredly. *One less thing to worry about,* he thought. His eyes flitted across the others. Exhaustion poked from dusty sunburned and sweat streaked faces waiting on Cotton to say or do something. His thoughts turned to Chad and Julie. Julie was going to be okay; she was even able to put her shoes back on to protect her tender feet. Julie was not able to walk much yet, but she was improving. Emma Sue seemed to be coming around too. Chad though was another thing altogether. The scrape on his shoulder had begun crusting over. The gash on his thigh worried on Cotton like a hound dog scratching it's fleas. They had nothing with which to clean Chad's wound properly. *No water, no medicine, nuthin',* Cotton thought. Without proper attention, the wound would likely become infected. *And then what...* Cotton's mind wondered. *What will I do then?* He physically shook himself, willing his brain to drop the sordid thoughts. Another poked through his exhausted brain...*Doc.* He'd remembered Doc mentioning wild plants used for medicinal purposes. But that was in Wyoming, he knew nothing about this stark land they traversed now. Dropping all other ideas, Cotton concentrated on placing one boot in front of the other with the little band following slowly.

Chad's chest and head resting on her back had pushed Emily Harrison forward over the neck of the sorrel they rode; the saddle horn gouged into her stomach. Two others, Julie Parks and Emma Sue, rode behind Chad on the back of the horse. Emily slowly pushed herself up. She really didn't want to disturb Chad, but her back had begun hurting.

190

Sitting upright, she tried to work the kinks out as Chad stirred with her movement. Staring at the heat shimmering across the white, buff and reddish colored landscape, Emily squinted against the glare. Tears pricked the back of her eyes making the landscape blur and shimmer even more. She wondered if she would ever see her Mama and Daddy again. Whisking the tears away, Emily concentrated on the plodding gate of the sorrel, focusing on the red-brown ears bobbing with each tired step. The rhythmic walk of the horse soon had Emily's eyes drooping and then her head sagged to her chest and rested there.

Suddenly Emily jerked awake realizing she had almost slipped out of the saddle. She blinked and concentrated on keeping her eyes open. Then she spotted it. Sitting straighter in the saddle, her hand rose to shield her eyes from the glare. *The wagon!* She pulled on the reins exclaiming excitedly, "The wagon...we're back at the wagon!"

Hearing a voice, Cotton dragged himself from the heavy concentration of just trying to put one foot in front of the other. Stopping, he looked at Emily. "What?"

Struggling to sit upright Chad realized he didn't feel so good. He finally peered over Emily's head closing one eye to focus better. The throbbing in his leg was making it difficult to concentrate on anything else. "She's right," he confirmed.

Dobie ran the few short yards to a sandy ridge and gave a whoop. Turning, he gazed back at the band of brothers and sisters. Dust cracked when he smiled, "It's the wagon alright, but tha mules is gone." Wheeling, he ran toward the wagon. Renewed energy seemed to urge exhausted bodies to quickly cover the distance following Dobie.

Cotton looked around, finding the out-cropping of rock they had hid behind allowing their escape. He slowly turned around; they had traveled in a big wide circle coming in from the east. "Damn..." he mumbled disgustedly.

Staring at the empty wagon bed Ben asked, "What happened to the supplies? There's nuthin' here."

Hanah sighed noisily. "Somebody come and took them," she said,

191

sticking grimy hands into britches' pockets while she also looked about.

Speaking from about ten yards away to the southwest, "Tracks lead that away," Dobie said pointing. " The mules is shod led by unshod ponies." He added, "Injuns."

Leaning his back against the sides of the wagon, Cotton braced his tired body. Feet splayed to remain upright, he sighed and closed his eyes. *Now what...Lord?* He wondered.

"Cotton?"

The soft words had him looking at Chad.

"We's gotta find some water soon, or else..." Chad trailed off leaving the rest unspoken.

All eyes zeroed in on their leader. A deep silence echoed against the blasting heat as they waited. Only the horses' tired shuffle broke into that silence.

With effort Cotton pushed himself away from the wagon. Walking over to Chad, he noticed the pain-etched cast that leaked through dust caked skin. Cotton nodded, asking gently, "You need to rest some Chad?"

Pain filtered through Chad's eyes. "No," he lied.

Turning Cotton announced, "Everybody off the horses, 'cept Chad and Julie." He reached up to help Emily down. Rustling noises spread through the little band as they did what Cotton ordered.

"I can walk," piped up Julie.

"You sure?"

Julie nodded.

Cotton helped her down and then Emma Sue, taking her hand he pressed it into Emily's to look after her. Looking around again, he saw an empty burlap sack left in the wagon bed. Removing a canteen from a saddle, he proceeded to moisten the burlap, then squeezed some of that precious water into the mouths of the two horses. Something in

192

the back of his mind told him to do that. Then he remembered old Luke giving him that tidbit. Something else flickered through his exhausted mind that Luke said; 'Animals can sense warder better 'n any human...let 'em have their head. Ev'ry time, theys dead on.'

Shielding his eyes from the blistering sun, Cotton asked Chad, "You 'member old Luke saying something like giving a horse his head and he'll find water?" He wanted some kind of reassurance that the sun hadn't fried his brain making him imagine stuff. One pain-filled eye cracked open as Chad nodded.

Breathing in the hot air that seemed to blister his lungs in the process Cotton asked, "Think you can hang on so these horses can find us some water?"

With difficulty, Chad looked at Cotton as he shifted in the saddle making the leather creak and pain soar through his injured leg. Words cracked through blistered lips, "I'll make it," he said firmly.

Cotton nodded. Looking around he saw his comrades had collapsed, sitting or sprawling in what shade the wagon offered up. *We're on our last legs,* he thought. *And dead, if we don't find water soon.*

As Chad nudged the sorrel brushing past Cotton, he led the way in whichever direction the sorrel wanted to go, which at that moment seemed to be southwest.

* * *

Ears pricked forward, nostrils flared as the gelding's steps quickened followed by the second sorrel. Sensing the change in tempo, Chad tried to sit straighter, casting eyes over the head of his mount. He tried to pull something out of the heat waves that shimmered across the distance. *Nothin',* he thought. *Nothin'.* His voice cracked when he spoke to Cotton, hanging onto his stirrup for support. "He's got something..." Chad's voice trailed off.

Cotton heard the words, but he didn't waste what little strength he

193

had left to answer. The others hung on to the two sorrels' tails or stirrups of the saddles, thinking of nothing else but putting one foot in front of the other, the back of their heads taking the brunt of the fiery sun.

* * *

Big Joe Kannon remained pissed. All of his men had deserted him or so it seemed. Shifting the wad of stale baccy in his cheek, he spat, emphasizing his thoughts. Brown juice was added to the dirty creases in his knuckles as they swiped at the dribbles. Only Biff and Dub remained. Kannon had sent the others off to find and follow sign and bring those kids back. None had returned as of yet, puzzling him further. Those kids were tender-footed, ain't no way they could have survived three days out here. *Damn...*his brain mouthed his frustration of the situation. Kannon's insides clenched instinctively thinking of Del Rio's reaction to the loss of his delivery should he arrive empty handed. Sucking air noisily through his dusty nose hairs. Kannon said, "Let's go back, boys...them kids is gotta be daid or close to it by now."

* * *

Two sorrels picked up their pace again. Cotton stumbled and fell to the hard-scrabble ground. He just lay there, the exertion of trying to get up remained beyond him at the moment. He was done.

Hanah dropped the sorrel's tail, quickly taking the few steps and knelt by her brother, "C'mon...Cotton, you gotta get up." Her hands dug through the sand under his arms, pulling as she pleaded with him. In desperation, Hanah called to Ben, "Help...me..." Another pair of hands landed alongside small freckled ones.

Cotton tried to form words, but they would not push past his swollen tongue. Thoughts continued to bounce against his skull, resembling lead ricocheting off rocks in a firefight. The words would not come. Cotton slipped into unconsciousness.

194

Fear tainted her voice as Hanah yelled, "Stop!" The exhausted band dropped in their tracks and flopped against the hot sand.

Reining up his sorrel, Chad glanced behind him at Cotton lying so still, fear reflected in his sister's face. Both horses shuffled, shaking their heads; they did not want to stop as they smelled water not far off now.

"Dobie...we need your help," Hanah called to him.

"Hep...yerself..." Dobie replied sourly.

Anger crackled from the freckled redhead.

Ben's brows shot skyward. He felt Hanah's temper as hot as the air surrounding them.

"Damn...You...Dobie Litchfield!" Hanah yelled. "When this is all over I'm gonna back you in a corner and give you a-licking...the likes ya ain't n'ver seen!" She threatened, "Now...git over here and help us!"

Easing off the right side of the sorrel, his good leg taking his weight and sparing the injured left limb, Chad stopped for a minute as the slight exertion made him dizzy. Blistering air seared his lungs as he took a big breath.

Rolling to his knees, Dobie rose. He knew that damned little redhead would do as she threatened. He sourly remembered when Hanah had been in the process of giving him a licking a few months ago when her Pa showed up and hauled her off him. Dobie slowly trudged through the thick sand toward Cotton.

His leg screaming in pain with each hobbled step, Chad dropped exhaustively next to Hanah. He roughly shook Cotton, receiving a groan for his efforts. "C'mon, Cotton..." he urged. "I think the horses are smelling water," Chad said, hoping to get a response from Cotton.

A white light appeared in Cotton's mind. A figure in a blue dress seemed to step from the light with flaming hair. Softly the voice spoke. *Rise son. You are strong, brave. The water is near. Rise son...it is not your time.* Then the figure disappeared into a door that closed out the light. Cotton stirred.

195

Retrieving the almost empty canteen from the saddle, Ben handed it to Chad, "There's not much left, but maybe it will help."

Unbeknownst to the others, Cotton had not drank any water when he'd passed the canteen around. Chad knew though. He poured a dribble through Cotton's parched lips. At first the precious water just slid out the corner and across his cheek, then Cotton's lips moved. Chad poured more into his friend's mouth and watched as he swallowed it.

Hanah shook her brother's shoulder, urging him "C'mon...Cotton! Wake up!"

Chad poured the last of the water between Cotton's lips. Hanah had tears rolling down her face as she kept shaking and speaking to him, "Please...Cotton...wake up! Please..."

Ben and Dobie stood silently staring at their leader.

In the commotion the children had forgotten the horses. Now the animals continued walking, side-stepping their reins as they moved toward the water they smelled.

Glancing up, Dobie shouted, "Hey, the horses...they're getting away!"

Chad shook Cotton harder, "C'mon...Cotton get up...the horses smell water!"

Looking at Ben and Dobie, Chad ordered, " You two lift him up between you and start following the horses." Gazing at Hanah, he asked, "Help me up and let me lean on you." He watched copper curls bounce in response.

With Cotton being held by Ben and Dobie and Chad leaning heavily on Hanah, the band of brothers and sisters moved slowly following the horses on the hunt for water.

* * *

196

Arriving back at the wagon, Kannon snorted disgustedly. With the mules gone and their cargo of kids that seemed to have disappeared into thin air, Big Joe was not happy. He spit the stale wad of baccy out, and bit off a fresh chew moving it around in his mouth softening it as he thought about what needed to be done next.

Biff slid tiredly out of his saddle and walked around loosening his limbs as did Dub. Both rested against the wheels of the wagon and stared back at their boss.

Dub squinted as he watched Big Joe loosen the cinch on his saddle. He spoke, "I gotta come ta believe them kids is got some kinda guard'n angel looking ober 'em. We ain't n'ver had this much trouble afore...."

"Shad-up...Dub!" Kannon said as he turned around. " I ain't giv'n up...'sides the split is 3-way now...might ought ta make ya want ta look harder."

"Fer what?" Dub argued, "We's plumbt went in a circle and them kids still ain't nowheres ta be found! I say we quit and go find some others!"

Remaining quiet, Biff had been studying the ground around the wagon, noticing the many fresh prints. "They's been here," he said abruptly.

Straightening, Dub mouthed, "Huh...?"

Kannon stared at the sand indicated by Biff's finger. Raising muddy eyes gazing into the distance, he spoke softly, "Well...I'll be damned...them kids doubled back on us." Spinning he strode toward his horse and re-tightened the cinch. Mounting and saying, "Let's go boys...them kids is headed fer water!"

197

Chapter Thirty-Nine

"Ma'am..." Lemony began. "...You know what yer gitting yerself into? Dealing wit Del Rio?" He asked.

Burnt coffee eyes above a sunburned face under a short crowned, dusty hat zeroed in on Lemony Jones.

He didn't flinch from her look this time.

"It ain't gonna be pretty," she replied.

"Ma'am...if I wuz you...I'd turn right back around...and go home," Lemony advised.

Lacy reined in Fancy, giving Lemony a hard, direct gaze. She made a point, "Mr. Jones...If you wish to leave, you may cut and run. But Becky stays because of the supplies."

Aged eyes narrowed at the girl when she challenged him. This one had a way about her that could set his hackles to arising.

Thad had reined up too. His eyes kept bouncing from Lemony to Lacy and back again. He'd witnessed Miz Lacy's temper before. But he also knew deep down she remained as warmhearted as they came. He waited.

Lacy prodded the old man. "Well...Mr. Jones?"

Eyes continued to squint at the redhead from beneath his battered hat. "We ride," he said, nudging the bay forward with worn boot heels towing Becky.

A smile framed by freckled cheeks arrived, "So be it...Mr. Jones."

Chapter Forty

A small mission sat on the outskirts of the village and three men headed toward that goal as they began traveling the street of Las Culebras. They felt eyes that remained hidden behind closed doors and shuttered windows following them while they cut glimpses at each other as they strolled toward one of the few remaining buildings not crumbling. Kelly carried his Henry 44/40 comfortably in his arms. Rawley's arms swung easily with his long strides. Hazel eyes shifted within Beckett's face as he too missed nothing in the quiet.

Tense bodies remained concealed, watching the men while they walked the eerily vacant street. Late afternoon turned 'dobe mud slightly grey with the impending shadows. Kelly, Lovett and Beckett's eyes continued to dart constantly as a low wind brushed against their cheeks and necks. The three men were alert to any slight movement as they made their way toward the church.

* * *

Standing on the crumbling steps of the mission, the three turned, looking over their shoulders. Rawley and Beckett rested hands on the butts of their weapons as they gazed at the quiet landscape. Kelly wrapped his finger around the half-moon trigger on the Henry, shifting the rifle into a firing position. They realized they were up to their ears in trouble invading Del Rio's territory. And they had a hunch that if they and the kids got out alive, it would mean they came out shooting.

Stepping into the coolness within the old adobe walls, they sought out the one man who might be able to help them.

The Padre heard the hombres behind him as he knelt in front of the cross praying. His stomach clenched. Crossing himself, maybe for the last time, he rose and slowly faced the footsteps, steeling himself to deal with Del Rio's men yet again. To his surprise, it was three strangers who stood silently in the aisle between pews. A sigh of relief escaped. The Padre's arms spread, resembling the open wings of a bird. "Welcome...welcome, gentlemen. You wish for a confession?" The Padre asked.

Three heads shook a silent no.

Walking a few steps, the Padre realized he felt no threat from these men. Sandal leather whispered against the stone floor as he moved closer asking, "Something else then?"

Three heads nodded.

Breaking the silence, Rawley spoke, "We're looking for Del Rio."

The Padre stiffened, his eyes shifted, becoming wary. He asked, "You wish to join Del Rio?"

"No," came Rawley's firm reply.

The Padre exhaled softly, "Then...why..."

"Another man, Big Joe Kannon..." Rawley saw recognition filter through the Padre's eyes at the name. "...Kidnapped all of our kids from the schoolhouse in our town in Wyoming to sell to Del Rio. We've come to take them back," he said. "We need to know where Kannon delivers to Del Rio and where they might go after that." Piercing blue eyes continued to gaze into the Padre's face. "Has Kannon brought any new kids to Del Rio that you know of?" Rawley asked.

Stepping closer to the three, his hand resting lightly on the back of a pew, the Padre said, "I know of no new children being delivered to Del Rio. You are brave. Many have died trying to rescue others," he warned them.

Kelly piped up, "Well...that wuz them. We aim to stay alive."

Staring at the flagstone floor, the Padre shook his head sadly, then his eyes rose, "It is an impossible task you have laid before you," he said softly.

"Padre..."Kelly began. "We're here to rescue some kids and mebe

200

set things right again."

The Padre's sad brown eyes brightened for a few seconds and then faded. He slowly made his way to a pew and collapsed into it, sighing heavily. Dull eyes again canvassed the three men who'd whisked off their hats in respect as they stood in this House of God. He smiled faintly.

"Gentlemen," the Padre spoke softly. "I'm afraid...you are too late. There is nothing you could do to save this village or it's people and find your children. Del Rio has many men. He controls many miles. You either work for him or you die, it is that simple."

The three glanced briefly at each other prompting Kelly to move to the pew in front of the Padre and sit. Hazel eyes touched on the Padre's face pulled tight and heavily lined with worry. Kelly spoke, "Oh...you can help us alright, Padre. You jus' don't know it...yet," he said.

The Padre shook his head, "No. We are held prisoners here. Only a few remain to work the fields to feed Del Rio's men. The others have left or died working the mine. We have nothing left with which to fight...our hearts and spirits are no more." Gaunt eyes canvassed three faces, pleading with the men. "You must leave. Spare yourselves the agony and go home. There is nothing more anyone can do to help you find your children." The Padre dropped his eyes to his hands clasped lightly within the folds of his brown robe.

Kelly looked at Rawley and Beckett, unspoken words seemed to pass between them.

Rawley ran his fingers through his hair as he pursed air between tightened lips. Moving closer, he began twirling his hat in his hands thinking, "Padre...tell us what you do know," he asked quietly.

Brown encased shoulders shrugged as palms raised. "There is nothing to share," the Padre said hopelessly.

Beckett stepped closer, "How many men?"

"Too many to count."

"Where does he get his guns and munitions...dynamite? Do you know where he keeps them? Near the mine? Someplace else?" Kelly asked.

The Padre looked up, "Why?"

Three men cut sharp glances at each other. "Because if we knew where he kept those, we might could break in and arm the villagers," Beckett offered.

Eyes grew round at Beckett's statement and then saddened. "No. No...you mustn't. It is too dangerous," the Padre said.

Kelly grinned. "Well...now Padre, you jus' let us worry 'bout that."

A tomb of silence filled the sanctuary. Kelly remained fixated on the Padre while Rawley waited patiently. Beckett shuffled his feet impatiently breaking into that stillness.

Worry lines worked deeper within the Padre's face as his eyes darted to each one of the men in turn sizing them up. A small ray of hope began to lighten the gloom he carried within his heart. "All right...gentlemen..." the Padre began. The soft folds of his garment whispered as he rose, "...I will help. Please follow me, I can draw you a map."

As the three grinned slapping hats on their heads, they followed the Padre out

Chapter Forty-One

The horses' shuffling steps quickened smelling water. Kannon and his men let the animals have their heads. The kidnappers were as parched as their animals and knew the life giving liquid couldn't come soon enough.

Reaching the cooling shade of cottonwoods feeding off a small stream, humans and their horses drank deeply.

Not a hundred yards away thirteen kids slept in exhaustion, their two horses grazing the green stalks along the watercourse.

Rousting what remained left of his men an hour later, Kannon spoke gruffly, "Let's go, sign sez them kids gotta be around here somewheres..."

"Awww...hell Big Joe, iffen them kids is anywheres near here, they ain't gonna be moving anytime soon," Dub answered rolling over planning to go to sleep.

Muddy eyes got ugly. " We's git 'em while they's too tuckered out to give much fite. 'N iffen ya want ya's share of tha payout ya better move ya's arses."

Giving each other a sharp glance, Biff and Dub rose following Kannon as he trekked along the stream.

Slowing and then stopping, Big Joe surveyed the scene. Pac and Wheat's horses were grazing and the kids laid sprawled sleeping. If the kids had his men's horses, what had happened to Wheat and Pac?

Turning toward Biff and Dub he whispered, "Go git our horses, we'll camp here tonight."

Silently the two backed away.

While they were gone Kannon looked over his ragtag cargo noting the boy with the bandaged leg, the torn dresses and...the rifles laying beside the boys. *Pac and Wheat must be dead,* he thought. For the life of him, he didn't know how those kids could have overpowered his men taking their weapons away. Sometimes his boys didn't have a lick of sense. His head swiveled hearing a twig crack behind him. He motioned for Dub and Biff to picket the animals near the other two horses.

When they sidled up next to him Kannon whispered, "They got guns, we take them first before we wake those kids up."

Sandy turf cushioned footfalls of the men as they silently gathered the weapons placing them out of reach of the kids.

Kannon motioned to Dub to get the rope off their saddles, he was bound and determined these kids weren't getting away this time. Pulling his weapon he fired two rounds quickly into the air. Girls screamed, scrambling and running only to be blocked by Biff and Dub. The boys reached for the rifles, grabbing sand instead. Hanah and Ben just sat there, rubbing their eyes. Cotton pulled his knees up, resting his head on them. Dobie kept blinking in surprise and Chad just laid there, fever racking his body with chills not caring whether he lived or died anymore.

Looking up Cotton gave their captors an exhaustive gaze.

"Ya kids thoughts ya wuz slick double backin' on us, din ya?"

We're dead, Cotton thought.

"Tie 'em up boys, they's aint getting away this time."

Whimpers came from the girls as they were shoved closer and rope was tied around everyone's wrists again.

Kannon watched as the kids were tied together, then his eyes zeroed in on the white-haired youth. "Sent Wheat and Pac after you'ns, what happened to them?"

"Dead," Cotton answered, twisting his wrists trying to loosen the bindings.

Shaking his head, Big Joe muttered, "Figures..."

"My friend...he's hurt...," Cotton announced. "Can you help him?"

Eyes narrowed in Kannon's face at the request. Walking over to Chad, he stared at the boy. Pulling his knife he cut the dried crusted bandage off Chad's leg. Dirty eyes narrowed at what he saw.

Cotton rose only to have Dub shove him back down landing him against Hanah as Dub pulled his weapon and aimed it at Cotton. His eyes flicked briefly at the gun, to Dub's face noting the sickening snarl and then to Chad and Big Joe.

Half-turning around Kannon said, "You kids is the damn 'dist thangs I ever did run acrosst...ya got sand I give ya that."

Cotton blinked; he didn't know what Kannon meant saying sand unless it signified they had grit.

Addressing the boy again, he asked, "What happened ta him?"

Cotton swallowed before answering. "Wild hog."

Nodding Kannon agreed, "Them things can be mean..."

Biff piped up, "I think we jus' need to leave 'im here and get a move on...we ain't got time ta be nursemaid'n."

"I do the thinking 'round here, youse jus' shad-up!"

Dub threw words, "Yep...be like babysitting a horse wit a broke laig...best ta put 'em right outta their miz-rey. 'Specially if they's get gan'rene," he finished saying as he stepped closer to Chad, pistol pointing at the boy's head. The hammer sounded it's metallic click, rolling the cylinder.

"Noooo...." Cotton cried struggling against the ropes that tied everyone together.

Kannon's fist came down hard and fast on Dub's wrist, making him yell in pain as the gun spit fire. The bullet splattered sand a few feet from Chad's head.

"Damn...you...you bastard! Ya like ta broke my wrist!"

"I will next time...ya sorry arse!" Kannon threatened. "I tol' ya we's don't hurt the merchandise!"

Stepping closer, Biff offered up, "I says we load 'em up ride to

205

Del Rio and git shed of 'em. They's caused us enough trouble as is."

Circling around Kannon and continuing to rub his wrist, Dub retrieved his gun. Stepping lightly he continued closer to Big Joe, giving a slight nod to Biff, his fingers wrapping around the barrel of his weapon.

Eyes huge, frightened to her very core, Hanah barely got the words out. "Cotton...what's going on?"

"Shush...I don't know, but be quiet!"

Watching Dub silently move on his boss, Biff continued to distract Kannon with his words. "Kannon we need to move, get rid of these kids, collect our money and git the hell outta this country...mebe head ta Canada or some such as that. We's prob'ly got us a damn posse on 'r tail rite now."

Dirty eyes hardened as Kannon glared back at Biff. "I runs this outfit and gives tha orders," his gravely voice gave warning.

Raising his arm, Dub let the pistol butt slam into Big Joe's head with all the force he could muster. Kannon crumpled to the ground.

Biff took the toe of his boot and pushed their leader on his back, Big Joe was out cold.

Dub and Biff looked at each other and smiled.

"Let's load these kids and get outta here."

Nodding, Dub's gun whispered faintly resettling firmly into it's boot.

Taking hold of Cotton's arm, Biff roughly pulled him and the string of kids into a standing position. "Move!"

"We ain't going nowhere's unless Chad goes too," Cotton stated firmly.

Towing the five horses, Dub stopped, "We's leaving him...no sense in dragging dead weight. Biff untie 'em then we'll re-tie 'em to tha horn."

"No."

206

A fist flew cuffing Cotton alongside the head landing him on his back; blinking and shaking his head, Hanah knelt next to him as she tried to help. He shook off her gesture, rose and advanced on the outlaw. "You bastard! Chad goes or we don't go!"

Abruptly, a gun appeared.

Hearing the sound of that familiar metallic click, Cotton stopped.

"We've had enough of youse kids sass', now mount!" Seeing no movement toward the horses, Dub added, "Cause iffen ya don'ts, one more of you'ns will be daid."

Sending one long look towards Chad, Cotton knew they had no choice but to do as told. *We're losing the fight,* he thought. Glancing back at the others he said, "Let's ride."

Pulling away from the stream, Cotton once again looked back over his shoulder at Kannon and Chad lying there knowing he may never see his friend again. He squinted at the heavens and whispered, "Please Lord watch over Chad..." A voice entered his mind. *I will...help is on the way...don't give up hope, little one.* Startled, Cotton looked around and found no one except the rag-tag little band and their two kidnappers leading them to only God knew where. A heavy sigh escaped as he focused between the ears of the sorrel he rode.

Chapter Forty-Two

Lacy, Lemony and Thad slipped out a back door of the mission, vanishing into the darker silhouettes of walls and trees in the night. She smiled faintly remembering the surprise of the Padre at their appearance and his exclamation that help might finally have arrived.

* * *

Lovett, Kelly and Beckett slip-knotted the reins of their mounts in a stand of mesquite should a quick getaway be necessary.

Scouting the area with the map the Padre had drawn them, they had found Del Rio's hacienda heavily guarded.

On their bellies they observed the activity below as the sun to the west slowly dropped beneath the horizon, a yellow ball that changed to red and then disappeared. Lanterns brightened with the incoming darkness showing spots of illumination within the compound. Sporadic voices and sounds lifted quickly in the cooling air reaching their ears.

Pulling his peeper from his belt, Kelly extended the telescope and then focused on the activity. Slowly making a sweep of the compound, he handed it to Rawley. "Take a look see," Kelly said quietly.

Adjusting it for his eye, Rawley slowly scanned the area, noting the amount of guards patrolling the grounds carrying Winchesters and wearing double braces of ammo that crisscrossed their torsos. He swept the peeper toward the corrals; several dozen horses and mules milled around within the confines of the rails. The telescope traveled to the hacienda observing slight movement within the lighted interior of the first floor. The scope rose and focused on windows that shed filtered light on the covered balcony of the second floor. A trellis covered in a vine of some sort grew to the top of the tiled roof, creating shade from the blistering sun. Rawley moved the peeper toward the back of the compound and focused on a couple of smaller adobe buildings. Finally he lowered it and handed it to Beckett.

Sighing exasperatingly Rawley asked, "Where could he be keeping the kids?"

"He's got a powder magazine in the back," said Beckett.

"What?" Rawley grabbed the peeper and focused where Beckett pointed. Pulling the scope down, he asked Beckett, "How ya figure that?"

"It's built like a dugout," he replied simply.

Taking the peeper from Lovett, Kelly examined the building, too. "He's right. Less chance of it exploding from the heat," he explained. Kelly grinned, "Lovett...you mean ta tell me, you didn't know that?"

Before Rawley could answer, a metallic click from behind had the three men rolling to their backs, palming their pistols.

A soft husky whisper broke into the stillness, "Damn...you, Lovett! I ought ta kill you where you lay...then divorce you!" Lacy said. "If you ever do something like that to me again...I'll..."

Her words made three men smile remembering the short conversation they had back in Top Notch.

"You'll do what...Sunshine?"

Hearing that warm caramel voice teasing her, Lacy stiffened; she was in no mood for her insides to turn to mush at the sound of his voice. "Oh...shad-up...Lovett!" she snapped and dropping to her knees she crawled toward him.

Slight rustling filled the air as pistols returned to their leather.

"How'd the hell you find us?" Beckett asked.

"The same way you found this place," she told him. Lacy weaseled her way further on her belly between Kelly and Rawley.

"The Padre?"

Ignoring Beckett, Lacy turned her attention to Rawley, "The kids...any sign of the kids?"

Rawley shook his head, "Not...yet..."

"Well...what the hell you been doing? Sitting with pretty girls in your lap!" She tossed out in a harsh whisper.

Kelly chuckled.

Lacy's head spun. "You jus' shad-up too, Kelly! You're jus' as dead as he is...you keep it up!"

Kelly shot a quick glance at Lovett over Lacy's head, but the smile remained under his horseshoe mustache. Beckett's hand slid over his mouth wiping his grin away.

"Simmer down, Sunshine," Rawley said, "We've been scouting out Del Rio."

Propping herself on her forearms with elbows dug into the scree, Lacy sucked in air trying to calm herself. Her whisper sounded loud in the quiet, "What have you found out?"

"Not much..." stated Kelly.

Lacy's head swiveled toward him.

"...Cept he's covered up in guns."

Scree clattered behind them, four bodies rolled, three pistols made an appearance again.

"Don't shoot! It's Lemony and Thad," Lacy told them.

Darkness masked the surprise that flitted across the men's faces. Rawley just stared at his wife. Lacy shrugged, "I forgot...to tell you. I brought reinforcements and supplies."

Lemony and Thad dropped to their knees, and crawled, scooting further on their bellies extending the line of faces watching the compound.

Lacy made the introductions.

When Thad slid in next to Rawley, the Marshal whispered patting the boy's shoulder. "Glad to see you son." Thad nodded. "The others...they okay?" Nodding again Thad filled in the Marshal, Kelly and Beckett on when they escaped and what had transpired after that.

Lacy explained, "Thad killed two of Kannon's men. So...when we find them we're only dealing with six now."

Rawley's eyes widened as he whispered, "That took some guts, son."

Thad shrugged, "Had to save Lemony..."

"'N he shor did too," piped up Lemony.

Five faces refocused on the compound below.

Beckett spoke, "From what I can tell, the guards pass each other every ten minutes or so. We need to break into that powder magazine."

As quietly as she could, Lacy pushed herself back from the others.

Rawley turned wondering were Lacy was going, "Sunshine...what are you doing...?"

"Nothing... I'll be right back," she answered swiftly.

Rawley watched Lacy disappear into the wash; he turned his attention back to the compound and the circling guards.

She slowly made her way closer to Del Rio's fortress. Squatting within the darker shadows of boulders, Lacy judged the distance to the wall. About twenty-five yards she figured and after she left the cover there was nothing to hide her presence whenever she decided to make her move.

Lacy glanced to her left, the long shadows continued and she moved toward them. The vague wall of darkness concealed her as she crept closer to the fortress.

A hand roughly grabbed her shoulder, swinging her around making her breath catch as she was shoved to the ground. Air escaped hoarsely when she realized it was Rawley.

"Damn you Sunshine!" Her husband hissed. "This is why I didn't want you involved! You got too many hair brained ideas!"

"I do not!" She replied tartly.

He plastered her lips with a kiss stopping another retort with his gesture.

Pushing away from him she snapped, "Cut it out Lovett, we got business to take care of."

Rawley grinned, teasing and reaching for her, "I can think of some pretty nice business right about now..."

Even in this tense situation, Lacy could envision being wrapped in his warm embrace as they made love. Instead she rolled away whispering, "We need to think about rescuing the kids."

Standing to a crouch, he pulled Lacy to her feet, "Let's go back to the others."

Resisting she argued, "I want to get closer."

"Not now, Sunshine," Rawley said. "We need to have a plan...a foolproof plan first." He took her hand leading her back to the others at the overlook.

Chapter Forty-Three

Stirring, Kannon rolled on his side. His head felt as if someone had been busting rocks with it. A hand reached toward the main brunt of his pain and gingerly touched a knot behind his right ear. Pulling his fingers away he glanced at the blood on them. Closing his eyes again, he didn't know how long he had laid there. He tried to focus on the sounds or the lack of them around him. He did not smell woodsmoke, he felt no bodies rustling. He did hear a few birds chatter above, but that was it. The uncanny silence continued. He drifted off.

Later the rock pounding headache had eased to where Kannon could open his eyes further this time. Realizing the camp was empty had him sitting up abruptly making his head spin and forcing him to close his eyes. When the dizziness had eased, his eyes swept the vacant camp. Everyone was gone including the horses except the boy, Chad.

Rising and planting his feet to keep from swaying, he muttered an oath, "I'll get you side-windin' sum-bitches or die trying," gazing at the numerous tracks heading southwest.

Swinging his head, Kannon focused on the boy some ten feet away. He stumbled toward the unconscious lad.

Staring at the sweat glazed face, watching the shivers that racked the boy's body, he pondered his predicament. Kannon could walk off now, leaving the boy to die or try and save him. No two ways about it; the boy was still worth money to him. He knelt next to the boy and cut away more of Chad's pant's leg exposing the gored flesh further. Retrieving his hat Kannon filled it several times, pouring the water over the wound and Chad's body in an attempt to cool the fever.

Pulling his gun, he removed two cartridges from the cylinder. Returning the weapon to its boot, he proceeded to pry the lead out of the brass tubes exposing the powder within and sprinkling the black

215

grains into the boy's wound. Staring at it for a moment he decided to add another. Kannon needed this boy well enough to walk some distance so he could collect the money he could get for the kid.

Striking a match, Big Joe stared at the flame a second before lighting the powder in the wound. Chad screamed when the grains ignited searing his flesh, then he fell silent. Kannon sat back on his heels; nothing more he could do now. It was a wait and see situation.

Chapter Forty-Four

"Padre..." Rawley began, "...We need you to gather all the able bodies you got left in this town."

"They will not come, they are too afraid."

"Do they trust you, Father?" Lacy asked softly.

"Yes, of course, but I do not understand..."

"You jus' get 'em here, Padre. We'll explain then," added Kelly.

"You will wait? It may take some time...to...convince them."

"We'll wait," Rawley said

* * *

Subdued shuffling accompanied the frightened residents of Las Culebras as they entered the sanctuary of the mission. They made rustling noises as they settled themselves in the pews. Wary time-worn faces stared at the five men and one woman along with their Padre, standing below the cross of their Savior. They only came because the Padre said these people offered hope. They waited for the words.

Stepping closer to the pews, Rawley spoke calmly, "We have not come to harm you, we have come to help you and to rescue our own children from Del Rio in the process. But we need your help to do this."

The Padre translated Rawley's words.

Continuing, Rawley said, "We need to know your schedules of when you deliver food and supplies to Del Rio and the mines."

Again the Padre translated.

Watching the skeptical glances dart amongst those in the pews, Lacy stepped forward. She spoke boldly, not mincing her words. "Are you so afraid of one man that it has left you spineless and cowering without vision? Do you not wish to gain your freedom back? To be free of fear? We are here to take our children back and restore your village. You must fight if you wish to live in freedom again otherwise you will die. To fight is to live."

The Padre translated.

Silence remained the answer. Beckett and Kelly stayed quiet as did Lemony and Thad, their eyes sweeping the pitiful few residents before them.

Speaking again, Lacy's words taunted them, "You wish the dreams of hell to be buried with you in your grave tossing you into the pits of fire because you had no stomach to stand up to the man who has destroyed your village?"

Swallowing, the Padre translated and then added, "Please, they have a plan...we must help."

With the silence still hanging thick in the sanctuary, Lacy grew impatient. She pulled on Rawley's shirt sleeve, "C'mon they're too yella to do do anything, Let's go." The six turned ready to walk away when a voice stopped them.

"Esperan!" An older man, Manuel stood and said, "We help!" Murmurs and nods of agreement passed amongst the residents.

Rawley and Lacy smiled briefly at each other. Kelly, Beckett, Thad and Lemony did too as well as the Padre.

Stepping closer to the first pew, Rawley sat and began, "Alright, here's the plan..."

* * *

Dusk it seemed took forever to arrive as Lacy's impatience continued to fester. Two carts had been loaded with dried grasses, the third with boards lying across the sides leaving room for men to hide underneath the chicken coops and produce from the fields. The Padre would lead the first cart telling Del Rio and his men they had brought their supplies. The other two, led by Manuel and Lemony, would also conceal the six who had come to rescue their children from the grip of Del Rio.

The few rifles were handed out to those willing to fire. Handing her Sharps to one, Lacy explained the workings of the rifle, with the Padre translating as she gave the man a handful of the linen encased powder cartridges and percussion caps. She left him with a warning, "Hold that stock tight against your shoulder, it can knock you on your butt if you don't." The man grinned and nodded. She didn't know whether he understood her or not.

The dynamite Lacy and Lemony were able to scrounge up in the dusty store in Top Notch had been given out with Kelly and Beckett tucking two sticks behind their belts and inside their boots with Rawley and Lacy doing the same. Matches were passed as were cheroots from Beckett's diminishing stash.

Donning raggedy woolen cloaks and flop brimmed straw hats for disguises, everyone waited to begin loading the carts.

Rawley hugged his wife close, "You 'bout ready Sunshine?" He felt her head nod against his chest. His gaze traveled to Thad, he would stampede the horses and mules out of the corral through the compound. "You sure about this, son?"

"Yes, Sir!" Thad replied firmly.

Nodding, Rawley looked straight at the Padre, "Father?"

"Yes," he replied, "And I feel the presence of others watching also...our Savior will protect and watch over us."

Abruptly, Lacy pushed away from Rawley hearing the Padre's words. Her eyes rose to the darkened skies above; she wondered if her Mama was one of those the Padre referred to. Lacy heard no voice speak to her as she tried to quell the barbed wire eating into her stomach in anticipation of what laid ahead. Her hand slipped to her tummy below the gun belt and rested there where a new life was growing. Her head said to stay back with the other women, but in her heart Lacy knew she couldn't.

Speaking to the hushed crowd, Rawley said, "Everyone know what to do?" Heads bobbed up and down. "Okay, let's go get those kids!"

Chapter Forty-Five

Bound hand and foot, Cotton tried to get comfortable. He heard Hanah's stomach growl in her sleep next to him. He looked up at the star studded sky; tears suddenly welled in his eyes, his hand quickly brushed them away. It was just because he was exhausted, they all were. Closing his eyes he sent a prayer, *Lord...please help us...and watch over Chad, too...* A voice entered his mind saying one word, *knife.* Cotton's eyes popped open, he blinked. He had forgotten about Hanah carrying a knife. He whispered, "Thank you..."

You're welcome, my little one.

Nudging his sister, he whispered in her ear softly, "Hanah, wake up...I need your knife."

Hanah didn't move. Cotton nudged her harder, she stirred this time. He asked again, "Punkin, give me your knife."

Blinking, Hanah tried to sit straighter. "What?"

"Your knife...can you dig your knife out of your pocket?"

"I don't know..."

Cotton hissed, "Well...try...damn it!"

Scowling at her brother's words, Hanah squirmed around. A snore and rustling sounds interrupted her movement. Both held their breath then exhaled slowly realizing their kidnappers continued to sleep. Fingers digging deep finally latched around the pocketknife. Pulling it out, she handed it to Cotton. Cupping it in his hands, he used his teeth to pull the blade out. He cut the ropes from Hanah's hands and feet. When he handed her the blade she did the same for him.

Crawling to Ben and Dobie, Cotton touched them lightly; they jerked awake. He put a finger to his lips silencing any comments from them. They nodded, understanding as they glanced over at their kidnappers sleeping. Cutting through the ropes binding them, Cotton whispered so softly they could barely hear him. "Get the guns and the canteens, leave the saddles, we'll ride bareback."

Ben and Dobie tiptoed, the sand cushioning their footsteps, while Cotton cut loose the others.

Slight rustling filled the night as the band of brothers and sisters made their way to the picketed horses. Taking the reins they led them off for a distance before mounting.

Out of earshot of their captors, Dobie asked, "Where we goin' now? I'm getting sick and tired of this..."

Out of patience, Cotton reined up and snapped, "Shad-up, Litchfield! I'm trying to save your sorry hide! We're going back and get Chad and then we're going home!"

"How in the hell do you know where we's even at?" Dobie asked sourly. "You don't...so how's we gonna find our way back home?"

Glaring at Dobie for a few seconds more, he didn't bother to reply. Cotton dug heels into his mount's ribs making it jump and pick up it's pace.

Hanah looked at Ben, he grinned. She shrugged and smiled back.

Chapter Forty-Six

The two-wheeled carts lumbered along, their wheels occasionally squeaking, piercing the darkness with muffled thuds from the oxen pulling them. Under the dried grasses, soft breathing was heard as those hidden waited in anticipation to make their move on the compound.

The plan...Kelly and Beckett would go around behind the corral, disabling any of Del Rio's men they found and try to gain access to the powder magazine. They needed what would be inside; cartridges that went with the extra rifles, dynamite, fuses and kegs of powder. Later the magazine would be ignited, allowing the small rag-tag army to invade and rescue any captives they may find. At least that is what Rawley, Kelly and Beckett wanted to happen. But they all agreed on one thing; they wanted Del Rio alive.

The carts rolled to a stop some one hundred and fifty yards out. Kelly and Beckett hopped out of one cart, Thad and Rawley another. They converged, talking in low tones. Then Beckett and Kelly took off running in a crouch toward the walls surrounding the compound with Thad sticking close behind.

Rawley knocked on the wooden sides alerting the men hidden in the cart to come out. He stopped when he saw Lacy's head poking through the hay watching. His hand reached out caressing her cheek. "You be careful, Sunshine." He then moved and silently began pointing for the men to space out ready to attack. He turned when he heard her words. "You be careful too, Lovett, I don't much like the idea of being a widow, especially now with..." her whisper trailed off. He grinned. Lacy hesitated and then added, "I love you, Rawley Lovett." The smile broadened, "Love you too, Sunshine..." Lacy's head disappeared into the pile of grass.

Gazing around Rawley realized it was a warm night as he felt sweat trickle behind his ear and run down his neck. His finger flicked at it like a pesky fly. Turning, he began leading the two men forward.

* * *

Sidling along in the shadow of the wall behind them, Kelly and Beckett both knew without speaking they were going to have to kill any man they ran across. Both looked at Thad with his wide-eyed innocence trying to control his heart banging against his ribs.

"You okay, boy?" Kelly whispered.

Thad threw a short but determined look. "I'll do my job, sir," he said.

Clapping a hand on the boy's shoulder and squeezing, Kelly smiled and replied, "That's what I like to hear, son." Looking at Beckett, he warned, "These hombres are mean and tough, you ready?" Beckett nodded, moving forward with the other two following.

* * *

The Padre with Manuel and Lemony pushed the carts nearer the adobe walls. The Padre was sending up silent prayers with each step taking them closer. The Padre knew when the time came, Manuel and Lemony would unhitch the oxen from the two grass filled carts, set them on fire and shove the carts into buildings within the compound. He wished he could calm his heart that was stampeding in his chest, but he couldn't. His heavy robe felt sticky with nervous sweat.

Abruptly, two guards blocked his path. Hearing footsteps behind him he turned and saw others alongside the carts poking their weapons into the pile of hay and rattling the chicken coops making the birds squawk. The Padre sent up another prayer for those hidden; if they were found it would be certain death for them all. He returned his attention to the guards in front of him and waited, his calm exterior belying the turmoil inside.

224

Hearing footsteps outside, Lacy held her breath trying to lay flatter under the hay. She heard rustling above her as she witnessed rifle barrels poking through the thick grass. A barrel touched her leg, her breath caught then slowly eased as the rifle disappeared. She heard the words, "*Todo claro!*" and the footsteps faded.

The head guard nodded in response, refocusing on the Padre as he said, "*Esta tarde, Padre?*"

The Padre spoke in English, "Yes, I know, please forgive our lateness..."

Lemony had his sombrero pulled low across his face keeping a low profile as he listened. Manuel's hand nervously rubbed the neck of his oxen waiting for the Padre to get them through.

The guard nodded, throwing a quick glance at the three carts. He stepped aside ordering, "*Entrada con los provisionales!*"

The Padre stepped forward guiding the ox and saying "*Muchas gracias,*" as he walked past the guards. Slowly the three carts moved into position within the compound. Manuel and Lemony stopped by the corral, unhitching the two oxen, Manuel walked them a few feet. The Padre continued to the side of the hacienda near the vine covered trellis and stopped. He gazed around; all was quiet except for the soft flow of voices coming from inside the hacienda. *The calm before the storm,* he thought.

Grabbing a hay fork, Lemony began tossing the grass over into the corral, his eyes constantly darting, appraising the situation. Stabbing for another forkful he whispered, "All clear Miz Lacy..."

Lacy emerged from the hay with a rustling sound. Crouching, she hung close to the cart, watching and listening.

The two knocks sounded loudly as the Padre alerted the three men in his cart. They slipped quietly to the ground then darted to the darker shadows of the hacienda pressing against the adobe and waited; their own nervous breathing loud to their ears.

* * *

Watching the guard come closer, Kelly whispered out of the corner of his mouth, "I'll take 'em, hide the boy behind you," he told Beckett. Thad was shoved behind Beckett as Kelly stepped out and toward the guard.

"Hey, amigo...*Tiene una luz?*"

"Si.." digging under the double brace of ammo that crossed his chest, he pulled out a match. Stepping to the wall and striking it he held the flame to Kelly's cheroot.

Drawing deeply, the smoke filling his lungs, Kelly said, "*Muchas gracias...*" as his knife plunged deep into the man's gut and ripped upward until it hit bone. The guard grunted and fell against Kelly's arm driving the blade deeper. Lowering him to the ground, Kelly pulled the knife from the body and wiped the weapon on his britches. Looking over his shoulder, he indicated for Beckett and Thad to move. Slowing for only a moment, Thad stared at the dead guard, remembering the two men he had killed. He swallowed and picked up his pace. The three encountered one more guard and he met the same fate as the other. The walls of the compound dropped off to only four feet making access easier as the three climbed over then squatted, eyes watching and ears listening. Crouching, they moved quickly and quietly, stopping behind the corral.

Whispering Kelly told Thad, "Okay kid...yer on yer own..." and with that he and Beckett silently moved toward the powder magazine.

Nervously, Thad kept darting his eyes about. He felt like gnats were chewing on his neck. His hand just wiped away sweat, it was the salt stinging his sunburn instead. He continued to peer through the legs of the horses and mules shuffling around in the corral. His boots felt tight with the sticks of dynamite in them. Thad's hand dug inside his pocket...the matches were still there. He briefly thought of his friends; Cotton, Ben, Emily, Hanah and his brother Chad and wondered if they were here or somewhere else...he just hoped they were safe.

Hearing a noise to the side, Thad threw himself flat against the ground and pulled his weapon. He aimed into the shadows cocking the hammer back. Lacy dropped down, Thad heaved a sigh of relief slowly easing the hammer back down and sitting up.

Pointing, Lacy whispered, "When I get to the top of that trellis...I want you to light that stick of dynamite and throw it into the corral."

He looked at Lacy, disbelief in his face. Thad stammered, "But...but that's not what Mister Rawley said, He said to..."

"...I know what he said, Thad." Lacy interrupted. "The kids may be in the house and I need to get to them before Del Rio disappears with them..." Her dark eyes probed Thad's face. "You understand?"

Dropping his eyes, he said, "Yes, Ma'am."

Increased restless shuffling and milling around with a few anxious nickers alerted Lacy and Thad to focus their eyes on the agitated animals. Speaking softly, Lacy said, "They know something is up..." She touched his face, "Be careful..." then she disappeared into the darkness. Thad turned around, glancing upward toward the trellis and then back down watching as more dust was being stirred into the air by the restless horses and mules.

* * *

The two older men with Rawley did not carry shooting irons but machetes instead. One guard had already lost his head to a powerful swing as they silently glided along the wall surprising and deftly disposing of the guards as they came to them.

Reaching the section of the four foot wall, the three climbed over and crouched, running to the opposite side of the hacienda and waited. The scent of rose bushes tickled Rawley's nose as he stretched over them and peered around the corner of the two story home. He saw the Padre waiting patiently by the cart while subdued voices and soft male laughter from inside floated through the open windows to mingle with the quiet clucking of the caged chickens. Glancing over at the corral, he noted the agitated milling about and dust kicking the animals were doing. Rawley's mind echoed Lacy's thoughts. *They know something is up...I just hope the guards don't pick up on it...*

Rawley didn't know how much time had passed, but it felt like hours. Suddenly he was exhausted, closing his eyes for a few moments. He shook it off, concentrating on the small army he knew lay in readiness. At that moment he only saw the Padre, Manuel and Lemony. He raised his eyes to the sky, offering a silent prayer, *Lord...keep everyone safe...and help us find the kids...* His gaze continued to sweep the dark compound; now all they had to do was wait patiently for Kelly and Beckett to ignite the powder magazine.

* * *

"Hurry...up!" Kelly whispered harshly as Beckett fumbled trying to pick the lock securing the door to the dugout.

"I'm not the one should be doing this, Lacy's the one who can pick locks smooth as silk," he retorted under his breath, struggling to make the hairpin work the tumblers.

Kelly suddenly reached out stilling Beckett's hands. "We got company..."

Sticking the hairpin in his mouth, Beckett swiftly turned and lounged against the door. Pulling the sombrero lower on his face, he stared at the ground. He'd let Kelly handle it.

The guard walked closer, *"Por que esta aqui?"*

Beckett hissed, "What did he say?"

Speaking out of the side of his mouth, Kelly whispered, "Asked why we were here." He took two steps closer to the guard, saying, *"El commandante dice que necesitamos comprobar las municiones."*

His body tense, ready to spring into action if needed, Beckett could pick out some of the words in Kelly's reply from his small knowledge of the language. El commandante, necessary and munitions.

228

"*El Commandante?*" The guard asked, confused. "*Revisamos ayer y es bueno.*"

Kelly translated in his mind, *The Commander? We checked yesterday and everything is fine.* Raising his hands palms up, Kelly chuckled, "Ahhh...Si." Offering another cheroot from his pocket to the guard and taking the dead one out of his mouth, he asked, "*Tiene una luz?*"

Shifting the rifle into a more comfortable position in his arm, the guard took the cigar, sniffed appreciatively and licked the end tasting the fine tobacco. Smiling he said, "Good...very good!" Striking the match he made sure to light his first and then Kelly's. Inhaling deeply, the guard let out a satisfied sigh that was abruptly cut short. Surprised eyes focused on Kelly before dimming with death, his body collapsing against Kelly. Pulling the knife out, he ordered Beckett, "Git a move on..." as he dragged the body behind the dugout.

* * *

Lacy sidled in next to the Padre making him jump nervously at her appearance. "I'm going in," she whispered tip-toeing past him. Her arms rose and hands grabbed the cross pieces on the trellis as she began climbing.

The Padre touched her leg as Lacy looked down. "God go with you..." he whispered. Nodding, she continued climbing. Reaching the top, Lacy quickly slid a boot over the railing and hopped down crouching, her eyes adjusting to the dark.

Rawley's head popped up hearing the slight thud from above. He could see a darker shape moving along through the cracks of the floorboards. *What the hell...*he thought. Looking at the Padre, Rawley noticed him staring up at the trellis.

Watching closely, Thad saw Lacy climb the vine and disappear. He pulled a stick of dynamite out of his boot and then dug a match out of his pocket as his stomach continued to roll making him nauseous.

229

He swallowed and struck the match on a fence post. His shaking hands finally lit the fuse; he tossed it high in the air to land in the middle of the corral. Frenzied nickers and snorts filled the night as the animals pushed against the corral barrier trying to get away from the fizzing tube in the center. Thad stuck fingers in his ears and squeezed his eyes shut and waited.

Lemony and Manuel saw and smelled the dust rising wondering what had the horses and mules so riled up. Cracking noises sounded as the animals broke through the barrier, running for the gate.

Kelly half turned, "What the hell..."

Beckett gave a sigh of relief as the lock popped open to the powder magazine. His fingers nimbly pulled it through the hasp and pushed the door open.

KAAABOOOMMMM!

Chunks of earth and sand showered the area.

Guards flew out of their quarters half dressed and trying to pull on their boots and juggle weapons as they yelled and issued orders. Men stampeded out of the hacienda and stopped short watching the bedlam around them.

One lean, tall dark haired man had black eyes that widened first in surprise then narrowed in anger as he watched the commotion reach a fever pitch within his compound. Suddenly, he was backing, turning and going inside.

All Rawley could think of was *Damn...damn...damn...*

Above Lacy smiled, thinking, *Perfect Thad!* She moved toward the double doors and tried the handle. It turned easily in her hand as she stepped inside, closing it softly behind her.

"Someone set off the dynamite too early...dammit!" Kelly groused shoving Beckett into the dugout. "We gotta move faster now..." He picked up a keg of black powder and started running outside with it.

Loading his arms with rifles, Beckett followed Kelly to where he had stashed the keg. Rifles clattered as he dropped them. He met Kelly

230

with another keg as he brushed past him. Entering the dugout, he picked up a box of dynamite and a roll of fuse and ran back out.

The Padre and the three men with him quickly emptied the cart setting the chickens to squawking louder amid the total confusion of the situation. They hurriedly drove and pulled the oxen to the kegs and rifles and began loading the munitions into the cart.

Manuel and Lemony hunkered down next to Thad. He had pulled another stick from his boot and was in the process of lighting it when Lemony said, "Boy, what the hell did ya set off that stick fer...we wuz ta wait till Kelly and Beckett set off the magazine."

"Miz Lacy told me to..." he replied simply, lighting the fuse, Thad threw it toward the main yard of the compound. Three sets of eyes followed the fizzing tube flying through the air, watched it hit and bounce. Guards saw the stick and began running away from it.

KAAABOOOOMMM!

Men flew through the air with the second explosion, landing with thuds as they dropped back to the packed dirt of the compound.

Clapping a hand on Thad's shoulder, Lemony chuckled, "Youse jus' as good at throwing as ya 'r at shootin', Sonny!" Motioning to Manuel he said, "Let's go set them carts afire!"

* * *

The window slid up silently, Rawley nodded to the two machete carrying men to follow him. He crawled through the opening and stood to the side so the others could enter. Then his long strides quickly took him to the closed double doors.

* * *

Running for his weapons, Del Rio was confused. How had

231

someone slipped past his guards? And how many were there? His head turned briefly when the second explosion rocked the walls and windows of his fortress. It couldn't be the people of Las Culebras, they didn't have any weapons, he had made sure of that. *So who had invaded his compound and what did they want and why?* He didn't have the answers yet. Joel found Del Rio and helped slip the double bandoleers across his commander's chest, asking, "What now, *El Commandante?*"

Chapter Forty-Seven

Stirring, Chad opened his eyes gazing through the leaves above him, shimmering a little with the low breeze. He tried to sit up but couldn't; he was too weak. Footsteps nearing had his head turning toward them. Chad saw Big Joe Kannon looming over him; he gave a silent groan, closing his eyes.

"Well...now boy...sure am glad youse decided not ta die on me."

Chad tried to swallow the mouthful of cotton that seemed to have wrapped around his tongue. "Water..." he whispered.

Kneeling Kannon said, "What's that...boy?"

"Water...I need some water..." Just the effort to say those few words deteriorated Chad's strength even more.

"It's jus' you and me, boy," Kannon began explaining as he held Chad's head to drink from the one canteen Biff and Dub left. "Them sum-bitches run off taking the rest of them kids and tha harses leavin' us afoot. Once youse gits better we's a walking."

Mumbling weakly, "No, you go on without me..." Chad said.

"Nope...youse still worth mebe hun'drt dollars ta me...we's goin' ta gither."

Too weak to think, Chad slipped into a deep sleep.

Rising, Big Joe's bulk moved toward the small fire and the snake meat sizzling over the coals.

* * *

Cotton didn't know how far they had traveled. All he knew is that they had been backtracking their two day old sign, heading to where Chad and Kannon had been left. He said a prayer that Chad would be still alive when they got to him. He also had no sense about what they should do next, except to rescue Chad and then find a town and a doctor and a way home. Thinking briefly of his Mom and Dad, he realized he had no way of contacting them. He thought of Thad and wondered if he made it out safely and found help. *But what good would it do now?* He asked himself, *We have no idea where we are or nuthin'!*

Refocusing his tired eyes on the ground, the little band continued to follow the partially sand filled tracks back to their friend Chad.

* * *

Dub moved restlessly in his sleep, his ears picking up on the unusual quietness of the camp wakening him. He abruptly sat up as his eyes swept the area. *Empty!* Except for Biff. He looked to where they had picketed the horses, *Gone!*

He stood quickly and kicked Biff in the ribs.

"Ow...damn you!" Biff mumbled.

"Git up," Dub yelled. "Them kids got away last night!"

"Wha... they wuz tied..."

Walking over, Dub picked up a piece of rope, "Cut! Them damn kids had a knife!"

Searching through their outfits, Biff spoke, "Took the rifles and the canteens, they did." Biff sat down heavily. "They done set us afoot wit no water..."

Whirling, Dub wanted someone to blame and Biff was it. "You...sum-bitch...why didn't you watch them last night?"

Stiffening, Biff's eyes hardened as his hand moved closer to the grip of his gun. "Now's not the time ta be pickin' a fite, Dub. 'Sides I'm faster than you," he warned.

Knowing he was outmatched even with Biff sitting took the bluster out of Dub. "Well...now what?" he asked.

"We's shuck of Kannon, so I sez we head ta Texas 'n hire on some outfit..sleep under a roof with food in 'r bellies 'n money in 'r pockets fer a change," Biff offered up looking at Dub.

Stretching out on his ground cover, Dub answered, "Yeah...that sounds like a plan after I get some more sleep." He pulled his hat over his face.

* * *

Gazing ahead, Cotton saw the odd shaped tree he remembered from before. He reined in the sorrel and waited on the others to pull alongside. He remembered how old Luke told his tales. Of how the Indians would bend small trees or twisting them into shapes as trail markers or water indicators.

Speaking to the others, Cotton announced as he slipped off the back of the sorrel, "We left Chad not far from here. Dobie bring that rifle, you and me are going ahead."

Blue eyes roamed the tired and rag-tag group waiting patiently for him to tell them what to do. "The rest of you get off the horses and rest awhile. But don't let them animals stray, we need them." Looking up, he saw a hawk sounding as it searched for it's next meal. Cotton watched the bird soar by them, his shadow passing quickly across the sunlit ground then disappearing.

Clicking the cocking lever down, Cotton saw the shell in the chamber. Dobie mimicked him and then said, "I'm ready."

A branch snapping had Kannon whirling and pulling his weapon.

Two boys stepped into the clearing, rifles pointing at the man who still wore the ratty buffalo hide even in this heat.

235

"Drop it, Mr. Kannon..." Cotton ordered.

Dirty eyes shifted toward the muzzle bores pointed at his gut and chest. Eyes lifted, thinking...*Them rifles could be empty,* he thought, *and them boys a bluffin'.*

"Them rifles loaded?" He asked.

Piping up, Dobie said, "They shor 'r and every last bullet is meant fer you!"

Kannon began laughing, chuckling at first, then a loud raucous sound filled the air.

Cotton and Dobie hesitated, unsure of Kannon's change in demeanor.

The man had the boys off their stride now, picking up on their uncertainty. "You kids is got ta be the damn 'dist things I ever did run acrosst," he said, taking a step toward them.

Dobie's finger convulsed pulling the trigger, fire spit from the bore of the rifle. Kannon grunted and spun to the side, still standing after the bullet caught him in the shoulder. The sound of a cocking lever was loud as Dobie injected another cartridge into the chamber.

Kannon fired blindly. Dobie gave a yelp, dropping the rifle and clutching his arm, watching the blood seep through his fingers. Cotton fired from the hip, catching Kannon in the chest, knocking him backwards. The cocking lever slammed down as Cotton took steps firing round after round into Kannon's now dead body.

A weak voice finally broke through his rage. "Cotton...that's enough..."

Footsteps and hooves clattered into the clearing, The others stopped and starred at the scene. Grey puffs of smoke from the weapons drifted in the slight breeze. The sharp scent of burnt gunpowder stung their noses.

Cotton continued to stare at Kannon who had turned their peaceful little world into a miserable and frightening existence. "No more..." he whispered, "No more will you be stealing kids...you bastard." He

236

jumped when Hanah touched his arm. "Cotton..." she began. He slumped with exhaustion but pulled his sister close. "It's over Hanah, we're finally free..." Cotton felt her head nod against his chest. Looking over the little band of ragamuffin kids, he suddenly felt proud at how they had all pulled together and made it outsmarting their kidnappers. His mind sent a *Thank you* toward the heavens.

A voice entered his mind. *I knew you could do it, my little one. So very proud of all of you.*

His arm still wrapped around his sister, Cotton just nodded. This time the voice didn't surprise him as it had in the past, but lent comfort instead.

Chapter Forty-Eight

Edging along the hallway upstairs, Lacy listened for any unusual sound she could discern over the commotion from outside. Reaching a doorway, the handle turned in her hand as the other pulled her pistol from it's boot. Cracking the door, she shoved it open and stepped inside; an empty room greeted her. Stepping out she tiptoed along the carpet runner, checking each room.

Arriving at the top of the stairs, the house suddenly rocked with a huge explosion knocking Lacy to her knees. Windows shattered and chunks of mud plaster rained down covering the stairs and floor below. Rising quickly, Lacy raced down the steps. Turning the corner, she ran smak-dab into a tall man.

"Rawley, the ki...." her words faded as she came face to face with a man she knew in her gut to be Del Rio. "You!" She rasped out hotly. In a split second Del Rio had disarmed Lacy, almost breaking her wrist and pulling her arm up high behind her back. "You...bastard!"

Black eyes became hostile as he pushed her along in front of him. Lacy tried to struggle, but it was no use; any movement would break her arm.

Crossing the stone floor, Rawley saw three people quickly disappear around the corner, one with a red braid swinging. He fired, his bullet missing it's mark. He heard Lacy call out to him, "Rawley!"

Del Rio ordered Joel, "Kill him!" as he opened a heavy wooden door shoving Lacy down the steps, then closed it behind him. Joel turned ready to face the intruders.

Sliding along the wall, Rawley motioned for the two men with him to do the same. Stopping, he listened for footsteps along the stone floor. He heard nothing except the gunfire and men yelling outside. Remembering his hat he took it off and holding the brim in his fingers, he edged his hat around the corner. A sharp retort sounded as a bullet whizzed by, catching the hat and sending it sailing across the room. Jumping out, Rawley fired back to back rounds into the figure and watched him crumple to the floor. Sprinting down the hallway he looked for tell-tale signs of Lacy.

Facing a man she didn't know but despised, she rushed him, ready to claw out his eyes. He cuffed her alongside the head sending her sprawling against a wine rack making the bottles clink. She tasted blood in her mouth when she tried to rise. Her hand reached around the neck of a bottle, but she wasn't quick enough. His pistol came down on her wrist making the bottle drop and shatter. A sweet smell engulfed the room. Del Rio grabbed her braid and roughly swung her up against him, his hand tightening around the back of her neck. The pistol barrel jammed under her chin as black eyes danced with anger. "I seemed to have caught a wildcat...I like spirited women..."

Lacy reared back against his hand and spat in his face. The next thing she knew her world went black.

* * *

Searching frantically through the hacienda, Rawley had yet to find Lacy. One of the men with him pointed at the heavy wooden door. "Senor...we haven't..."

Rawley jerked the door open, hurrying down the steps into a dimly lit wine cellar. Reflected in the glow was a smashed wine bottle. One of the men opened another heavy door. "Senor, a tunnel..."

"Where does it go?"Rawley asked.

Shrugging the man replied, "The mines?"

"Alright, you go up and tell Kelly and Beckett and the others I'll meet them at the mines. I'm going after Lacy." He started down the tunnel, but the man's next words had him slowing and hesitating.

"Senor? God be with you..."

Nodding, Rawley sprinted further into the tunnel.

* * *

Dashing outside the hacienda, the two men searched for the Padre finding Beckett and Kelly instead, rounding up what was left of Del Rio's men in the center of the compound. Breathlessly, they told them what happened - that Del Rio had the Senorita Lacy and that Senor Rawley had gone after her. Faces turned grim hearing the news.

Turning to Lemony, Kelly asked, "Where'd the Padre go with the munitions?"

"Back to town."

"Alright," Kelly said. Refocusing on the men being tied into a circle by the townsmen, he announced. "When you are done, follow us back to town."

"But Senor? You plan to just leave them here to bake like bread in the sun?"

Turning, Kelly focused on the man who spoke. "And that amigo, would be much kinder then what I'd really like to do."

241

Chapter Forty-Nine

Walking off by himself, Cotton leaned against a boulder, he needed to think. His eyes strained against the glare as he looked around. He was worried and not knowing this country he was reluctant to wander far from the water source. Cotton didn't know if there might be a homestead or town just a few miles in either direction and he was missing it. Sighing heavily from his burden, he stared glumly at his grimy and broken fingernails, his mind reliving the horrors they had been subjected to. Lifting his head, he realized a bright side to it all. They were safe, their captors dead. Chad was going to make it and they were all still together. His mind drifted to Thad and he wondered if he was okay.

Squinting against the blue expanse of sky that seemed to go on forever, Cotton spoke softly, "Gramma? What now? What do we do now?" He sat patiently waiting on an answer but none came. He rose, despair clinging to his shoulders like a heavy cloak. Cotton began walking slowly toward his comrades.

Do not fret my little one. Travel east to the town of Top Notch. Wait there, the voice said.

Stopping in his tracks, Cotton asked, "How far?"

Not far, was the reply.

"But why wait there, we want to go home..."

*No. You wait, you will see in time...you must wait...*the voice faded from Cotton's mind. Spinning around, he once again looked for someone standing nearby and again there was no one.

The next morning thirteen kids packed the backs of five horses and   headed   east.

Chapter Fifty

Rawley's pace was slowed by the dark tunnel. Lighting a match, he held it up and found a lantern. Lifting the lamp from the braces holding beams at intervals across the ceiling, he lit it and continued to sprint in a crouched position down the narrow, low ceiling passageway. His footsteps echoed against the hard packed path.

He continued to cuss his wife and Del Rio as he ran. In the ten years they'd been married Lacy never did catch on to the knack of listening, even when it was in her own best interest. *And now with a baby on the way...*he kicked that thought out of his head. He needed to focus on just getting out of this tunnel and reaching Lacy before any harm came to her or their baby.

The passageway seemed to go on forever; when making a turn Rawley saw the tunnel abruptly end. Standing and looking up the makeshift ladder, he stared at a crude wooden cover. Setting the lamp down, he tested the lower rung; it would hold him. Hands reaching above he moved the cover enough to peer out. Not seeing anything with his limited vision, he listened. Voices seemed to be distant, coming from the outside. Shoving the cover out of the way, he quickly pulled himself up to the packed dirt above the tunnel. Rawley seemed to be in a small cavern-like area. Sprinting towards the stacks of wooden boxes toward the back, he hid. He explored what they were; dynamite and coils of fuse along with kegs of black powder. He ran around and flattened himself against the sandstone wall and peered around the edge. Rawley was surprised to see that dawn had broken, he felt as if only minutes had passed since they began the raid on the compound. A sloped road from this cavern led to the mining area below. Men were posted every twenty-five feet or so below, guarding the workers and a guard tower with a Gatling gun that could shoot out the whole area. His eyes narrowed, realizing most of the workers were young boys and men. He looked for Cotton or Chad. To his right he saw what looked like cages with metal gates swung open.

Automatically he knew this is where the prisoners were kept at night. *But where is Lacy?* He thought.

Turning, he ran back towards the munitions. Rawley knew how to make Del Rio show himself.

* * *

A terrible pounding in her head brought Lacy back to semi-consciousness. She tried to rub her aching head but couldn't. She opened her eyes and realized her wrists tied to the arms of a chair. Looking across the room, she saw Del Rio sprawled in another chair staring lewdly at her.

He rose and stepped toward her, a wicked smile on his lips that did not reach his eyes. "It seems...my little red-bird has awoken from her nap."

Lacy's mouth clenched, making her jaw hurt where he had clubbed her. Her throat dry and parched sounded raspy. "Where are my children?"

Cocking his head arrogantly he repeated, "Children?"

Seeing her struggle against her bonds made Del Rio smile.

Dark eyes snapped with fire. Her voice low, packed with venom, she said, "Yes. The children you pay Kannon to steal and bring to you to be sold into this hell."

A questioning gaze flitted across his face. "Kannon? I know no such ma..."

"Liar!" Lacy shouted. "I've come to rescue my children and take them home!"

Surprised, Del Rio asked, "Alone?"

"There are others..."

"Ah...the compound..." he walked over to the table and picked up

246

a cheroot and a match. Striking the phosphorous, it flared. He sucked the flame into the tobacco, then released a plume of smoke into the air. Turning, he sat on the edge of the table and studied her. The smoke floating lazily across his face made him squint. "So...it appears you think this Kannon has stolen your children and...."

Lacy cut him off, "I know he did! I've come over a thousand miles to find them and take them home." A sly smile showed as she added, "And to put you where daylight will never reach."

Del Rio smiled and stood and walked back to Lacy. "A threat..from someone as beautiful as you?"

"Not a threat...a promise," she said.

Blowing a plume of smoke into her face, Lacy sneezed and coughed as he grinned. Spinning, he walked a few steps then turned back, gesturing with the cheroot. "A large and unfathomable task for one of your..." he obscenely allowed his eyes to roam her body, "Of your stature."

Lacy stiffened recalling that same type of look her grandfather would give her before violating her. *Skeletons*, her mind said. Mentally she shook herself before replying. "I've met men like you before."

"Oh..."

"Yes. They no longer grace this earth."

A black brow cocked, "You have killed before..."

"Yes."

"You hold onto big dreams...no one can stop me." Del Rio stepped closer. His hand suddenly gripped her face as he leaned toward her.

Lacy tried to shake his painful hold.

Del Rio roughly pushed her head back to where she thought it would snap, making sure her dark eyes focused on his. This man wore evil like a strong perfume, Lacy realized. She kept her face flat which belied the turmoil within. She refused to let this man know she was scared witless. *Where are Rawley and the others?* she thought, staring into the face of the devil himself.

247

KAAABOOOMMMM!!!

The room shook with tremors. Del Rio quickly ran to the door; smoke continued to roll from across the way. Guards and workers were scrambling in fear. He turned away glancing at Lacy as she smiled. Crossing the short space, he backhanded her hard enough to make the chair flip over. Her head banged against the floor. Lacy gasped and tried to keep from passing out.

* * *

As Kelly sat on his black striped dun mule, he heard the explosions and waved his arm saying to the small army on foot, "Let's go!" He and Beckett on his chestnut raced toward the mining complex, lit cheroots gripped tightly between their teeth, their saddlebags filled with sticks of dynamite.

The small army swarmed the hills of scag from the mines with heightened intensity. The miners running out of the mine shafts recognized their families and friends and realized their opportunity for freedom was upon them. They picked up anything they could lay their hands on to use for weapons and joined with the villagers.

Beckett and Kelly split directions, lighting and tossing the dynamite as they rode.

Lemony and Thad lay above on a small rise, picking off the guards with their rifles.

Bullets riddled the ground sending up pockets of dust from the Gatling gun in the guard tower. Rawley dove behind a metal cart just as lead peppered the side.

Elbowing Thad, Lemony said, "Sonny? Think ya could pick off off that one manning that repeater in the tower?"

"Don't know, all's I can do is try..."

"That's a start," Lemony said.

Kelly stopped by Rawley for a moment and yelled, "Find Lacy?"

"No!"

Lighting the fuse from his cheroot, "I'll try ta keep 'em off ya's arse till then!" Kelly grinned as he dug his heels into the mule.

Hearing quickened footsteps behind him, Rawley turned and seeing a guard ready to bayonet him, he fired. The man crumpled. Crouching, studying his position through the acrid scent of dynamite and black powder burning his nose with the plumes of dust choked air irritating his eyes, Rawley tried to think like Del Rio. *Where would I go with Lacy?*

More bullets skimmed the ground as another burst came from the Gatling gun, pinging the cart's side. Rawley hunkered down, emptying his gun's cylinder of casings and refilling it with the spare cartridges in his gun belt.

Shifting into a more comfortable position, Thad tucked the butt of the rifle tightly into his shoulder, pulling it closer to his cheek. He sighted the man in the tower and gently pulled the trigger. The guard's arms flew up as he flopped over the back of the repeater then slipped out of sight.

Lemony chortled, slapping Thad's back, "I knew youse could do it!"

Thad grinned.

Riding by the now quiet tower, Beckett threw a sizzling stick into the air and kicked the chestnut hard. A few moments later the guard house blew up into a pile of toothpicks.

Kneeling, one of Del Rio's men took aim at the man riding by and pulled the trigger. Beckett spun out of the saddle, hitting dirt hard.

Firing his pistol, Rawley saw the guard flop forward and remain still. Beckett struggled to his feet and ran to Rawley.

"You hit bad?" he shouted over the din of the fighting.

Grimacing, "Shoulder...find Lacy?"

"Not yet, but will...you stay here," Rawley ordered.

Beckett nodded.

Edging his head around the cart Rawley stared at the cages and a few shacks near there. He moved toward them.

Inside, Del Rio had released Lacy's bonds and jerked her up roughly.

Kicking at his shins with her boots, she aimed a knee at his crotch, but he whirled her around, locking his arm around her neck. Jerking her hard against him Del Rio began cutting into her air supply.

Lacy's hands gripped his muscular forearm trying to pull it away from her throat. He was too strong, it wasn't working. She went into defense mode slumping as if she had passed out. His arm wrapped around her waist as he positioned her in front of him to take bullets meant for him. His pistol in his other hand, Del Rio stepped out of the building.

Stopping abruptly seeing Del Rio carrying his limp wife, Rawley's heart skipped a beat. Recovering, he yelled, "Del Rio!"

Lacy's breath caught as she tried to remain limp and seemingly unconscious tucked against Del Rio's torso.

His pistol whipped up toward the voice, Del Rio stood still.

"Release my wife!"

"This is your wife?" He answered. "Then you have quite the prize here, she carries spirit. But I'm afraid amigo, she is mine now..."

The silence between the two men became a chasm, the focus so deep they could almost hear the other breathing.

Beckett had moved around to the other side of the cart, but his angle here was no good either; Lacy remained in the way.

The sweat continued to bead across Rawley's forehead, dripping into his eyes stinging them. He refused to blink, not wanting to lose sight of Del Rio even for a second. More sweat rolled down Rawley's arm dampening his gun hand. His finger around the half-moon trigger felt greasy from the moisture. He knew he had only one chance to make his shot good. He continued to steady his breathing using every ounce of control he had.

Astride his mule, Kelly saw Lovett facing off against someone. The din of hearing celebratory yells and shouts faded when he realized it must be Del Rio with Lacy in his arms. Looking, he saw no way to get behind the shack; it was built into a cliff, maybe he could go through the side and come in behind Del Rio? He swung the mule around.

Beckett decided to try something. He remained hidden, throwing words toward Del Rio. "You don't want her," he said.

Startled by Beckett's voice, Rawley kept eyes on the man holding Lacy.

Keeping his pistol on the man fifteen feet in front of him, Del Rio tried to see where the voice came from.

"She can be mean as a snake," Beckett continued to talk from behind the cart. "With a temper to boot."

Beckett, you rat! Lacy thought.

"That's right, you don't want her mad at you," Rawley said.

Lovett, I'm gonna kill you, she thought. *If you boys are just going to chat...*Lacy curled her fist and threw it backwards nailing Del Rio between the eyes. He yelled, stepping back and dropping Lacy. She quickly crawled toward the side of the building away from flying lead.

Del Rio fired blindly, then backed into the building slamming the door shut ending the short firefight.

Rawley ran to Lacy and swung her into his arms carrying her out of harm's way and sat her down. Touching the bruises on her face he asked, "You okay, Sunshine?"

Lacy nodded as tears brimmed over and ran down her cheeks. She launched herself into his arms wrapping her own around his neck, buried her face in his shoulder and sobbed. He just held her, smoothing that copper braid he loved so much.

251

Replacing his spent cartridges with fresh, Beckett kept glancing over at Lacy and Rawley. He sighed, knowing he still carried a torch for the woman, but also knowing he could never have her. He glanced up when Kelly edged around the building, holding his Henry. Beckett nodded in response when Kelly indicated that Del Rio had holed up in the building. Kelly walked silently toward him.

Rawley's thumbs wiped the moisture from freckled cheeks as he listened. The words tumbled from her mouth, "Rawley...that man is pure evil, it sweats out of his pores he's so vile. I mean, I thought Lowell Taylor was evil, but...but this man is worse." Lacy stopped only long enough to haul in air, "Did you find the kids?"

Rawley shook his head, "No...not yet."

Glancing around she stammered, "But...but...they're not here?" She stood quickly, Rawley pulled her back down. "You stay put...maybe now you will listen..." He glanced up when Kelly and Beckett's shadows fell across them.

Kelly squatted in front of of the pair. "I say we drop a short fuse into a crack."

Lacy's mouth dropped open. "But...that'd kill him! We need to find out where the children are first!"

As much as he wanted to find the kids, Rawley ordered Kelly, "Rig a short fuse, a couple of 'em in case the first doesn't shake him out of there.

"No! He has to know where the kids are...let me talk to him," Lacy rose only to be pulled back down again. "Damn...you Lovett! Let me talk to him!"

"No!" Rawley used the tone Lacy tended to listen to, *sometimes.* "Those boards are like tinder and thin to boot. A bullet would cut through that wood like paper, hitting you. The answer is no, Sunshine."

Lovett nodded at Kelly, "Do it." He took Lacy's arm and pulled her up walking away.

Sweat was pouring in streams down Del Rio's face as he listened

252

from within the shack. He heard a few mumblings and then all became quiet. Nervously he checked and rechecked his pistol.

Lacy wandered in a frantic daze through the crowd of freed miners, looking for the children. Turning to her husband as tears once again formed and fell, "They're not here, Rawley...and we traveled a thousand miles to find them and bring them home and they're not...here. What do we do now...where do we search?"

Pulling his wife to him he held her close, "We won't stop searching until we do find them, Sunshine."

"Fire in the hole..." Kelly yelled.

Everyone dropped; Rawley placed his body over Lacy.

Beckett and Kelly placed themselves to grab or shoot Del Rio as he came out.

Hearing those words from outside, Del Rio frantically searched the the interior walls. Finally he heard it; the slight sizzling sound a fuse makes. He bolted for the door, opening it and ran out shooting as he swerved to his right. Kelly's 44/40 slug cut him down and that's when the building blew. Shards of debris rained down along with a portion of the bluff behind.

When silence prevailed again Rawley helped Lacy to stand. She stared at the empty hole left by the dynamite. Her heart felt like that hole, empty. The tears began to roll down her face. Lacy sat down cross-legged and buried her face in her hands crying silent sobs.

"Hey...Lovett," Kelly called. "You wanna talk ta this sum-bitch before he kicks off? He ain't doing so well, right 'bout now."

Hearing that, Lacy raced to Del Rio's side. Not even noticing his battered and bloody body, she grabbed a handful of hair and pulled his face close to hers. "Where are my children?"

Glazed eyes stared at the redhead.

"Kannon was to bring you more children...wasn't he?"

"Never came..." were the last words Del Rio uttered.

253

Lacy let go of his hair and stood. "I hope you rot in hell...you sick bastard!" She whispered. Turning she walked into Rawley's arms.

Chapter Fifty-One

A column of thirteen solemn riders entered the outskirts of a town, their horses plodding wearily in the high noon heat. Cotton was leading the way and had found a town, but it didn't look much like a town. He searched frantically for a name, hoping it was Top Notch. Spotting another sign over the front of a jail, he rode toward it. He exhaled a sigh of relief when he read the words *Top Notch:* he reined his horse in front of the water trough. The others followed, their mounts dropped noses into the tepid water and guzzled the moisture.

Pedro had stepped outside his open air Cantina and watched the strange sight of kids packed liked sardines on the backs of horses riding into town. He scratched his head and wandered back inside. A few others also wandered through doorways to see the odd visitors then returned to their cooler interiors.

Helping Chad off his horse, Cotton and he made their way inside the adobe walls away from the blistering heat. Settling Chad on a bunk in one of the two cells, Cotton looked around. The others trooped in and settled on the floor, backs against mud plaster walls, heaving sighs at the coolness.

As much as he would like to rest also, Cotton moved to the door and and stepped onto the short walk. His gaze roamed the street. *Gramma told us to wait here,* he thought. *But I don't understand...wait for what?*

A voice answered, *You will my little one, just wait.*

Cotton jumped, looking around; no one was there, once again. Stepping into the bright sunlight, Cotton trotted toward the Cantina hoping to find some answers.

Pedro looked up when the sunburned white-haired boy walked in. Watched as the kid looked around and then came toward him.

Cotton measured the swarthy individual on the other side of the planks set atop three wooden barrels and wondered if he could trust him. Reluctantly deciding he had to, Cotton cleared his throat and spoke, "Mister, we..."

"Pedro...call me Pedro," the man said.

Nodding, Cotton continued, "Mister Pedro, we...my friends were kidnapped from Wyoming and we need some help...we escaped and two are wounded and..."

Interrupting, Pedro asked, "...You the ones the Marshal and his red haired wife looking for?"

Now it was Cotton's turn to be surprised. "You mean they were here?"

"Si...Senor Buckshot and another they call Beckett with a big man...Lovett?" He tried to recall the name. "They went to the border to rescue children. The wife they leave here. Then old Lemony Jones and a boy...I tink they call him Thad come and the wife and those two also rode to the border."

Astounded, Cotton couldn't believe their luck! Thad was alive and with his Mom! His Dad too had come to rescue them! He slumped against the planks and then passed out from relief and exhaustion, sliding into a heap on the dirt floor.

Scooping the boy into his arms he ran into the street calling, "Lupita...Lupita!"

Hearing her name, Lupita stood in the doorway of her father's store. She quickly descended the steps running to Pedro. Her hand gently caressed the boy's forehead.

Speaking in a rush, Pedro explained, "This boy...the others, the children Buckshot is looking for...are here."

"Where?" She asked.

"Come..." he led the way into the jail.

Lupita stopped suddenly as she saw all the children laying about on the floor, sleeping, dirty, exhausted and terribly sunburned. She uttered softly, "Dios mio!"

Pedro looked up after placing the boy on the other bunk in the cell. "Look...Lupita...another one is hurt."

She had knelt by another boy with a dried bloody bandage on his arm. Lupita rose quickly and went to stand at Pedro's side. Eyes wide in her chubby face, "Go get Sophia and plenty of hot water, I will get fresh bandages, medicine and blankets," she said brushing past him, hurrying out the door.

Chapter Fifty-Two

Holding the reins lightly in one hand while the other shook the Padre's. Rawley said, "Father, you have your town back and a mine to work. I expect Las Culebras will prosper."

"Senor, it will...it will, but not under the name of Las Culebras, but under the name of Santa Maria."

Smiling, Rawley stepped into his saddle. "By the way Father, what does Las Culebras mean?"

"The Snakes."

"You do well to change the name to Santa Maria, Padre."

The six reined their mounts around and began trotting out of Santa Maria. Arms were lifted and voices cried out their goodbyes.

The Padre waved as he called out, "God..be with you!" Then he stepped inside and pulled on the bell rope. The toll of the bell rang for the first time in years, he sighed happily.

* * *

Conversation was lighthearted as they all sat around the campfire, with Lemony and Buckshot regaling everyone with their tales. Even Thad's laughter was music to his ears. But Rawley couldn't bring himself to enjoy the light banter. He was becoming more worried by the second about Lacy. Her face had become drawn and pinched and she was barely touching her food, even though Lemony's chow wasn't half bad as trail chow goes.

Standing, Rawley moved toward his wife sitting off by herself with her back turned. Rawley was oblivious to the fact the voices had ceased as eyes followed him nearing Lacy.

"He shor do love that little upstart...don't he?" Lemony asked of no one in particular.

Heads nodded.

Stopping in front of his wife, Rawley tucked thumbs into his back pockets as he gazed at Lacy. She'd been crying again he noticed, as she quickly tried to wipe the tears away. Stepping closer he squatted in front of her and took her small freckled hands in his big one.

Lacy focused on how gentle those big hands were and yet could handle a pistol or rifle with deadly accuracy. She looked up. "Rawley, what are we going to do..."

"First, we are going back to Top Notch. And then when you are rested enough, you and Thad are going home."

Lacy opened her mouth to protest and Rawley wagged a finger in her face. "At-ah...Sunshine. You have someone else to think of besides yourself and I want both of you healthy." He gave her a stern gaze, "You understand me?"

Chewing on her bottom lip, Lacy finally nodded.

Standing, Rawley pulled Lacy close and kissed that flaming mop he loved so well. "Think you could eat some of Lemony's chow?"

"I'll try," came her soft reply.

His fingers tilted her face up. Lacy's burnt coffee eyes held a questioning and frightened gaze. "Sunshine...I promise you, I will find them and kill Kannon so those skeletons can be put to rest once and for all."

Dark eyes filled with tears, making Rawley's heart turn to mush. "I love you so much, Rawley Lovett."

He smiled, "I know you do, Sunshine. I love you too."

Chapter Fifty-Three

Restless and becoming bored, Cotton sat in a chair by the jail's door, one leg thrown over the arm and swinging his foot as he chewed on a stalk of dried grass. They had been here a week best as he could recollect. Time seemed to stand still in Top Notch.

Chad was walking a little more each day with the aid of a crutch. Dobie was being his usual charming self; claiming bragging rights about everything that had happened to them. Ben and Hanah spent most of their time across the way at Lupita's and her father's store helping in exchange for a piece of candy, not getting into trouble like they used to in Ezra's store. His gaze drifted to the two sitting on the steps with their heads close, whispering and giggling. Julie's feet had healed and Emily and Emma Sue were stilled glued at the hip. Where you found one, you found the other.

Cotton sighed, he didn't know how they could repay the kindness of these strangers who took them in when they needed a helping hand in the worse way. They had no money and he had no idea how they would make it back to White River...The soft voice entered his mind making him jump, *Look up, my little one and you will see the reason I told you to wait.*

His leg slid off the arm of the chair as he sat straighter and then stood walking to the edge of the boards. Coming in from the west, rode six riders with one pulling a burro.

Hanah and Ben also watched the newcomers come closer. Then something piqued her interest. There in amongst the dusty men and their alkaline covered hats, mixed with the bays, chestnuts, sorrels and a mule was a dirty greyish-white horse. Hanah sat straighter. *Fancy? Naw...* then she saw her Mother with her copper colored braid draped across her chest as she rode Fancy. She stood and let out a squeal, "Cotton...It's Mama!" tearing past him running toward the riders.

Hearing the squeal and the words *Mama*, they jerked hard on their mounts' reins, pulling them up short.

Cotton stepped out and shouted, "Dad!" as he too took off running.

Lacy, her mouth hanging wide open, couldn't believe she just heard the word *Mama*. Then she saw Hanah, arms wide running toward them. Lacy couldn't get out of the saddle fast enough. Pushing through the horses, she ran a few feet, knelt and engulfed Hanah in her arms crying so hard she could barely see her daughter.

"Mama...Mama...I was so afraid I'd never see you again..."

Smoothing copper curls so very like her own, Lacy whispered, "I know...honey...I know..."

Rushing to Cotton, Rawley picked him up and swung him around then hugged him close. Setting him down, Rawley's palms kept squeezing Cotton's shoulders which seemed to have gotten wider and taller as both gazed at each other with tears glistening.

Chad hobbled out of the jail when he heard all the commotion. As soon as he recognized Mister Rawley, that hobble became a scramble. The others flowed into the street and followed behind Chad.

Thad spotting his brother yelled, "Chad!" He hopped off his saddle and ran toward his brother grabbing him in a bear hug, crutch and all, yelling, "Waahooooo!"

The other riders dismounted and gathered around, jostling the kids and teasing them. Smiles and tears flowed freely. Even old Lemony sniffled and wiped his nose.

Chatter rose as each one tried to tell their story.

"Yeah...Mama, that dirty old man said they wouldn't stop, I had to pee in my britches..."

"Yeah...and then there was this fight in the wagon...and I stole his gun..."

"Then we escaped..."

262

"I killed one..."

"We were in this huge sandstorm..."

"Chad got gored by a..."

"Wild hog..."

"Yeah and then we killed two more...and..."

"Chad's leg got sick..."

"Julie's feet got hurt..."

"We got captured again..."

"Then we escaped...

"Then Dobie got shot..."

"Yeah and Cotton killed Kannon...and..."

Stunned, Rawley said, "What? Wait a minute...say that again?"

Chad filled in the Marshal, "Cotton killed Kannon. Ya see Mister Rawley, Kannon's men took the others and left me for dead and Kannon afoot. Cotton and them came back for me and shot him dead."

Hanah added with arms thrown wide. "Yep and here we are...all back together again," she twirled and gave a skip-hop. "One big happy family!"

Thad stepped toward Lemony saying, "Thank you for rescuing me back yonder."

Squinting at the boy turned man in a short time, he replied, "Sonny, I's got rite fond of youse. Ya got a rite pow'ful aim...jest don't let it git youse inta trouble."

Nodding, Thad looked around, then he brought his eyes back to the old codger. "Lemony, why don't you come back with us...it's a nice place to live and I know you and Luke would hit it off..." Letting his words trail.

"Ta...Wyoming? Hell...I'd freeze..." Lemony stopped, realizing Thad had grown fond of him too. "Sonny, them's awfully nice words ta hear. Don't think me 'n Becky could take tha cold."

263

"But who'd look after you...I mean..." Thad looked down and scuffed the dirt with his boot toe.

A smile poked through Lemony's grizzled face. "Buckshot keeps an eye fer me," he replied.

"I'll write...okay?"

"You do that Sonny, ain't got a real letter in a long time."

Reaching Lacy's side, Cotton whispered, "Mom...I need to tell you something."

Giving Cotton a quizzical look, Lacy answered, "Okay."

He took her arm and led Lacy to where it was a bit quieter. "Mom...I don't know how...but Gramma was talking to me out there."

Lacy gasped.

Nodding Cotton said, "I know, unbelievable...she brought this sandstorm to cover our tracks from Kannon or someone did...and told us when water was nearby...and then she told me to wait here, in Top Notch and well it was and still is unbelievable. But every word is true, Mom."

Lacy hugged Cotton, "I believe you. She spoke to me too...in a dream. That's how we knew to come here." Her fingers smoothed his white hair. "She will always be with us, watching and protecting and loving us, Cotton."

He smiled then went to talk with Thad and Chad.

Tears were rolling down Lacy's cheeks as she smiled at Rawley. He opened his arms and she went to him. "What was that all about?"

"Mama." She looked at her husband, "She was out there protecting them, Rawley."

"Ahh...Happy now, Sunshine?"

"Yes."

"Looks like we can really lay those skeletons to rest for good..huh?" As Rawley kissed that copper mop.

Lacy nodded.

Pedro shouted at the crowd gathered in the center of town. "Buckshot! I see you lived ta see another sun!"

Kelly glanced at Pedro. "Ya better git out the good stuff, Barkeep! I see a celebration coming on!"

Waving his arms Pedro urged them toward his Cantina. "Come...come...!"

Rawley whispered in Lacy's ear, "Let's go home...Sunshine!"

Lacy remembered the first time Rawley had uttered those words. When he had fought through a blizzard arriving at the cabin madder then a wet hornet at her for running away. He came after her because he loved her and to bring her *Home* to White River. "Yes...home," she whispered smiling at the man she loved.

Chapter Fifty-Four
December 1888

Ben pulled the door shut on his Pop's mercantile, stepping to the edge of the walk, he pulled the collar of his coat closer around his ears to ward off the blustery cold wind. He stared at the dusting of snow on the steps, then looked off toward the town cemetery.

They had all been back in White River for a month now and in that time he hadn't been able to bring himself to visit his Mom's grave. But today was the day, Ben had decided. He slowly took the steps one by one until he stood on the street.

"Ben!" Hanah, called racing to his side and sliding to a stop.

He looked at her. Ben felt they had both grown up during their ordeal. The mischief they used to create seemed childish play now.

"What are you doing today, Ben?" She asked.

Ben's gaze traveled toward the cemetery. "I..I was thinking on visiting my Mom's grave."

"You haven't done that, yet?"

He stared at the ground and shook his head, "No..."

"Oh..." Suddenly Hanah understood. "It would be hard for me too...if it was my Mama. You want some company?"

Ben looked at Hanah, "Yeah, that would be nice." He was rewarded with a smile as Hanah slid her hand into his. They headed toward the knoll that housed the town's cemetery.

* * *

The second day of June 1889, Victoria Rose Lovett was born to Rawley and Lacy Lovett. She had a cap of black hair just like her Daddy and they weren't sure what color her eyes would be, but right now looked to be a dark grey.

And there wasn't one tawny colored freckle on her tiny body...anywhere!

The End

Juliette Douglas and *Noon At Night Publications* Thank you for reading *Freckled Venom Skeletons.* We hope you enjoyed the ride of *The Freckled Venom Series.*

*Ms. Douglas would like to introduce you to her next series: Perfume Powder & Lead * Holy Sisters. Three high priced sportin' gals from Black Jack's Ten-Cent Saloon where all drinks are always ten-cents. Enjoy!*

Dealer Kip Rogers looked away from her sorry hand, her ears registering the dull roar that permeated the Ten-Cent Saloon, where all drinks were always ten cents. It appeared that she just might lose this game. She sighed inwardly. Brown eyes flicked over the faces seated at her table. *These jackasses couldn't maintain a poker face if their lives depended on it.* She thought of the dust caked, stringy cowhands that surrounded her, swilling down cheap, watered down snake-tail whiskey and losing a month's wages in the process. Kip sighed again.

Weak light filtered in from two dingy front windows, spreading over and under the bat-wing doors. Dust motes floated through the stringy sun, it's fingers reaching into and breaking through the hazy darkness of the saloon's interior. A smoky fog hung near the ceiling with heavier pockets that swirled above each table and the scarred bar.

Raucous, harsh laughter exploded every once in a while, followed by the other girls' squeals who also worked for Black Jack, cutting into the low murmur of male voices. The swift sound of cards being shuffled, chairs scraping against wood planks, boot heels thunking across the cheroot and cigarette littered floor, mingled with the scent of smoke, dusty, sweaty bodies and the sweet smell of cheap perfume and whiskey.

Turning tricks and dealing for Black Jack Hennessy in his Ten-Cent Saloon had become old...real old. The brunette flicked pecan shell colored eyes upward through the fog toward the balcony where her two best friends stood gazing down on the motley crowd of

269

creeping crud that littered Black Jack's establishment. Tall, walnut-eyed Audrey Mitchell had long ebony hair that spilled over her shoulders and fell almost to her waist. Daisy Stone, her other friend, was petite in contrast and had a pretty round face, two constantly present dimples, blonde locks and hazel eyes that carried more green then brown. Their forearms rested on the railing of the balustrade edging the balcony. The girls leaned forward, showing off their best attribute to the men below...*boobs*.

Mitch straightened, casting dark eyes around as they landed on Kip. Mitch rolled those eyes and tilting her head, she drew her finger across her throat in a cutting motion, sticking out her tongue as she did so. Kip's mouth began to form a curve, then she quickly doused it. Eyes flicking back to the cards she held in her hand, her face resumed it's deadpan expression. She tried to concentrate.

"Hey...whore," a voice broke into her thoughts. "I need three..." that same voice said.

Looking up, Kip's eyes zeroed in on sandy brown ones peeking out from under a shaggy head of sun-bleached brown hair above a weathered face. The man across from her was probably only twenty-four or so...but the sun and harsh climate had created an aged look. Her eyes tapered when the man called her whore. Laying her cards face down, she silently dealt him three more. Picking those three up, he gazed hard at them, then exclaimed harshly, "Aww...hell...I'm out," he said, tossing his cards across the table toward her.

The game proceeded downhill from there. Kip who was not able to concentrate on the game, had dropped out, too. Finally a winner emerged, dirty paws scraped the puny winnings toward him.

Scraping her chair back and rising, Kip told the men at her table, "I'm taking a break...gentlemen." She pushed the stack of cards toward the center of the table. "Play on," she said, beginning to move through the smoke drenched room, causing it to swirl.

"Hey...whore."

Kip spun at the word. Her eyes lit on the sandy-eyed kid.

"Since ya made me lose most of mah money," he began. "Ya owe me...sometin' in trade."

Twitters danced around the table as eyes flicked cautiously at her, waiting on her reaction. The sandy-eyed kid allowed a devilish smile to crack through the dust.

Kip's peacemaker rested snugly in it's boot strapped securely around her waist, in plain view for everyone to see. She sipped air quietly realizing what the kid was trying to provoke. Kip had two options; she could let the kid screw her...which she sure as hell didn't feel like doing. Or wait and see what he would do when she turned him down. *Damn...pip-squeak,* she thought. *Wanting to show off for his buddies.* Her eyes narrowed, throwing him a warning before she spoke. "The game was played fair and square...mister," she said, quietly and calmly.

Dark eyes grew round. *Ut...ohhh,* thought Mitch. She touched Daisy's arm. "Let's go...'fore Kip kills someone else," she whispered to the flyspeck blonde. Both scurried down the steps arriving alongside the sandy-eyed kid. Their hands reached under his arms as they pulled him up and out of the chair.

A big grin plastered his dust-caked face, as he threw an excited look over his shoulder at his comrades.

Daisy and Mitch ushered him up the stairs toward their room, telling him he could have two whores for the price of one. Kip just stared after them. She knew what was going to happen next. Number one...they'd get him really drunk, with a little help from knock-out drops added to the watered down snake-tail whiskey; he'd then pass out. Number two...roll him, taking what few dollars and valuables he had. And three...shove him out their two story window where he'd land on a pile of dirty, old, bug infested mattresses inhabiting the alleyway. When he'd finally come to, he wouldn't remember a thing...except that he thought he'd got his tube greased by two whores for the price of one and that he carried a whopping hangover.

Kip turned to her table addressing those who remained saying again, "I'm taking a break...gentlemen." Giving them all one last, long

271

threatening look, Kip moved toward the bar.

The four at the table raised eyebrows at each other, then one picked up the stack of cards and the thin sound of shuffling filled the air. Orville Rayburn stared glumly at the girl as she walked behind his bar, small beady eyes peeked through the fat folds encasing his face. Kip's hand reached for the good rye he kept under the counter. Picking up a glass, she held it up to the hazy light, checking to make sure it was half-way clean. Satisfied, it lightly tapped the scarred, dirty top. The cork tweaked as she pulled it out of the bottle. Two fingers of amber liquid splashed into the glass. Settling the bottle on the bar, Kip placed the cork in the hole, then the heel of her hand drove it home with a solid tap. Picking up the glass she threw her head back, opening her mouth and poured the liquid in. Kip swallowed and waited for the warmth to begin spreading through her gut, and into her veins. Her eyes settled on the now empty balcony. The empty glass tapped the bar and without even a backward acknowledgment thrown at Orville Rayburn, Kip began weaving her way through the dusty, stinky, creeping crud Black Jack called patrons, toward the stairs.

A hand gripped the door knob twisting it as Kip pushed through into the room's interior. Shutting the door, she leaned against the wood, closing out the din from below.

Continuing to lean out the open window, Mitch and Daisy glanced briefly over their shoulders when they heard the latch click softly open, then close.

Pushing herself away from the door, Kip wandered across the planked floor, high-topped shoes creating a soft, quiet cadence. Peering over Mitch and Daisy's shoulders, she spied the sprawled body resting comfortably down below. Straightening, she asked, "How much did you get?"

Mitch turned and sat her fanny on the sill. Folding her arms, she replied. "Couple of dollers and a gold watch." Fingers reached into her bosom, pulling the watch and chain out of her corset encasing two full breasts. She let it dangle between the three of them.

Daisy glanced from one woman to the other as she waited.

Author Juliette Douglas is shown here with Arctic Bright View who played one of the Silver's in the 2013 remake of 'The Lone Ranger'. Both hail from Marshall County, Kentucky.

Visit our websites: www.juliettedouglas.com
www.megsonfarms.com

Visit Juliette Douglas via www.facebook.com/author.juliette.douglas

SADDLE UP...LET'S RIDE!
Photo by Lois Cunningham, Benton, KY

Made in the USA
San Bernardino, CA
13 August 2016